Mari Jungstedt lives in Stockholm with her husband and two children. This is her fifth novel set on the island of Gotland.

THE DEAD OF SUMMER

Mari Jungstedt

Translated from the Swedish by
Tiina Nunnally

CORGI BOOKS

TRANSWORLD PUBLISHERS
61–63 Uxbridge Road, London W5 5SA
A Random House Group Company
www.transworldbooks.co.uk

THE DEAD OF SUMMER
A CORGI BOOK: 9780552159951

First published in Great Britain
in 2011 by Doubleday
an imprint of Transworld Publishers
Corgi edition published 2011

Addresses for Random House Group Ltd companies outside the UK
can be found at: www.randomhouse.co.uk
The Random House Group Ltd Reg. No. 954009

The Random House Group Limited supports The Forest Stewardship
Council® (FSC®), the leading international forest certification organisation.
All our titles that are printed on Greenpeace approved FSC® certified paper
carry the FSC® logo. Our paper procurement policy can be found at
www.randomhouse.co.uk/environment

Typeset in 11/14pt Giovanni Book by Falcon Oast Graphic Art Ltd.
Printed and bound by CPI Group (UK) Ltd, Croydon, CR0 4YY

2 4 6 8 10 9 7 5 3 1

For Ewa Jungstedt, my dearest sister

From the lighthouse-keeper's diary, the island of Gotska Sandön, August 1864

In the early-morning hour of 25 August, at ten minutes after midnight, on the south-east side of the island, the Russian steamship *Vsadnik* ran aground with a crew of one hundred and forty, of which three officers and twelve seamen drowned; all of the others were rescued. A hard easterly storm with rain.

MONDAY, 10 JULY

As night gave way to morning a solitary car was driving north on the main road that cut across the island of Fårö. The rain had stopped. Heavy clouds were still covering the sky in grey sheets. The birds had been singing since three a.m.; the light of dawn was spreading across the fields and meadows. Through the haze it was possible to glimpse juniper bushes, the crooked trunks of dwarf pines, and stone walls dividing the fields. There were also farm buildings made of Gotland limestone, seemingly scattered about haphazardly, along with an occasional windmill, though the sails had long since disappeared. Flocks of black sheep could be seen in the pastures. Indolently they got to their feet, one after another, and began grazing on the meagre grass offered by the mostly bare earth.

Calm still reigned at the Sudersand campsite in the north of Fårö, although the area was fully occupied now, in the middle of summer. The campsite extended for three kilometres along the beach with its fine-grained sand. Caravans and tents were decoratively lined up in a meticulously ordered pattern. The Swedish flags adorning the entrance drooped limply from their poles. Here and there round grills had been set up, along with plastic tables, which still had wine glasses standing on them, left over from the dinners served the previous evening. Bath towels, soaked from the night-time rain, had been fastened with clothes-pegs to the improvised clotheslines. There were striped, collapsible deck chairs in bright colours, inflatable mattresses and beach toys. A few bikes.

In the centre of the grounds stood a low wooden building with several doors leading to a kitchen, laundry room, toilets and showers. A well-organized holiday community, just a stone's throw from the sea.

In one of the caravans parked near the perimeter of the campsite, Peter Bovide abruptly came wide awake. At exactly five a.m. he opened his eyes. Out of old habit he checked the time on his watch, which lay on a shelf next to the bed.

Always the same thing. Sleeping late in the morning was not part of his world.

He lay in bed, staring up at the ceiling for a while, but soon realized that he wasn't going to be able to go back to sleep. Not on this morning either. All those years working construction had taken their toll on him, and the habit of getting up early was hard to break. Although he really didn't mind. He appreciated having some time to himself before Vendela and the kids got up. He usually went out for a run and then did some callisthenics.

During the night he had lain in bed for a long time listening to the pattering of the rain on the metal roof of the caravan. He hadn't slept well. Now the rain seemed to have stopped, and faint morning light was seeping through the thin cotton curtains.

He looked at his sleeping wife. Her blanket had slipped off, and she was lying on her side. At five foot eleven she was slightly taller than he was. He found that sexy. He ran his eyes over her slender legs, the curve of her hips, and he could just make out her small breasts. He felt himself getting an erection, but this was not the right time for it. The kids were lying nearby in their narrow bunks. Five-year-old William with his mouth open and his arms comfortably stretched above his head, as if he owned the whole world. Mikaela curled up in a foetal position, three years old and holding her teddy bear in her arms.

They had four weeks ahead of them, with very few obligations or demands. First here on the island of Fårö and later two weeks in Mallorca. The company had been doing well lately.

'Are you awake?' He heard Vendela's clear and slightly drawling voice behind him, just as he was about to open the door.

'Yes, sweetheart. I'm going out for a run.'

'Wait. Come back here.'

Still lying on her side, she stretched out her arms towards him. He burrowed his head against her breasts, warm with sleep, and wrapped his arms around her. In their relationship she was the strong one; in spite of his robust appearance, he was actually fragile and vulnerable. Nobody who knew them realized how things really stood. Their friends never saw Peter Bovide when he wept like a child in his wife's arms during one of his recurring panic attacks. Or how she soothed him, comforted him and helped him to get back on his feet again. The anxiety came in waves, always unexpected, always unwelcome, like an uninvited guest. It suffocated him.

Each time he felt the onset of symptoms, he would try to suppress them, pretend they weren't there, think about something else. For the most part his attempts failed. Once the attack had begun, it was usually impossible to stop.

It had been a long time now since the last bad episode. But he knew that the panic attacks would inevitably return. Sometimes they occurred at the same time as the epileptic fits that had plagued him since early adulthood. These days the incidents were rare, but the fear of another one was always in the back of his mind. Underneath his self-confident façade, Peter Bovide was a frightened man.

When he met Vendela, his life was in a hell of a mess. Alcohol had taken an ever firmer hold on his life, leading him to neglect his job and increasingly lose his grip on reality. He had no steady girlfriend, and he never managed to maintain any long-term relationships. He neither dared nor wished to get too close to anyone. But everything had been different with Vendela.

When they met six years ago on the boat going to Finland, it was love at first sight for him. She was from Botkyrka and worked as a croupier in a casino in Stockholm. They decided to marry when she got pregnant after they'd been dating for only six months, and then they bought an old farm in the country outside Slite. A fixer-upper that they were able to buy cheap; since he was a carpenter, he could do most of the remodelling work himself.

Their two children were born two years apart. Everything was going well. For the past five years he had run a construction company along with a former work colleague, and they had gradually been able to hire several employees. The company was doing better and better, and at the moment they had more work than they could handle. New stormclouds had recently appeared on the horizon, but they were nothing he couldn't cope with.

His demons were haunting him less and less.

Vendela hugged him hard.

'I can't believe that we're going to have such a long holiday,' she murmured, with her lips pressed against his neck.

'I know. Damn, it's going to be great.'

For a moment they lay quietly, listening to the even breathing of their children. Soon the old, familiar uneasiness began creeping over him.

'I'm going to take off now.'

'OK.'

She gave him another hug.

'I'll be back soon. Then I'll put the coffee on.'

It was liberating to leave behind the close confines of the caravan. From the sea came the fresh smell of seaweed and salt. The rain had stopped. He inhaled the air deep into his lungs and stopped to take a piss at the edge of the woods.

Going out jogging every morning was a must. He didn't feel human if he couldn't start his day with a run. When he cut back on his alcohol consumption after meeting Vendela, he started running instead. Strangely enough, running seemed to have the same kind of effect on him as alcohol. He needed some kind of drug to keep the anxiety at bay.

The trail felt spongy under his feet. On both sides of him were sand dunes spreading out between grass-covered hills. He quickly reached the shore. The sea was rough, the swells moving every which way, without direction or purpose. Farther out, a flock of seagulls balanced atop the crests.

He started running north along the water's edge. Clouds swept across the leaden sky, and it was hard to run on the sand after the rain. It didn't take long before he was soaked with sweat. Out by the promontory he turned round. His thoughts became clearer as he ran. The jogging seemed to provide him with a respite of some sort.

On the way back, off in the distance he noticed somebody coming towards him, but suddenly the person stumbled and toppled over on to the sand. Then just lay there, apparently without making any attempt to get up. Feeling uneasy, he ran forward.

'Are you all right?'

The face that turned towards him was expressionless, the eyes cold and indifferent. The question remained unanswered.

For several seconds time stood still, as Peter froze in place. A disturbing churning started up inside his stomach. Deep down inside of him something came alive, something he had tried to bury for years. Finally it had caught up with him.

The eyes that were fixed on him changed; now they were filled with contempt.

He couldn't manage to utter a word, though he was breathing hard, and the familiar pain in his chest was back. He struggled not to collapse.

His body felt limp, loose-jointed.

Then he saw the muzzle of the gun. It was pointed straight at him. He automatically sank to his knees; everything in his mind went still. His thoughts stopped.

The shot struck him between the eyes. The report made the black-backed gulls lift up from the surface of the water with frightened shrieks.

Detective Superintendent Anders Knutas was pottering about in the spacious country kitchen that belonged to his parents-in-law while the rest of the family slept. He was planning to surprise them with his special breakfast: American-style pancakes with maple syrup. They tasted almost like sponge-cake, and when they were hot, they melted in your mouth. Knutas was no master in the kitchen, but he had two specialities: macaroni cheese, and pancakes.

After he had finished mixing the batter, he decided to let it sit in the bowl for a while. He picked up his coffee cup and went outside to sit down on the steps. The house stood on a promontory surrounded by the sea at the edge of a little coastal town on the Danish island of Fyn. The sun had shone non-stop ever since they'd arrived. At first Knutas had been only moderately enthusiastic when Lina suggested they go to Denmark for two whole weeks. He would have preferred to spend his holiday lazing about at their own summer place at Lickershamn in the north of Gotland, but Lina had succeeded in persuading him. For once her parents were away, and they would have the house all to themselves. And besides, she was homesick for Denmark. No matter how happy she was living in Sweden, her heart would always belong to her native country.

After a week on Fyn, Knutas was grateful that Lina had stood her ground. He hadn't felt so relaxed in years. An entire day could pass without him giving a thought to his job. And the weather was fantastic, much better than back home. They swam, fished and gorged themselves on shellfish, which tasted even more delicious here. In the evening they took strolls through the town, sat by the sea, drank wine and played cards on the porch after dark. Their twins, Petra and Nils, were having a blast. The kids had made lots of friends during their many summer visits to their grandparents, and they were gone most of the day. They would soon be sixteen, and spending time with their parents wasn't exactly a high priority.

At the moment, that was a good thing. Knutas and Lina needed to have some time to themselves. He loved his wife, but during the spring it felt as though their marriage had gone stale. He had felt exhausted and run down after yet another complicated murder investigation; for a long time afterwards, he had been plagued by guilt and spells of brooding, with no energy left whatsoever, not even for Lina.

She complained that he seemed distant and uninterested, which of course was the truth. Both of them had probably been expecting their love life to heat up now that they finally had some time off together, but that hadn't happened. They just kept plodding along in their familiar routines, and their sex life wasn't amounting to much; neither of them was particularly interested in taking the initiative.

It wasn't that he found Lina unattractive; that wasn't the problem at all. She was just as beautiful as ever with her long, fiery-red hair, freckled complexion and warm eyes. But she had almost become like a piece of furniture, like a marvellous armchair in the house. Serene and secure, comfortable but not especially exciting. Lina was a midwife at the hospital in Visby, and she loved her job. She still told stories about the mothers and their troubles with the same fervent enthusiasm. He'd heard stories like these thousands of times. In the past he'd found them entertaining and interesting, but now he would merely listen politely as he thought about something else. The feelings he had were upsetting him. Maybe he was just in a slump. It wasn't that he was looking for someone else, not at all. His sex drive had diminished; he just didn't think it was worth the effort. Sometimes he wondered if it was his age, but he was only fifty-two.

It had been a difficult spring in general. The weather was cold and rainy. At the office he'd had to deal with a ton of paperwork and other administrative tasks, which he detested. He'd felt he would never get it all done. On the other hand, he was pleased that Karin Jacobsson, the colleague he felt closest to, had been named his deputy. And she was definitely putting her best foot forward. She was such a ball of fire that she could make him feel like the least efficient and most slow-witted and lethargic person on earth. But that didn't bother him. Anders Knutas admired Karin; he had felt that way about her ever since they started working together, more than fifteen years ago.

The surly expressions that appeared when her appointment was announced had finally begun to fade. The only person who still seemed to have a hard time accepting Jacobsson's promotion was the police spokesman, Lars Norrby, who had considered himself the most likely candidate for the position. Even though they'd been colleagues for many years now, Knutas sometimes wished that Norrby would leave the Visby police department. His attitude towards Jacobsson since she'd become the deputy superintendent was very hard to take.

He hoped that things would go well for Karin while he was away on holiday. Everything had seemed calm when he left. The tourist season was in full swing, of course, but it was the same old story. The biggest problem they had was with the kids from Stockholm who arrived on the ferries in droves, intent on partying in Visby. Every summer their presence meant drunken sprees, fights, drugs and, unfortunately, more rapes. It was unpleasant, but nothing that Karin couldn't handle.

In a week he would be back on the job. He hoped that nothing major happened while he was away.

At 9.42 on Monday morning the call came in to Visby police head-quarters. Two young boys had discovered a dead body in the water near Sudersand beach on Fårö. One of the boys had swum right into the body as it floated twenty or so yards from shore.

By the time acting Detective Superintendent Karin Jacobsson and Detective Inspector Thomas Wittberg arrived at the crime scene a crowd had gathered on the beach. After a rainy night, the sun was peeking out. Crime-scene technician Erik Sohlman had managed to get help in cordoning off the area and setting up a white plastic tent over the body to protect it from both the sun and the gawking of curious bystanders. Over by the tent, Sohlman took Jacobsson's arm.

'He was murdered, no doubt about it. And that's not just a shot in the dark, if you'll excuse the expression. You need to sound the alarm immediately. After that, I'll show you.'

Jacobsson took out her mobile to summon more police officers and the dog patrol to Sudersand; she also ordered all cars on the ferries leaving Fårö to be checked.

She turned to the officers who were setting up the police tape and shouted, 'We need to cordon off a much bigger area!'

Jacobsson and Sohlman then went over to look at the body, which was covered with a cotton cloth inside the improvised tent.

'Are you ready?'

Sohlman cast a glance at his colleague's pale face. Jacobsson always had difficulty looking at dead bodies. For her to throw up at a murder scene was more the rule than the exception. As the crime-scene tech lifted off the cloth, she pressed a handkerchief to her mouth.

The dead man was about her age. He had a very striking appearance, with deep-set eyes that were an unusually bright blue. Almost non-existent eyebrows. He had high cheekbones and a slightly protruding jaw. If not for the bullet hole in his forehead, his face would have seemed quite peaceful.

'The shot was fired from a distance of a few inches, maximum. It's obvious from the entry wound that the murderer was very close. The guy never had a chance.'

'How can you be so sure he didn't do it himself?' muttered Jacobsson from behind the handkerchief as she struggled to fend off the nausea.

'There's more. Prepare yourself.'

Cautiously Sohlman lifted off the rest of the covering. Jacobsson groaned when she saw what was underneath. The man's stomach was riddled with bullet holes.

'Shot to hell. I've counted seven shots to the abdomen. It's completely insane.'

Jacobsson turned away and threw up.

Johan Berg was standing in a cow pasture interviewing a farmer who was complaining about the cutbacks in EU subsidies when the call came through. He had forgotten to switch off his mobile during the interview; it was just the type of stupid mistake that TV reporters were not supposed to make. But the damage was done. His camera person, Pia Lilja, rolled her eyes and threw out her hands, then left the camera on its tripod as she went over to pat a cow while Johan took the call. It was Max Grenfors, the head of Regional News.

'Have you heard?'

'No, what is it? I'm in the middle of an interview.'

'Yeah, OK,' said Grenfors impatiently, 'but a man was found shot to death over on Fårö. Right next to the campsite. Sudersand. You know it, right?'

'Of course. What happened?'

While he talked Johan fixed his eyes on the farmer, who was looking unhappy about the interruption. No doubt he wanted nothing more than to continue his complaints about the bureaucrats down in Brussels.

'He was found this morning, in the sea near Sudersand beach.'

'How do you know he didn't drown?'

'I'm just reading what it says on the TT wire service. According to their report, the body was in the water, but he'd been shot several times.'

'Bloody hell.'

'So stop what you're doing and get over there as fast as you can. Ring me when you're in the car. I'll give you the latest news update while you're on the road.'

Johan quickly said goodbye to the disappointed farmer, explaining that they would have to finish the interview some other time.

Luckily they were in Lärbro in the north of Gotland, not far from Fårösund. Pia Lilja's face shone with excitement as she stomped on the accelerator, making the car tyres squeal as they took the curves at high speed. Her black hair was sticking out in all directions, as usual. Her eyes, with their heavy coating of mascara, were firmly fixed on the road ahead.

'Fabulous,' she exclaimed. 'Finally something is happening.'

'Fabulous?' Johan looked at her in surprise. 'The fact that a human being has been shot to death?'

'Come on, you know what I mean. Of course not. But it's much more exciting to report on a homicide than to film a story about unhappy farmers.'

Pia loved it when things got cracking and stuff was happening. Gotland was really too small a place for someone as news-hungry as Pia Lilja. She was twenty-five and wanted to get out into the world, to accompany one of the TV foreign correspondents and witness wars and famines.

But so far she was considered too young and inexperienced. For the time being she had to settle for documenting more ordinary domestic events, such as disputes about putting in a new road in Burgsvik, or the complaints of students about the poor quality of the food served in the school cafeteria in Hemse, or the drama of the local championship match in throwing the *varpa*, a flat round stone, to get closest to the pin.

But no matter what the news report, she somehow managed to take all sorts of exciting pictures. Pia always did her best. In addition, she had a huge network of contacts that was truly astonishing. She was the youngest of seven siblings, and her extended family was spread all over Gotland. Thanks to them, and her highly developed social skills, she seemed to know absolutely everyone.

In the car on their way over to the Fårösund ferry dock, Johan listened to Grenfors with one ear and to the local radio station with the other, all the while taking notes at lightning speed. The news had come over the TT wire ten minutes earlier. The press was always cautious if there was the slightest suspicion of suicide, but a witness had managed to catch a glimpse of the body and had seen first-hand the bullet hole in the head, as well as the wounds in the abdomen.

Anybody could work out that the dead man couldn't possibly have caused such wounds all on his own. The witness had been interviewed by a journalist from Radio Gotland who just happened to be on Fårö with all of his equipment. The police had confirmed that they were dealing with a suspected homicide.

The ferry crossing to Fårö took only a few minutes. The sky had cleared and the sun glittered on the surface of the sea. The road north towards Sudersand took them through the rocky landscape of Fårö. Along the way Johan and Pia encountered bicyclists, camping caravans and cars filled with families on holiday.

When they reached the intersection of four roads near Sudersand and turned right towards the campsite, a picture of Emma's face flashed through Johan's mind. If they had turned left at the intersection instead, they would have eventually ended up at Norsta Auren, the beach near her parents' house.

Emma Winarve was the great love of Johan's life. Or at least she had been. They had spent so many wonderful days in that house by the sea when her parents were away, there on the beach between Skärsände and the Fårö lighthouse, on the extreme tip of Fårö. It was the most beautiful of places. But now their relationship was non-existent.

He was roused from his thoughts as they reached Sudersand campsite. The police had blocked off the entire area. Officers were everywhere, but there was no one available to speak to journalists. Neither Karin

Jacobsson nor the police spokesman, Lars Norrby, answered their mobile, and Knutas was on holiday in Denmark with his family.

'Typical.' Johan stared with dismay at the campsite as they stood outside the police tape. 'What do we do now?'

'I've got an idea,' said Pia as she finished shooting one last panorama of the area. 'Come with me.'

They jumped back in the car. Pia drove back to the intersection that would take them to Sudersand East and headed for the nearby colony of summer cottages. She turned on to a small side road, no bigger than a cow path, and the car began jolting along through the woods, thick with underbrush, and across a meadow filled with flowers and tall grass.

Several times Johan thought they were going to get stuck, but Pia managed to make the car forge its way onward. When she finally stopped next to a big shrub that was blocking their way, he could hear the sea. It was three thirty in the afternoon, and they still had about an hour left to file their report. Johan patted Pia on the shoulder.

'You're damned good at this.'

It took them all of two minutes to walk down to the shore. In one direction they could see the promontory that marked the end of Sudersand bay, and in the other direction was the campsite. Close to the shoreline a small tent had been set up, and a group of people was gathered around it. Suddenly a whirring sound was heard overhead. It was the police helicopter from Stockholm, probably with the medical examiner on board.

Pia immediately began filming. Even though Johan was well aware that he was inside the area that had been cordoned off, he walked over to see if he could talk to the pilot when the helicopter landed. It was worth a try. A man got out and hurried over to the tent. That had to be the ME.

'We're from Swedish TV,' he shouted to the pilot. 'Is that the ME who just arrived?'

'That's right. We came straight here from the helipad at Karolinska hospital.'

'When are you heading back?'

'They said we'd be taking off in half an hour. I can't keep the chopper here any longer than that. It's needed at Berga.'

'OK.'

Johan waved his thanks to the pilot. He'd found out what he wanted to know. Now he just needed to try talking to the police. He noticed Erik Sohlman, who had stepped away to get himself a cup of coffee.

'Hi, Erik. What's going on here?'

Sohlman nodded to Berg. Johan had been a crime reporter on the island for quite a while now, and on several occasions he'd actually helped the police, once when his daughter's life was at stake and once when his own life was in jeopardy. So Sohlman felt compelled to repay the favour. He hesitated before answering, taking a moment to decide what he wanted to say. Then he came over to Johan.

'I can tell you this much: a man was found dead, and we suspect foul play. The ME is doing his first examination right now. Later the body will be moved to the morgue in Visby, and from there it will be transported by ferry to the forensic medicine lab in Solna.'

'I understand, but . . .'

'I'm afraid I can't tell you anything else. And you're inside the police tape, so I'm going to have to ask you to leave.'

Johan and Pia headed back to their car. Both were more than satisfied. Now they even had time to shoot some reactions from people at the campsite.

Their story was in the can.

Late that afternoon the investigative team gathered for a meeting at police headquarters. Besides Karin Jacobsson, Thomas Wittberg and Erik Sohlman, the group included Lars Norrby and chief prosecutor Birger Smittenberg.

Jacobsson started by welcoming everyone.

'So it looks like we have yet another brutal murder on our hands. You might call it an execution, pure and simple. The victim has already been identified down at the beach by his wife. His name is Peter Bovide, born in 1966, married and the father of two, from Slite. He's been on holiday with his family at Sudersand campsite since Friday – in other words, he'd spent three days there. Early this morning, around five thirty according to his wife, he went out for a run. Apparently this was not out of the ordinary for him. The victim appears to have had a stable family life. He and Vendela Bovide have been married for six years. They have two children, a boy, five, and a girl, three. We interviewed the wife very briefly when she was asked to identify the body. She's suffering from severe shock, so she was taken to the hospital, where they've decided to keep her over-night for observation. I'm hoping to be able to talk to her tomorrow.'

Jacobsson paused for a moment to glance down at her papers before she went on.

'The body was found around nine thirty by two boys from Stockholm. They're both thirteen years old, and their parents rent a cabin nearby. They were playing soccer on the beach and ended up quite a distance away. Then they decided to go for a swim and dis-covered the body in the water a short way from shore. They shouted for help and several people came to their aid. The man who rang the police is the father of one of the boys. The call to the emergency number 112 came in at nine forty-two. The first officers to respond arrived forty-five minutes later.'

'How long had he been dead?' asked Prosecutor Smittenberg.

'At least a couple of hours, but five or six, max,' replied Sohlman.

'Precisely,' said Jacobsson. 'So there's no sense in setting up road blocks or stopping the ferry traffic. Of course, all day we've been checking everyone who leaves the island by ferry, and we'll keep doing so into the evening. Does anyone here happen to know the victim?'

All those seated around the table shook their heads.

'So what do we know about Peter Bovide?'

Jacobsson answered her own question.

'He actually has a police record, but just for a minor crime. A charge of assault and battery from back in the eighties, when he was twenty. A fight at Burmeister here in town. The bouncers refused to let him into the disco, so he punched one of them. Because he didn't have a prior record, he got off with a fine. Nothing since then. He's done construction work, and now he runs his own building company along with a partner. Slite Construction, with six full-time employees. The partner's name is Johnny Ekwall, and we're going to interview him tonight. In short, that's all we can say about the victim right now. When it comes to the crime itself, I'm afraid we don't have much to go on. We've been knocking on doors in the area, but there are no eyewitnesses. On the other hand, somebody did hear the shots. A couple that lives nearby heard first one shot and then several more bangs that they thought might have been gunfire. The sound woke them up, and according to them, it was around six this morning. They thought it was either rifle practice or someone who was out shooting rabbits illegally. Apparently that's common in the area. We're continuing to interview visitors and employees at the campsite and at the nearby restaurants. Some people left the campsite during the course of the day, and we're trying to track them down. Since we need to do a large number of interviews, I've contacted the National Criminal Police. Martin Kihlgård and some of his colleagues will be here early tomorrow morning.'

'Good,' said Lars Norrby. 'Sounds like we'll need their help.'

Jacobsson gave him a quick look. It was impossible to tell whether his remark was intended to be sarcastic or not. Her appointment as Knutas's deputy had taken place only six months earlier. When her older colleague realized that Karin was going to be given the promotion, he had loudly voiced his objections, devoting a large part of his work days to bad-mouthing both Knutas and Jacobsson. Norrby was also suspected of having leaked information to the press. Finally he had been removed from the investigative team. Today he was present solely because of his role as spokesman; this was their first meeting, and he needed to be kept informed, at least to some extent, regarding the progress of the investigation.

Jacobsson wanted to believe that all grudges had been forgotten, but she wasn't sure whether that was true. Norrby's expression revealed nothing of what he was actually feeling. She had to admit to herself that because Knutas was away, anybody who still wished to oppose her authority now had free rein.

She was looking forward to Martin Kihlgård's arrival to help with the investigation. Jacobsson had always liked the inspector from the NCP in Stockholm, ever since the first time they'd met in connection with a manhunt for a serial killer several years earlier.

She turned to Sohlman.

'Erik, would you like to take it from here?'

'Sure.'

He sat down in front of the computer, signalling for Jacobsson to turn off the lights. On the white screen at the front of the room a map of the campsite and Sudersand bay appeared. Peter Bovide's presumed jogging route had been marked with a red line.

'Here you can see the area. The campsite itself covers the whole top half of the map. The Bovide family caravan was parked at the very edge. On the other side of the fence is the path that leads to the beach restaurants and the summer cottage colony. Peter Bovide didn't take that path; instead he ran straight down to the shore and then turned left and followed the shoreline north. He turned around out by the promontory, and on his way back he encountered the perpetrator, only a kilometre from the actual campsite.'

'How do we know this?' asked Smittenberg.

He was the chief prosecutor for Gotland's district court, and he'd worked with the investigative team on so many cases that it felt as if he were a regular member. He still spoke with a distinct Stockholm accent in spite of the fact that he'd lived on the island and been married to a Gotlander for more than twenty years.

'We've identified Bovide's footprints. We found them both on the path from the caravan heading down towards the sea, and along the beach. It was easy to follow his route.'

'Did you find footprints from the perpetrator as well?' asked Jacobsson.

'There are a bunch of different prints in the area where the victim was found. The most interesting are from a type of trainer, size 7½. We're working on that. Otherwise we haven't found much evidence in the area so far.'

'No bullets or empty casings?'

'No, but it looks like he has a number of slugs still in his body. He was shot no fewer than eight times. The ME has been here and examined the body at the scene, so what I'm telling you about now is the first impression we both had. In other words, nothing has been confirmed yet, so take it all with a grain of salt. We're hoping that the post mortem will be done in the morning, and then we should have a preliminary report by tomorrow evening.'

'Good,' said Jacobsson. 'At this stage, how would you interpret the wounds?'

'In terms of the shot to the forehead, we can see that the bullet penetrated the skull and entered the brain, where it stopped. Judging by the appearance of the entry wound, we think that the shot was fired at very close range. Either the perp pressed the gun to the victim's forehead, or the muzzle was only a few inches from Bovide's head.'

'How can you tell?' asked Wittberg with interest.

'We know that it was fired at close range because of the type of entry wound in the victim's head. It's quite large and star-shaped. You can see how jagged it is if you look at the photo. That's because the bullet carries a cloud of hot gas that follows it into the body when the shot is fired at close range. The gas collects under the skin like a bubble which bursts when the bullet penetrates farther inside – rather like a zit, actually – and that results in this type of star-shaped wound. Carbon particles also collect around the entry hole, and there are some traces left on his forehead.'

'Even though he was floating in the water for several hours?' asked Wittberg.

'Yes, it's rather like a tattoo.'

'Good lord,' groaned Jacobsson.

She couldn't understand how Sohlman could sound so unmoved when he talked about a victim's wounds.

'The shot to the forehead should have been sufficient to kill him, since it was fired so close to his body,' Sohlman continued. 'So it's a mystery what the hell went on after that.'

The next picture showed the bullet holes in the abdomen.

'If the shot to the forehead was fired first, the murderer must have gone crazy afterwards. He seems to have emptied an entire magazine into the body. Seven shots fired at the man's gut, also at close range.'

'What does it mean?' muttered Jacobsson. 'Why would he do that?'

'The first thing that comes to mind is rage,' said Wittberg. 'It must have been somebody who was really furious with the victim.'

'Yes,' Jacobsson agreed. 'It seems very charged with emotion. Maybe they knew each other.'

'Unprofessional is what I'd call it,' Sohlman interjected. 'If you want to kill somebody, you don't fire a bunch of shots at the stomach. There's a good chance the victim might survive, as long as the bullets don't hit the aorta or the heart. A pro would have fired another shot to the head if he wasn't sure that the first bullet had been fatal.'

'So an amateur then. Somebody who hasn't killed before,' said Jacobsson. 'At the same time, it seems incredibly cold-blooded. I mean, not everyone would be able to shoot a man standing right in front of them, and in the forehead at such close range.'

'But why do you think he was shot in the head first and then in the stomach?' asked Wittberg. 'Wouldn't the opposite seem more reasonable? The perp shoots the victim in the stomach, and then to make sure he dies, he fires a shot at his head.'

'It's just a feeling I have,' said Sohlman. 'We really won't know until after the post mortem. I'm sure the ME will be able to determine in what order the bullets were fired.'

'Can you tell us anything about the weapon?' asked Jacobsson.

'Nothing except that we're talking about a small-calibre pistol. I won't know more until we've taken a look at the slugs.'

'The question is how the murderer knew that Peter

Bovide was going to be out running so early,' murmured Wittberg. 'In other words, was the murder premeditated?'

'It seems most likely that it was planned,' said Norrby, crossing one long leg over the other. 'How long did you say they'd been at the campsite?'

'Three days,' replied Jacobsson.

'The perp must have followed Bovide to the campsite and observed his routines.'

'Apparently, he always went running every morning at the same time,' interjected Jacobsson. 'Every single day of the year.'

She reached for the flask of coffee standing on the table.

'What I can't understand is why the perp would choose to commit the murder so close to a campsite swarming with people. Doesn't that seem a bit crazy?'

'Maybe he was staying at the campsite himself,' said Wittberg. 'It might have been someone that Peter Bovide had just met.'

'Or maybe there's some reason why the perp didn't want to kill Bovide close to home,' said Smittenberg. 'A neighbour, a work colleague, or someone else with strong ties to Bovide's life back in Slite. Killing him on Fårö could serve as some sort of diversionary manoeuvre.'

'That doesn't sound very likely,' said Jacobsson. 'The MO seems to indicate that a lunatic is on the loose. We need to do everything we can to catch this person as soon as possible. One way to proceed is to look for the gun. The perp might have thrown it away somewhere nearby. We'll use metal detectors and get the coast guard to bring in divers who can search the area where the body was found.'

Jacobsson silently reminded herself that she needed to make sure the Swedish Crime Laboratory, the SCL in Linköping, gave priority to examining the bullets to find out what type of gun was used. She turned to Sohlman.

'Erik, could you see to it that the SCL puts a rush on this case, both the post mortem and the examination of the bullets? We can't rule out that we're dealing with someone who's mentally ill, and in the worst-case scenario he may have developed a taste for killing. There's a good chance he'll strike again.'

Peter Bovide's partner, Johnny Ekwall, looked pale and upset when he arrived for the interview at police headquarters on the night of the murder. His muscular body slumped, and he was obviously having trouble holding back the tears. He sank heavily on to the chair across from Jacobsson, who was already sitting at the table in the cramped interrogation room. He smelled strongly of sweat. Jacobsson wrinkled her nose but decided she'd have to overlook it, since the man's colleague had just been murdered, after all.

'I realize that it's tough to have to come here,' she said sympathetically, 'but I'm afraid it's necessary. We need to gather as much information as we can about Peter Bovide, and do it quickly, so that we can catch the murderer.'

She switched on the tape recorder and ran through the standard statements. Then she leaned back in her chair and studied the man sitting in front of her. She knew that he was fifty-two, but she thought he looked older. His hair was thinning, and he had deep lines on his face.

'How long have you been running the company together?'

'Five years. Peter had dreamed of doing it for a long time – starting his own company, I mean – and recently things have really taken off. This is too bloody awful.'

He stared down at the table.

'How did you divide up the work?'

'Peter mostly handles the administrative and financial sides of the business, plus he goes after more jobs and writes bids. I take care of the practical matters. Meaning, I find the men to do the work and things like that. Make sure that everything is going smoothly. I also get more personally involved in the operational side than Peter does. I spend as much time as I can out at the construction sites. Peter mostly stays in the office. You might say that he's the brains of the company while I'm the heart.'

Jacobsson raised her eyebrows at this use of metaphor. She felt an instant empathy for this man who spoke of Peter Bovide as if he were still alive.

'How did you happen to meet?'

'It was back in the nineties, when there were very few construction jobs to be had. We were both working extra hard as longshoremen at Slite harbour. After that we often ended up working at the same building sites, and we became good friends.'

'Why did you decide to start a company together with Peter?'

'I've spent my whole life working for other people,

and I thought it was about time for me to run my own business. Peter was always a driving force at the construction sites. He inspired the other guys to work more efficiently and pick up the tempo, so I trusted him. If I was going to try starting my own company, I wanted to do it with him. And I'd saved up a fair amount of money, so that was enough for our initial investment.'

'Are you married? Do you have children?'

'No.'

'Could you describe Peter? What was he like?'

'Everybody liked him. He was the quiet type, very meticulous. And he was a workaholic, he really was. Never stopped working.'

'How was his marriage?'

'Vendela and the kids were everything to him. He was one of the few guys I know who actually had a great relationship with his wife. He put in long hours, but he always went straight home when the work was done.'

Johnny Ekwall sighed heavily and rubbed his eyes. Jacobsson paused for a moment before asking her next question.

'And the business was doing well, you said?'

'Yes. It was tough in the beginning, but for the past year the work has been pouring in. People are building like crazy. We've also had some big jobs that paid really well. Things are going better and better. We've even been thinking about hiring a couple more guys. And now this happens. It's so damn unfair.'

'Do you have any idea who might have wanted to harm Peter?'

'Not a clue.'

'Have you noticed any changes lately? Somebody new he'd made contact with, or anything like that? Think carefully. Every detail is important, no matter how small.'

Johnny Ekwall hesitated before replying.

'Well, actually, Peter told me that sometimes he felt like he was being watched. Just recently, not long before he died.'

Jacobsson gave a start.

'What do you mean by "watched"?'

'As if someone was literally tailing him, shadowing him.'

'When did this happen?'

'Once when we were having coffee at the company office, as usual. He suddenly got up and went over to the window to look outside. I asked him what was going on, and he told me that he thought he'd heard something, and then he saw a shadow pass by outside.'

'Did you see anything?'

'No. It happened again when we were doing some grocery shopping in Slite. He kept turning round, and he said that he had the feeling somebody was after him.'

'When did all this start?'

'A few weeks ago, maybe in early June.'

'Did he ever show this sort of behaviour before?'

'No. But lately he started getting strange phone calls as well.'

'What do you mean?'

'Someone would ring him up and then just put down the phone.'

'Did you get these kinds of calls too?'

'No, but I know it happened to Peter several times.'

'What did the person on the phone say?'

'I don't think they said anything. Maybe it was just a wrong number.'

'What time of day did these calls take place?'

'Any time at all, I think.'

'Do you know whether he got these calls at home too?'

'He never mentioned it.'

'Did anyone else at the company get these types of phone calls?'

'No.'

'Do you think it had something to do with your business?'

'Haven't the foggiest. I don't even know whether he was really being followed or whether it was just his imagination. He was a bit fragile from a psychological standpoint, I have to admit.'

'Fragile? What do you mean by that?'

'Sometimes he'd get depressed and hardly say a word all day. He seemed to retreat inside himself. It was obvious that he was feeling low.'

'Do you know what caused it?'

'No.'

'Did you ever talk about it?'

'No. I did try to bring it up a few times, but I could tell that he didn't want to talk about it, so I dropped the subject.'

'How much do you know about the company's finances?'

'Not a thing, as a matter of fact. As I said, Peter handled everything to do with the account books. I have no sense for numbers.'

Johan and Pia were working to get their report ready in time for the first evening news broadcast. They were sitting in the editorial office of Regional News, housed in the Swedish TV and Radio building on Östra Hansegatan, just outside the ring wall. For the past few years Gotland had been included in the area covered by Regional News, but there was no permanent staff on the island. Johan had been forced to get used to commuting back and forth between Stockholm and Visby. It had been very trying, not just professionally but also in terms of his personal life. His relationship with Emma Winarve was complicated enough, and it had been that way from the very beginning. She was married when they first met, and she had two young children. They instantly fell in love and carried on a passionate affair in secret. When Emma was pregnant with Johan's child, she got a divorce and gave birth to their daughter, Elin, who was now a year old. Emma had been too bewildered after the divorce to move in with Johan right away, which had greatly upset him.

But eventually he was allowed to move into her house in Roma.

Their familial happiness was short-lived, because soon afterwards they had landed in the middle of a kidnapping drama, and for a few terrifying hours Elin was held captive by a murderer on the run from the police. While carrying out his reporting duties for Swedish TV, Johan had come too close to the perpetrator. Emma had accused Johan of putting their daughter's life in danger, even though deep inside she knew that he hadn't done it on purpose. After Elin was found safe, Emma had broken off the engagement. Several months had passed since then, and the contact between them was still chilly. They saw each other only when picking up Elin or dropping her off.

During the whole turbulent spring, Johan had rushed back and forth between Stockholm and Gotland, trying to spend as much time with Elin as he could.

Swedish TV had rented an apartment for him on Adelsgatan in the middle of Visby so that he didn't have to stay in a hotel. Just a little cubbyhole, of course, but the location couldn't have been more central.

Emotionally, Johan found himself in a miserable state. His body was screaming for Emma, and he constantly felt an aching yearning to be with Elin. It was like having a black hole inside him. Right now he had no idea what he was going to do; it was probably merely a matter of accepting the situation. He had wanted to demand to see his daughter at least 50 per cent of the time, as was his right, but it was actually his own mother who had made him change his mind.

'One thing at a time,' she had said to console him. 'One thing at a time.' Making demands in the midst of such chaos would just make everything worse. His mother thought that, with time, Emma would calm down and listen to reason. And he wanted to believe in her.

The situation couldn't be described as anything but disastrous, yet the kidnapping drama that occurred in the early spring had also taken its toll on Johan, and he didn't have the energy to deal with the conflict with Emma right now. For the time being, he made do with the few days he was allowed to spend with Elin.

Dark had fallen by the time Karin Jacobsson walked home from police headquarters. She crossed Norra Hansegatan and continued along the main street down to Östercentrum. The shops were closed, but some young guys were sitting at tables outside McDonald's, bellowing into the warm July night. Teenagers walked past, on their way down to the ring wall and the old town looming inside. It was close to midnight, and she still hadn't been able to get in touch with Knutas. Now it was too late to call. Instead, she sent off a brief text message:

'Murder on Fårö. Man shot to death, execution-style. Ring when you have time.'

Just as she passed Ali's barbecue stand outside Österport, her mobile rang.

'Hi, it's Anders. Are you kidding?'

'I wish I was.'

She couldn't resist smiling a bit when she heard how flabbergasted he sounded. She realized he must be frustrated at being so far away.

'I tried to call you several times.'

'I know. I was recharging my mobile, so it was switched off. Then I forgot about it. I'm on holiday, after all,' he joked. 'So tell me what happened.'

Jacobsson quickly outlined the sequence of events as she walked through the gate in the Visby ring wall at Österport and down Hästgatan.

The restaurants she passed were packed with people enjoying the warm night. Music poured out of the bars and eating establishments. Visby had a lively entertainment scene in the summer, and it was high season right now.

She had reached Mellangatan by the time she had finished her report.

'Bloody hell,' said Knutas. 'What are you doing now?'

'I've talked to Martin Kihlgård, and he and a few colleagues from the NCP will be here tomorrow.'

There was silence on the line for a moment. Jacobsson was at her front door. She felt a pang of guilt. Partly because Knutas was having a well-deserved holiday, which he really needed. Partly because it was so late, and he should be spending time with his wife instead of talking shop with her.

'OK,' she went on. 'So now you know what happened, at any rate. But you're on holiday. We can handle things here, Anders.'

'I have every confidence that you can. Ring if you need anything. It's no bother.'

'Thanks. Good night.'

'Good night. Give my best to everyone else.'
'Sure.'

When Karin went to bed that night, she felt lonelier than she had in a long time.

HAMBURG, 22 JUNE 1985

Vera sat in the kitchen, staring with yearning at the other side of Friedenstrasse. The building directly opposite was six storeys tall with a light-coloured façade. She no longer needed to count the rows of windows to know where he lived. Gotthard Westenfelder – she tried out the name. Said it aloud. Never before in the twenty years of her life had she been so in love. They had met at the university just after she had completed her first year. Both of them were studying to be teachers, and they were in the same class. Even on the first day she thought there was something special about him. Not just in terms of appearance, even though he was very attractive with his blond hair and green eyes. It was a week before they spoke to each other. He asked her if she knew where to find one of the textbooks required for the course. She knew at once that his question wasn't solely about books. They went out to a café and the next day to the cinema, and that was when he kissed her. That had been two weeks ago, and she was so in love that she couldn't think about anything else. When she wasn't with him, she still saw his face everywhere.

Now she was sitting here and trying to concentrate on the

last exam before the summer holidays, but her eyes kept shift-ing to the window to stare at his building. Unfortunately, his bedroom window faced the other direction.

She looked down at her book, but the letters forming the words swam before her eyes, merging and separating and taking on a life of their own. She sighed and glanced out at the street one last time before she got up and went to the bathroom.

She stood in front of the mirror, studying her face. Vera was quite pleased with how she looked, even though she thought her sister Tanya was prettier. Tanya had their mother's beauty, while Vera had inherited her features from their father's Russian ancestors. Her parents had met in West Berlin, and after a few years there the family had moved to Hamburg, where her father, Oleg, had found a new job as a biologist at a large company while her mother, Sabine, worked as a teacher in a secondary school.

Vera ran her finger over her forehead, followed the curve of her cheekbone down to the tip of her chin. She had big grey eyes with dark lashes and eyebrows. The door slammed downstairs, startling her out of her reveries, and she heard her little sister's voice saying: 'Hello?'

Vera went back to her place at the kitchen table.

'I'm so hungry,' said Tanya.

She yanked open the refrigerator door and began pulling out one thing after another: cheese, salami, Sabine's home-made meatloaf left over from dinner the night before.

'Haven't you eaten anything today?' asked Vera, watching with amusement as the pile of food on the table continued to grow.

'I didn't have time.'

Tanya stopped what she was doing and gave her older sister a coy smile and a wink.

'What is it? Tell me,' said Vera with a sigh. 'Who is it now?'

Her younger sister possessed a bewitching charm, and she knew how to make use of it. She regarded it as a sport to make men fall for her.

'Wouldn't you like to know?' Tanya gloated as she plunked herself down on the chair across the table and began spreading peanut butter on a slice of bread.

'Come on, cut it out. Tell me,' Vera insisted. 'I won't say a word.'

Tanya leaned forward, as if to confide in her sister.

'Promise?'

'Yes, I promise.'

'Peter.'

'Which Peter?'

'Peter Hartmann, my philosophy teacher.'

'Are you mad? You must be out of your mind – a teacher! How did this happen?'

'Oh, you know, I stayed after school today to find out more about what's going to be on the exam tomorrow. While we were standing there talking, I suddenly felt a tension between us. He must have felt the same thing because he touched my arm and asked me whether I'd like to go out for coffee. And then . . .'

She stopped what she was saying as the door opened. Their father always came home earlier on Fridays, and it was out of the question to tell him anything about amorous adventures. Especially if they involved a teacher.

'Hi, girls,' *cried Oleg cheerfully, standing in the kitchen doorway and smiling. He was holding an envelope in his hand.*

'What's that, Pappa?' *asked Tanya.* 'Have you got good news?'

Oleg slapped the envelope against the door frame.

'You might say that,' *he replied gleefully. He came in, gave each of his daughters a kiss on the cheek and then sat down on a chair across from Tanya.*

'But I think I'll just wait until Mamma comes home,' *he said.*

'No!' *they both protested.* 'Tell us what it's about!'

'OK.'

All three of them pushed aside the food to clear a space on the table.

Oleg opened the big envelope and took out a brochure and several photographs.

He held up the brochure so the girls could see it. Vera leaned forward to get a better look.

The picture showed a sandy beach with a bunch of reeds in the foreground. The sky was cornflower blue. It looked like a lovely beach somewhere in the Canary Islands. Then they read the text. 'Gotska Sandön,' *it said.*

'What's this all about? Are we going there?' *asked Tanya eagerly.*

Without replying, their father showed them the photographs, one after the other. A sunset over a shimmering sea; long expanses of shoreline, sandy beaches and pebble-strewn shores; deserted forests; enormous flocks of exotic birds; a ravine; and plump grey seals lazing on the rocks in the sunshine.

'Yes,' he said with a sigh. 'At last.'

'But foreigners aren't allowed there,' Vera objected. 'You said it was a restricted military area.'

'It is, but I've been granted special dispensation. The county administrative board in Gotland has given me permission to go there because that's where my great-grandfather is buried.'

'That's fantastic, Pappa.'

Tanya gave him a big hug. Vera studied her father. Oleg had been talking about Gotska Sandön for as long as she could remember. He was a biologist and an active member of an ornithological association. In her eyes he seemed incomprehensibly obsessed with nature. Gotska Sandön was a nature reserve, and he had told them countless times about the amazing natural setting and the wealth of flora and birdlife on the island. Otherwise, she really didn't know much about it. Except that it was part of Sweden, just off another island called Gotland.

'Do we get to go with you?'

'Yes, of course. I haven't said anything to your mother yet. I want to surprise her.'

'Oh, what fun,' said Tanya. 'When are we going?'

'In about three weeks. We leave for Sweden on 16 July and we'll spend the night in Stockholm. It's supposed to be such a beautiful city. From there we catch a plane to Visby

on Gotland, and we'll stay there overnight. Then we take the boat to Gotska Sandön for a week.'

'But where are we going to stay?' asked Tanya. 'Is there a hotel there?'

'No,' said Oleg with a laugh. 'It's a protected nature reserve. There are only a few little cottages. The rest of the island is uninhabited. Nobody lives there year-round.'

Vera was touched by the fact that he looked so happy. He'd been dreaming about this trip all his life.

Now his dream was finally going to come true.

TUESDAY, 11 JULY

Karin woke with a jolt and reached for the clock on the nightstand. 6.55. She lay in bed for a while, thinking about the events of the previous day. The image of Peter Bovide's lacerated body appeared in her mind.

Outwardly there seemed to be nothing remarkable about his life. Bovide was an ordinary father of two and part-owner of a construction company. The answers that his partner Johnny Ekwall had given seemed perfectly straightforward. Karin was looking forward to hearing the results of the search the police had carried out, both at Bovide's home and at his company offices. The police had still been hard at work late last night.

Jacobsson climbed out of bed. She and Knutas were both morning people. She wondered what else they shared. How would he have handled the investigation? She realized that she wouldn't be able to resist ringing him again later in the day.

She opened the window. Since she lived on the top floor, she could look out over the rooftops to the sea.

Off in the distance she saw one of the Gotland ferries on its way out of Visby harbour.

The floorboards creaked under her feet as she went out to the kitchen. Her cockatoo, Vincent, was awake, and he said, 'Good morning,' to her, in English. He was the only bird she knew who was bilingual. Karin had inherited him from an Australian friend who had moved back to her home country a few years earlier.

She made herself some coffee and a couple of open sandwiches on rye. She fetched the newspaper from the letterbox and switched on the radio. The murder of Peter Bovide was of course the top story. She noted with relief that the news reports contained no surprises, only the information that the police had already revealed. After carefully reading everything written about the murder, she quickly scanned the rest of the newspaper. An article in *Gotlands Tidningar* caught her attention.

The Russian ships bringing coal to the cement factory in Slite were going to double their deliveries in the autumn. They would be arriving in Slite harbour once a week instead of every two weeks, as they did now. The factory was apparently increasing its production, and coal was used in its furnaces. The stone quarry in Slite was one of the largest in Sweden.

She poured herself another cup of coffee. Something about this article bothered her, but she couldn't work out what it was. She read it again, this time paying more attention, but didn't notice anything special.

No doubt it would come to her later on.

The phone started ringing even before Karin Jacobsson stepped into her office. She recognized at once the agitated voice of the director of tourism. No matter what the issue, Sonja Hedström always sounded as if it was a matter of life and death. Just the sound of her voice could raise the blood pressure and cause heart palpitations in even the calmest of people.

'Hi, this is Sonja Hedström. We've got our hands full here with nervous campers and visitors. The public seem to think that this terrible murder has something to do with the fact that the man was staying at the campsite!'

As usual, the tourism director took it for granted that whoever she happened to be calling had all the time in the world to talk to her. She didn't ask whether she might be interrupting anything, even though the police were in the middle of a homicide investigation. Jacobsson did her best not to sound too annoyed.

'Is that right?'

'Yes. It had already started yesterday morning, and since then it has escalated, getting worse and worse.

And now the cancellations have started rolling in too. What if people decide they don't dare come over here? What if the murderer strikes again, at some other tourist destination?'

The high season was not very long on Gotland; it lasted about six weeks, from Midsummer's Eve until early August. During that time, between 300,000 and 400,000 tourists visited the island, which had only about 60,000 permanent residents. So of course the income from these tourists was essential. Jacobsson could understand why Sonja Hedström was so concerned.

'Tell the people who call that there's no indication that the murder has anything to do with camping or that particular campsite,' said Jacobsson. 'On the other hand, we really can't rule out anything, since we've just started the investigation.'

'The only thing that will calm the public down is if the police catch the murderer. How close are you to making an arrest?'

'Impossible to say at this point. The murder was committed only yesterday, you know.'

'And you really have no idea what this is all about? There must be some sort of clues at the crime scene, and I'm sure that lots of people must have noticed something. I mean, he was shot, after all, and the shots must have been heard in a wide area, and Sudersand was fully booked. Now lots of campers have decided to cut short their holidays and leave. Nobody is going to want to camp there after this. Do you realize what a disaster this is for the owner of the campsite?'

Great. Now it seemed Sonja Hedström also wanted to tell the police how to run a murder investigation.

'At the moment my primary sympathies are not with the owner of the campsite,' said Jacobsson dryly. 'And of course there are witnesses and evidence. That's exactly what I need to concentrate on right now instead of wasting time on unnecessary phone conversations.'

'You don't need to be so rude,' said Sonja Hedström, clearly insulted. 'Peter Bovide was a frequent visitor to the campsite, so it's not so strange that rumours have been spreading; they say the murderer must hate people with caravans, or something like that. I just wanted to know what I can tell people to reassure them, at least a little bit, but I guess I'll just have to wait until Anders gets back.'

The tourism director's voice was quivering with indignation, and with an abrupt click she hung up.

The blood instantly raced through Jacobsson's body, and with a flushed face she went out into the hall to get some water. That usually helped if she was feeling upset.

As she was drinking from her plastic cup, Thomas Wittberg showed up in the hall. As usual, he was more suntanned than anyone else; he wore a white T-shirt to show off his tan, and a pair of worn jeans. His curly blond hair was longer than normal and hung down into his eyes, which were barely visible.

'Hi, how's it going? You're looking like a thunder-cloud.'

'Don't ask,' Jacobsson said between clenched teeth. She turned her back to him as she filled another cup with water from the drinking fountain.

'That bad, huh? Well, I've got some news. Would that help?'

A couple of minutes later they were seated in Jacobsson's office. Wittberg had dropped on to the chair facing her desk.

'I just talked to the man who was captain of the Fårö ferry yesterday morning. He told me that on the first crossing at four a.m. there were only three cars on board. He always finds it amusing to study the passengers on the ferry, so that's why he remembers exactly who was sitting in those three cars. If the perp wasn't already on Fårö, then he would have had to take the four o'clock ferry across the sound. There aren't any earlier boats, and the one at five o'clock would have been too late.'

'And?'

'In the first car there was a young couple who looked as if they'd been partying in Visby all night. The driver of the second car was a pregnant woman, and in the third was a man with a horse trailer hitched to his car.'

'Does the captain remember what kind of cars they were driving?'

'That's what's so amazing. He not only remembers the colour and type of car, he can even tell us the licence plate numbers. He usually memorizes at least the letters.'

'What a guy! He should be a detective,' said Jacobsson with a laugh, forgetting her earlier annoyance. 'What's his name?'

'Bo Karlström. Sixty years old. From Fårösund.'

'Good. Get him in here ASAP. He might have actually seen the perp. And get started on looking for those people in the cars. We need to find out why they were going out to Fårö so early in the morning.'

When Emma Winarve drove into the car park near the Almedal library, part of her wanted to turn round and go straight back home. She cast a glance at her face in the mirror. She could see how pale she was under the sunburn, and there were bags under her eyes. Never mind. She was just going to leave Elin with Johan for a little while so she could go to the dentist. Nothing to get excited about.

She got out and opened the boot of the car. With some effort, she hauled out the pushchair and unfolded it. On the rack underneath she put Elin's bag, containing nappies, a baby bottle filled with water and a stuffed animal. Then she lifted her daughter out of the car and kissed her neck before she put her in the chair and stuck a dummy in her mouth. She straightened the child's cotton dress and patted her hair, which was pulled back in a ponytail. It had grown long and now reached all the way down her back. They headed toward Almedalen. The lovely park was right outside the Visby ring wall, an oasis between the town and the harbour.

The sun was blazing, and it was already hot. The park

was relatively deserted this early in the morning. An elderly woman was sitting on a bench, tossing bread-crumbs to the ducks in the pond, and a couple of early-rising mothers and their toddlers had settled on blankets which they'd spread out on the grass. Otherwise Emma saw mostly tourists who were on their way to the boats in the harbour, or to their cars, carrying all their beach paraphernalia as they headed for the sea.

Everything seemed so carefree in the summertime. The people she passed all seemed happy and relaxed as they chatted and laughed. It made her feel even more lonely and miserable. Was life so much easier for every-one else? Was there something wrong with her, something that somehow made her life more difficult?

They had agreed to meet outside the Packhus restaurant on Strandgatan, but as she approached the ring wall she had already caught sight of Johan as he came through the gate opening. He was looking the other way and hadn't yet seen her. She couldn't help it if she still found him attractive. His dark hair, those sinewy arms, his unshaven cheeks. He was wearing shorts, which revealed that his long legs were slightly bowed, and of course the obligatory trainers. Johan had never been interested in fashion.

For a few moments she pretended that nothing had changed between them, that they were simply about to meet and take a walk in the park with their daughter. That everything was fine.

She had just managed to convince herself how that would feel when he turned his head and saw her. She flushed when she noticed how his face lit up.

He waved and started towards her.

'Hi!'

'Hi,' she replied, sounding a bit strained.

He gave Elin a hug and planted a light kiss on Emma's cheek before she managed to pull away.

'Do you have time to keep us company for a bit?'

Of course she did; her dentist appointment wasn't for another half-hour.

'So how are you doing?' asked Johan as he took over the pushchair.

'OK, I suppose.'

They walked on in silence for a moment.

'It's so awful about that murder. Do you know anything more than what was reported in the papers?'

'And on the radio and TV, you mean?' he teased her. 'No, not really.'

'Pappa phoned. They were really upset because it happened so close to their house.'

'Yes, well, I'm not surprised at their reaction. Although I don't think they need to be scared. The murderer has probably left the island by now.'

The house belonging to Emma's parents was quite isolated, located on Fårö's north-eastern promontory.

'So I guess you're really under a lot of pressure right now.'

She studied his profile.

'Yes, but don't worry. We've got to do a follow-up report today, of course, but we'll make it. You'll be done around eleven, right?'

Emma noticed a trace of impatience in Johan's dark-brown eyes, which annoyed her. He always seemed to think his job was so damn important.

'Sure, probably even a little earlier.'

'All right. That'll be fine then.'

Emma took a pack of cigarettes out of her purse and lit one.

'I thought you'd given up.'

'I did, but I've started again,' she snapped.

She hadn't intended to sound so sharp, but it was too late now. She avoided meeting his eye.

'You don't need to be so grumpy. I didn't mean it as a criticism.'

It was impossible to ignore the resignation in his voice. And it drove her crazy. As if all it took was for her to light up one cigarette to ruin everything. That's how bad things were between them. They just couldn't get along. After five minutes, it was all spoiled.

They had reached the path that wound its way along the harbour. The waves were rolling in, calmly and steadily lapping against the pebbles on the beach. Now and then they met a bicyclist heading towards town.

Suddenly Emma had a great urge to be somewhere else. She stopped abruptly.

'I've got to go now.'

'Already?' Johan cast a glance at his watch.

'Yes.' She pressed her lips together for a second. 'Just keep on going, it's great for Elin to be near the water when there's a cool breeze blowing. I'll see you around eleven, back at Almedal library, OK?'

'Sure, that's fine. I'll tell Pia to meet me at the office so we can drive out to Fårö.'

'OK.'

In his mind he's already making plans to be on his way, she thought. She turned round and dashed off.

When she was out of sight, the tears came.

On the day after the murder Vendela Bovide was still in Visby hospital. Jacobsson gave her name at the reception desk and was asked to take a seat and wait until she could be allowed into the patient's room.

The sight of the young widow was distressing. She was sitting up in bed with several pillows behind her back. Her eyes were closed, and her face looked almost transparent. Her hair hung limply, dull and lifeless, the gown she was wearing was too big, and her hands were clasped on top of the blanket. Her despair filled the room like a heavy cloud.

Jacobsson greeted the woman without getting a response and then glanced around the room, feeling a bit lost. There was a chair standing in the corner. Cautiously she pulled it forward and sat down next to the bed.

'Where are my children?' asked Vendela Bovide, her voice weak.

'They're with your husband's parents.'

'Where?'

'They live in Slite, don't they?'

Jacobsson fidgeted, feeling uneasy as she considered

whether to call a nurse. The woman in the bed seemed rather out of it. Barely twenty-four hours had passed since she'd learned that her husband had been murdered.

Her expression scared Jacobsson. During all her years in the police force, she had talked with a great many people who had lost someone they loved, but she'd never before witnessed such complete withdrawal and bottled-up despair as that exhibited by this woman in the bed. It was so strong it actually made the air hard to breathe.

Jacobsson wanted either to leave at once or else take the woman in her arms to console her. Just sitting there doing nothing seemed absurd.

'I'm sorry to have to bother you,' she began. 'My name is Karin Jacobsson, and I'm in charge of the investigation. We spoke on the phone yesterday.'

Almost imperceptibly, Vendela Bovide nodded.

'Let me start by offering my condolences. Are you ready to answer some questions?'

Silence.

'Do you know what time it was when Peter left to go running yesterday morning?'

'It was 5.35.'

'How can you be so precise?'

'I glanced at the clock when he left.'

'So you were awake? Did you talk to him before he took off?'

'Yes.'

'How did he seem?'

71

'The same as always.'

'How was that?'

'Cheerful. He was going to make breakfast when he came back. And put the coffee on. That was the last thing he said.'

'Did he usually go running in the morning?'

'That was his regular routine, all year round.'

'And at about the same time?'

'Yes.'

'Both weekdays and weekends?'

'Every day. He was a man of habit. Peter liked routines.'

'Why was that?'

'Because he was insecure.'

'Do you know why?'

'No, he never talked about it.'

'But there was something worrying him?'

'I think so.'

Her voice faded. Vendela turned her head so she could look out of the window.

'What do you think it might have been?'

'I don't know. Maybe something to do with the company.'

'Why would he be worried about that?'

'It's not easy running a company, you know . . .'

'According to his partner, Johnny Ekwall, Peter thought he was being watched. Do you know anything about that?'

A faint twitch of an eyebrow.

'No, nothing. Watched? No, he never said anything about that.'

'Are you sure?'

'Yes.'

'And apparently he'd received some anonymous phone calls at the office. Did you know about that?'

'No. I think we did get some calls that were wrong numbers, but that was a long time ago.'

Vendela's hands were picking nervously at the covers.

Either she was telling the truth or there was some reason she didn't want to admit that her husband thought he was being spied on. More likely the latter, but Jacobsson chose not to ask any more questions on that subject until later.

'How was the company doing?'

'Good. At least that's what he told me.'

'OK. But you don't know anything about company operations or the book-keeping?'

'No.'

Jacobsson paused for a moment and glanced down at the notepad she was holding on her lap.

'Could you tell from your personal finances that things were going well at the company?'

'Yes. It meant that we could take a holiday. This time of year we usually go camping, but we've never been able to afford a trip abroad. We were supposed to go to Mallorca after two weeks on Fårö. He'd booked a four-star hotel. I thought it was too expensive, but he was so determined, and he said we could afford it.

He thought we deserved it after all the work involved in starting the company. The years when our kids were babies were really tough for me; he was working almost all the time.'

Vendela began sobbing. She took a tissue from a box on the bedside table and loudly blew her nose.

'Why did you happen to choose the Sudersand campsite?'

'We've gone there for several years, every holiday. Peter loved that campsite. He knew the owner. He reserved the same spot for us every year.'

'Did you also socialize with the owner?'

'No, almost never. Mats – that's the owner's name – works at the campsite all summer long, and as soon as the holidays are over, he and his wife go somewhere on the Black Sea. She's from that area.'

Jacobsson's pen raced to keep up as she took notes. For a moment she pondered what Vendela had just told her. The woman's answers to her questions were quite lucid, considering her condition only a few minutes ago.

'When Peter left the caravan yesterday morning, was that the last time you saw him?'

'Yes.'

'What did you do after he left?'

'I couldn't sleep any more, so I got up and made coffee. I decided to stay inside the caravan because it had rained all night. I drank my coffee and did a cross-word puzzle.'

'And after that?'

'A couple of hours must have passed, and then the kids woke up.'

'What time was that?'

'Maybe around eight.'

'Didn't you wonder why Peter hadn't come back?'

'Yes, I did, but sometimes he stayed down at the beach and did callisthenics and then took a swim. I didn't think it was so strange. The sun had come out rather quickly, you know.'

'When did you start getting worried about his absence?'

'I ate breakfast with the kids. They were watching a children's programme on TV. By the time I'd cleaned up and made the beds it was eight thirty. That's when I started to wonder where he was.'

'Were you worried?'

'Not really. But around ten o'clock the kids and I walked down to the beach, and there we saw that a big crowd had gathered. Later the police rang.'

In a matter of seconds the controlled façade had shattered, and Vendela Bovide again started sobbing loudly.

Jacobsson put her hand on the woman's arm. Vendela yanked her arm away as if she'd been burned.

'Don't touch me,' she snarled so vehemently that saliva sprayed from her lips. 'He's the only one who's allowed to touch me. Do you understand?'

Jacobsson gave a start. She had been completely

unprepared for such an outburst. She shoved her chair back as far as it would go, and for a while she didn't say a word. There were still some questions that she wanted to ask. She sincerely hoped that Vendela wasn't about to lose all control.

The woman's sobs gradually diminished enough that Jacobsson dared continue the conversation.

'Do you know whether your husband had any enemies? I mean, did he ever receive any threats, or was there anybody who was particularly hostile towards him?'

A shadow passed over Vendela's face.

'No. I don't know.'

'You don't know?'

'I don't think so. Peter was a very generous man, and everybody liked him. He was kind and helpful and hardly ever disagreed with anyone. He hated any sort of conflict. It was the same in our relationship. We hardly ever argued.'

Vendela Bovide's voice was fading, and Jacobsson could tell that it was time to stop. The woman's thin body slumped lower on the bed.

'So what was Peter like? Was he happy?'

Vendela hesitated before answering. She looked as if she were seriously mulling over the question. As if it were something new to consider, and unexpected.

'I think he was happy, at least as happy as he could be.'

'I realize this is difficult for you,' said Jacobsson

sympathetically. 'But I'm afraid I have to ask these questions so that we can catch the person who did this as soon as possible. Has anything unusual happened lately?'

'No.'

'Did the two of you, or maybe just Peter, happen to meet anybody new?'

Vendela Bovide seemed to be considering what to say. Again she answered in the negative.

'Do you have a job too?'

'Yes, I work part-time at a beauty salon in Visby, every other Saturday.'

'What's it called?'

'Sofia's Nails and Beauty.'

Jacobsson wrote down the name in her notepad.

'Is there anything else?'

Jacobsson noticed a momentary hesitation before Vendela replied.

'Sometimes I work as a croupier at the Casino Cosmopol in Stockholm.'

'I see. How often?'

'Once a month. I go over on Friday afternoon, work all weekend and then come back home on Sunday afternoon. My sister and mother live in Stockholm, so I usually stay with my sister in Söder.'

'OK.'

'And my mother-in-law helps out with the children while I'm away.'

'I understand.'

It was time to stop. She thanked the woman for her help and left the room.

By then Vendela Bovide had slipped down until she was lying flat on the bed, gazing vacantly out of the window. She already seemed to have forgotten all about Karin Jacobsson.

After Johan had handed Elin back to Emma when she returned from her dentist's appointment, he walked up the hill from the harbour and through the town's winding lanes, then out of the gate on the other side. The Swedish TV and Radio building, which also housed the editorial office of Regional News, was located on the south-east side of town, a short distance beyond the ring wall.

He paid no attention to any of the passers-by; he was still seeing Emma in his mind. He passed the Café Vinäger on Hästgatan, where he had kissed her for the first time. A fleeting kiss, but the memory was etched into his body. Back then neither of them had any idea what was in store for them. Would he have subjected himself to all this trouble if he'd known ahead of time? Yes, of course. If nothing else, because of Elin.

He took the road past Söderport and bought an ice-cream cone at the kiosk. Standing in front of him in the queue were two kids about the same age as Sara and Filip, Emma's other children. He'd managed to build a relationship with them over the past two years. Were all his efforts now going to be in vain? And most important of all: Elin. He loved his daughter. Was she going to grow up seeing him only every other weekend? The thought was unbearable.

Why did it have to be so difficult? Emma was still holding back, and the situation with her seemed deadlocked. He found it impossible to talk to her. He could make no headway, even though he'd tried every imaginable tactic. Everything from being gentle, positive, sweet and undemanding to behaving like a shrill martyr who complained that she didn't care about him at all. Finally he'd tried to be as distant and indifferent as she was. Nothing worked. Did she have no feelings for him any more? In the spring, when she broke off the engagement, she had gone to stay with her parents on Fårö, taking Elin with her and refusing to see him. Johan's life had fallen apart. For the first time, he sank into what felt like a depression, and he lost all interest in life. He sought help from a counsellor at the corporate health service who had steered him through the crisis. Now he didn't know whether he even had the energy to try again.

When he arrived at the TV and Radio building he paused to smoke a cigarette. He had to push all of these thoughts aside. Maybe he should just stay away from Emma for a while and focus on his work. The murder investigation should keep him busy, at least for the next few days.

He went in through the front door, said hello to the

receptionist and went up the stairs to the Regional News office.

Pia Lilja was already there. Her eyes were fixed on her computer screen.

'Hi,' she said, taking a pinch of snuff without shifting her gaze.

Her hair was pinned up in a sort of straggly knot that strongly resembled a bird's nest. Her eyes were heavily made up, as usual, and a fiery red gemstone glittered on one nostril. Her lips were painted as red as the gemstone.

'Hi, how's it going? Nice hair-do.' To tease her, Johan tugged on one of the wisps of hair sticking straight up. 'Now what could we use this for? A pen holder?'

'Ha, ha. Very funny,' she muttered, although she couldn't help smiling a bit.

'It looks cool. I mean it.'

Pia had her own style and attitude, which he liked.

'Anything new turn up yet?' He looked over her shoulder.

'No, not really. But check this out. These pictures were on the front page.'

Photos of the police helicopter on the beach were spread all over the evening newspapers.

'You should get paid for those.'

'Fat chance. But I'm happy to get the photo credit. Oh, by the way, Grenfors rang. He wants to talk to you.'

'So why doesn't he ring my mobile?' scoffed Johan. The editor-in-chief was not his favourite person.

Pia took her eyes off her computer and turned to face him.

'Because it's switched off. I tried ringing you too.'

'Shit.'

He dug out his mobile from the pocket of his jeans and plugged it in to recharge.

'OK, what's on the schedule for today?'

'Hopefully we'll find out more about who the murder victim is and how he was killed. The police have announced a press conference for three o'clock this afternoon. Before then, I think it would be a good idea for us to drive up to Sudersand. Find out what the mood's like on the day after, you know. Talk to people, and not just those staying at the campsite, but people who work there too. Apparently the victim had been there several days with his family. Maybe they'd made friends with somebody; I'm sure plenty of people will have something to say. But ring Max first and find out what he wants.'

'Sure.'

The editor-in-chief sounded stressed.

'Good you rang. So what do we know now?'

'No more than we did yesterday. I just got to the office. Haven't even had a chance to check the TT wire yet.'

'I've had a meeting with the national news guys, and everybody wants to use your report again today. Preferably before lunch.'

'Excuse me for laughing. Not a chance in hell.'

'Couldn't the two of you put together a quick interview with the police? So we have something to give them?'

Johan could feel the heat rising to his cheeks. It always upset him that Regional News had to kowtow to the more important national news division, supplying them with all sorts of material at the expense of their own broadcasts.

'If we do that, how do you think we'll have time to drive up to Fårö? To take day-after pictures and do interviews and try to ferret out some of our own information? Besides, the police have announced a press conference for three o'clock. How are we going to attend that if we have to put together some shitty report to keep the national news guys happy? They should send over their own reporter.'

'Take it easy. It was just a thought. I'll talk to them. They've already mentioned sending somebody over. So I suppose they might as well do it sooner than later. With a camera person. I realize it's too much for you to handle. I'll get back to you.'

Johan ended the conversation and glared at Pia, who patted him on the shoulder.

'Come on,' she said, trying to console him. 'Let's get going.'

At Sudersand campsite on Fårö, there was hardly any sign of the murder drama from the previous day. At least not at first glance. Tourists were picking up brochures from the check-in desk, taking the path down to the beach and going to the cafeteria. No police officers or police tape in sight.

An elderly grey-haired woman sat behind the front desk.

'Hello,' she greeted them automatically. 'How can I help you?'

Johan introduced himself and Pia, causing the woman to raise her eyebrows with interest.

'We'd like to know more about the man who was shot yesterday,' Johan began. 'Who was he? And how long had he been here?'

'The police told me not to say a word to any reporters.'

The woman pressed her lips together as if to demonstrate and gave them a suspicious look.

'Of course, and we respect that. But maybe you could tell us something about the sort of reactions you've witnessed here today. When we arrived, Pia and I were surprised to see that nobody seems the least bit upset. Everybody here seems very calm and collected. If nothing else, surely it can't hurt to do a report for TV on what the day after the murder is like. To show that the campsite is functioning normally, I mean. Have you had any cancellations?'

'Not very many, actually.'

'Would you mind talking about that while we film? I'd think it would be in your interest to show the viewers that everything is OK here, right?'

Johan was ashamed of stooping to this sort of veiled threat, but he felt no sympathy for the stern-looking woman sitting behind the counter.

He watched as she debated with herself for a few seconds.

'No,' she said, pursing her lips. 'Not interested. And I'm going to have to ask you to leave now. And take that camera with you.'

The same instant she made her decision, a man came inside. He was tall and lanky, with tousled hair. He was carrying a stack of cigarette cartons. He introduced himself as Mats Nilsson, owner of the campsite.

'Hi,' said Johan, ignoring the scowling elderly woman. 'We're from Regional News. Have you got a minute?'

'All right, sure.'

'Could we go outside to talk?'

'OK. I need a smoke anyway.'

Outside, they explained what they'd like to film, and after they had talked to the campsite owner for a few minutes, his face lit up.

'Now I know who you are,' he exclaimed, jabbing Johan in the stomach. 'I recognize you from TV.'

'Oh, really?'

Mats Nilsson let out a bellow of laughter, displaying his nicotine-stained teeth. Johan stared at him, un-comprehending.

'You and Emma are an item, right? Emma Winarve?'

'Well . . .' Johan said, hesitating.

'You even have a kid together. I read all about it in the newspaper. I dated Emma in the ninth grade; she was in the other class. She was damned cute back then, a lot prettier than she is now. Even though she had rather small . . . well, you know what I mean.'

He pointed at his chest.

Johan wondered if he'd heard this guy correctly. He felt Pia looking at him, and sensed how close she was to delivering a crushing remark to the unpleasant campsite owner. Even Johan had to make the utmost effort not to punch the guy in the face. He made a lightning-quick decision about which tactic would be best in this situation, and he chose to focus on their report, which meant assuming an ingratiating attitude. Even at his own expense.

'Right. How cool. So I guess we have something in common.'

He managed a strained smile. Nilsson didn't seem to

notice his sarcastic tone of voice, and Johan quickly changed the subject.

'How are things going here after that young man was shot yesterday?'

The campsite owner's face clouded over.

'I wouldn't call him young. Peter was over forty. Bloody awful, the whole thing.'

Johan was all ears. The police hadn't yet revealed the victim's identity. It was important to tread lightly.

'Did you know him?'

'Yes I did, quite well in fact. He and his wife have come here several years in a row, and after a while I get to know all the regular campers. It's a bleeding shame he had to go and get himself shot. Makes me wonder what was behind it.'

'Is it OK if I film you while we're talking?' asked Pia.

'Sure, go ahead.'

'What's Peter's last name?'

'Bovide.'

'How long had he and his family been here before this happened?'

'Just over the weekend. They arrived Friday night and were supposed to stay two weeks. They do that every year. And they like to have the same camping spot each time. Before they left, he would always reserve it for the following year.'

'Where is it located?'

He nodded towards the campsite.

'It's number fifty-three, the very last space, you know,

and the one closest to the beach. There's a sign, but right now the area is blocked off so you won't be able to see it. It's the space they had the first summer they were here, and since then they've never wanted to park their caravan anywhere else. Even though there's no electrical hook-up over there; they have to run everything on liquefied natural gas, but that works fine.'

'So he was married and had kids?'

'Of course. His wife's name is Vendela, and they have two children, a little girl and a boy.'

'How old are they?'

'Not very old. Maybe three and five, something like that. But how the hell would I know? I haven't got any kids myself.'

'Where are they from?'

'Slite, so they didn't have far to drive, you might say.'

'Do you know what kind of work he did?'

'Sure, he was a carpenter, and he had his own construction company. He was really good at his job. And always willing to lend a hand. He did quite a bit of carpentry work for me, so I gave him a good discount on the camping fee and made sure he got the spot he wanted. I felt like I needed to pay him back in some way. I know that he also helped out other people here at the campsite if they were having trouble with something. He could fix almost anything.'

'What's the name of the company?'

'Slite Construction.'

'What was Peter like as a person?'

'A real decent guy. There's no doubt about that. But he did have some odd habits.'

'Like what?'

'Well, he went out running every single morning, for example. And it was always so damn early. I used to see him sometimes if I had to be here extra early for the bread delivery or something like that. You'd always see him out running before six.'

Johan was so fascinated by all the information that came pouring out of the man standing in front of him that he almost forgot that he was doing an interview. He pulled himself together and changed direction.

'How did you react when you heard about the murder?'

'I was shocked, you know. To think that somebody could end up getting killed here. And to top it off, it was somebody that I actually happened to know. And to think he was killed in such an awful way. Shot dead, and with multiple bullet wounds. A gangster-style execution right here in our little campsite.'

'How has the murder affected the other campers?'

'Of course they're nervous. I've been forced to keep the check-in desk open round the clock since it happened. Lots of campers have been over here to ask questions.'

'What are they asking about?'

'They want to know what happened, how he was killed, and whether the murderer has been caught. They think I have all the answers. I have to supply information and also play the roles of psychologist and master detective. And I really don't know much. At any rate, I don't think it was anyone who's been staying here at the campsite.'

'Why not?'

'Well, who would it be? The campers are all completely ordinary citizens who just want to spend their holiday in peace and quiet. Why would any of them go around with a gun and start killing people? You can hear for yourself how unlikely that sounds.'

There was a plaintive note in the man's voice, and Johan gave him an encouraging nod so he'd keep talking.

'You must have given the whole episode a lot of thought. Has anything happened lately that might have some bearing on the murder?'

'No, nothing. Everything has been the same as usual. The weather hasn't been great, but most people have seemed perfectly happy, at least I think so. We haven't had any complaints or anything like that.'

'No strangers acting suspiciously?'

Nilsson shook his head, looking gloomy. Johan had the feeling that the reality of what had happened so close to his peaceful campsite was just beginning to sink in.

'Have you had any cancellations since the murder?'

'A bunch of people left as soon as they found out what had happened, and we've had about twenty or thirty phone calls with cancellations. But plenty of people have actually stayed, especially our regular campers. About 80 per cent of the campers are regulars, you know; they come back year after year. Most of them are from Gotland, and they probably realize that this was a one-off occurrence.'

'What about you? How sure are you of that?'

'Of course you never know, but I have a hard time imagining that we're dealing with a serial killer who's only interested in killing campers on Fårö. What do you think?'

Johan left the question unanswered.

By the time Karin Jacobsson got back to police head-quarters after her interview with Vendela Bovide, Thomas Wittberg had already located the passengers who had been aboard the first ferry to cross Fårösund the previous morning.

The captain of the ferry had remembered enough of the licence plate numbers to allow the police to track down the vehicle owners.

'It was easier than I thought to get hold of these people,' Wittberg told Jacobsson with satisfaction as they sat down across from each other in her office.

He brushed the shock of blond hair out of his eyes and began his report.

'Let's start with the young couple. They're from Gotland and had been spending the past week on holiday on Fårö. They'd been out partying in Visby and were on their way back. That's why they took such an early ferry. They're renting a cottage from a farm family. We've asked the couple to be here at one o'clock for an interview. They'll be going home on a boat this afternoon.'

'OK, we'll have to wait and see whether we should let them go.'

'The woman travelling by herself is married and lives in Kyllaj.'

'All year round? I thought there were only summer homes out there.'

'No, she and her family actually live there permanently, but I think they're practically the only ones. There might be one other family.'

Karin had been out to Kyllaj only once in her life. It had been for a summertime party when she was thirteen, and she'd had her first kiss down at the beach. It was a lovely memory, and the little village by the sea had a special place in her heart.

She pushed the thought aside.

'Will she be coming in too?'

'No. She's pregnant, and fairly far along from what I understand. She asked if we could do the interview on the phone, but I explained that wasn't possible; we need to see her in person. Apparently she has a hard time getting around; she said something about pelvic girdle pain.'

'If she's about to give birth, she probably has other things on her mind besides our investigation, but of course she might have seen something,' said Jacobsson. 'I'd be happy to go out to Kyllaj; I haven't been there since I was thirteen. But I can't make it today. Find out if she noticed anything out of the ordinary, and we'll have to make do with that for the time being. By the way, what was she doing on the Fårö ferry at four in the morning?'

'She said that she can't sleep at night now that she's pregnant and it's so hot, so she likes to drive around and take a look at the countryside when there's no traffic. She hasn't lived here very long. And it's still light almost all night long.'

'That sounds a bit odd, but I've heard that pregnant women can come up with all sorts of weird ideas. What about the third car, with the horse trailer?'

'It belongs to a farmer on Fårö. His son had gone over to the mainland to buy a horse, and he arrived by the night boat from Nynäshamn. The family has run their farm on Fårö for many years.'

'Darn it.' Jacobsson spun her chair around. 'I had high hopes the perp would turn out to be someone on the ferry. But I suppose that would have been too easy. How often do we run into someone who's as observant and has such a good memory as that captain?'

'But we don't have to give up hope yet. We still have to interview the passengers.'

'Sure, but the most likely scenario is that Peter Bovide's killer was already on Fårö on the morning of the murder, meaning that he had slept there overnight. And we can't rule out the possibility that he's still on the island. Let's keep checking everyone leaving on the ferries for a few more days.'

Jacobsson had just finished a phone conversation with the fraud division, asking them to look into the finances of Peter Bovide's company, when she heard voices out in the hall. Her colleagues from the NCP had arrived. She smiled to herself when she recognized Martin Kihlgård's bellowing voice mixed with the laughter and happy shouts of the others. As soon as the inspector made his appearance in the corridors of police headquarters, the mood always improved considerably. The mere sight of him brought smiles to the faces of his co-workers. Martin Kihlgård was close to 6 foot 3 inches tall and he weighed well over 220 pounds. He never bothered to comb his hair, which stuck out in all directions in the strangest way. His eyes were big and round, giving the impression that he was staring attentively at whoever he happened to be talking to.

'Hi, Karin,' he exclaimed heartily when he caught sight of his significantly smaller colleague. A foot shorter and weighing only half as much as Kihlgård, she practically drowned in his embrace.

'Hi, it's great you're here.'

Jacobsson returned his bear hug as best she could, glimpsing several more colleagues from Stockholm standing behind the huge inspector.

The entire investigative team immediately gathered in the meeting room. A tray of coffee and cold drinks was brought in, along with a platter of fresh fruit. Jacobsson had specifically requested a more healthy alternative for refreshments at their meetings, instead of the usual cinnamon rolls and *Wienerbröd* pastries. She noted with amusement the look of disappointment on Martin Kihlgård's face.

'I heard that Knutie is on holiday,' said Kihlgård as they all sat down.

'Yes,' said Jacobsson. 'He's in Denmark with his family. His wife is Danish, you know.'

'Lina, yes. Terribly attractive woman. And what a sense of humour. They're a lot of fun, those Danes.'

'Right.'

Jacobsson felt a sudden stab of annoyance. She wasn't sure why. But it was gone as abruptly as it had appeared.

'When will he be back?'

'In a week.'

'Uh-huh.'

Kihlgård ran his eyes over the table. Presumably in search of a treat, thought Jacobsson. He was the most voracious glutton and had the biggest sweet tooth of anybody she'd ever met.

She asked each of her colleagues to introduce themselves briefly before she turned to Wittberg.

'You've compiled all the interviews, Thomas. What do they tell us?'

'The murder took place just after six yesterday morning. We can pin that down with some certainty because a couple living in a cabin near the crime scene heard the shots while they were listening to the news broadcast on the radio. They both heard at least five or six shots. They didn't call the police because they were convinced somebody was just out shooting rabbits. A lot of that goes on in the area – poachers hunting rabbits, that is,' he said, turning to his colleagues from Stockholm. 'In the peaceful terrain of Fårö we would hardly expect somebody to be murdered.'

'They still could have called the police,' objected Kihlgård. 'It's illegal to shoot rabbits!'

'I know,' admitted Wittberg. 'But the people who live on Fårö are so used to it that nobody pays any attention any more.'

'At any rate, there's nothing to contradict the witnesses' statement as to the time of the murder,' said Sohlman. 'Peter Bovide probably died instantly from the first shot, the one that struck his forehead. And he'd been dead for three and a half hours before he was found.'

Sohlman got up and pulled down the white screen at the front of the room. He turned off the lights and switched on his computer. A detailed map of the bay and the campsite at Sudersand appeared on the screen.

'If he left the caravan just after five thirty, he should have reached this point no later than five or ten minutes before six o'clock. It takes about fifteen or twenty minutes to run to the other end of the beach.'

Sohlman pointed with his pen to indicate the route that Bovide must have taken. Nobody said a word.

'Somewhere along here on the beach, at the water's edge, he encountered his killer. His footprints were still in the sand when we searched the area. Judging by the bloodstains on the sand and the way the body had fallen, it seems that the victim was first shot in the forehead. He toppled over on to the sand, then the perpetrator took a few steps forward and continued to fire – we're talking about no fewer than seven shots to the abdomen. After that the body was dragged into the water, where it drifted out quite a distance, at least twenty to thirty yards. That's not so strange, considering the offshore wind that we had yesterday morning.'

Sohlman tugged at a lock of his hair, a habit of his, and then went on.

'We've found two empty shell casings on the beach, but no bullets. They're probably all still in the body. The post mortem is being done right now, so we'll have to wait for the preliminary report.'

'Yes, I'm hoping to get it some time this evening,' said Jacobsson. 'Now I think we should discuss what the motive might be for the murder. What sort of options do you see? I'd like all of us to do some brainstorming on the subject. Feel free to voice your opinions.'

Her colleagues, who had worked with Knutas for aeons, now looked at her in astonishment. They weren't used to anything like this, being asked to speculate about possible scenarios with so few facts on the table. Knutas detested speculation. Wittberg was the first to respond.

'If he was shot just after six o'clock but arrived at the site five or ten minutes before six, then the question is: what did Peter Bovide do during the last minutes of his life?'

'Maybe he injured himself while he was running and had to stop. Or maybe he was simply tired and needed to take a break,' suggested Jacobsson.

'Why would he be tired after only a few kilometres?' objected Wittberg. 'He'd been going out to run every day for years. Maybe he stopped to talk to the perp before he was shot to death.'

'That sounds to me like a more plausible explanation,' interjected Kihlgård. 'The victim and the perp might have known each other.'

'Another possibility is that he happened upon an armed madman who was bent on killing somebody,' Jacobsson went on. 'Any random victim.'

'The question we need to ask,' said Kihlgård, 'is why would a carpenter and the father of two young children from Slite be shot in cold blood at a campsite while out for his usual morning jog? It sounds completely unbelievable when put into words. Especially since it all takes place on peaceful little Fårö.'

'Don't say that,' Wittberg protested. 'Keep in mind that we had the manhunt of the century on Fårö just a few years ago. You remember Emma Winarve, don't you? You were really taken by her.'

'Oh, that's right,' said Kihlgård, his face lighting up. 'By the way, is she still together with that pesky TV reporter?'

'I have no idea.' Wittberg threw out his hands. 'They had a baby together and everything but apparently things kind of fell apart for them.'

'All right then,' Jacobsson interrupted her colleagues. 'Let's keep on topic. You can do all the gossiping you want later on.'

She gave them a stern look.

'According to Peter Bovide's partner, the victim had recently felt that he was being watched. Johnny Ekwall couldn't say exactly what was going on, but Peter had mentioned several times that he thought somebody was tailing him. He had also received anonymous phone calls at the office. Apparently there was nobody on the line, but from what I understand, the calls gave Bovide the jitters.'

'When did all this start?' asked Kihlgård.

'Several weeks ago.'

'And he'd never received any threats before?'

'Not as far as I know.'

'If the phone calls and the feeling that he was being

shadowed began at the same time, there must be something to it,' Kihlgård went on. 'And of course it reinforces the theory that the perpetrator had specifically targeted Bovide. We need to find out if anybody else can confirm this information. I'd be happy to follow up on the lead.'

'Fine,' said Jacobsson. 'The strange thing is that his wife denies knowing anything about it, and yet they seem to have had a good relationship.'

'Maybe he didn't want to worry her,' Wittberg interjected. 'Maybe he was mixed up in something shady and wanted to keep her out of it.'

'That's possible, of course,' said Jacobsson. 'Or maybe we should be focusing our efforts on the wife. She works in a casino in Stockholm. And in the gambling business there are plenty of sleazy characters, as you well know.'

'So you think it could be some sort of revenge directed against her?' said Kihlgård.

'Maybe, maybe not. Or the wife could be the next victim. How do I know? We need to ask Stockholm to help us by interviewing Vendela's co-workers at the casino.'

'Wasn't Peter Bovide found guilty of assault and battery?' Wittberg tossed out. 'Of course it was a long time ago and it happened only once, but you never know. I'll check up on it.'

Jacobsson nodded pensively and scribbled a note on her pad of paper.

'How long had he been at the campsite? A few days?' Wittberg went on. 'And he went out at approximately the same time every morning to run practically the same route?'

'Yes,' said Jacobsson. 'His wife confirmed that when I interviewed her earlier today.'

'So it seems very likely that the perp was keeping an eye on him and took note of his usual routines. That would also confirm what his partner said about Bovide feeling he was being watched. The murderer then chose the most advantageous time and place to kill him, meaning down near the end of the beach and at six in the morning when everybody was in bed asleep.'

'In other words, the killer was presumably at the campsite, at least during the weekend, and he may have even been staying there,' said Kihlgård.

'Naturally we'll need to keep that possibility open,' said Jacobsson. 'If you look at the layout of the area, you can see that you have to walk downhill a bit to reach the beach.'

Erik Sohlman stood up and pointed to the map.

'Evidently the perp was on foot. We're continuing to interview witnesses, and it seems likely that somebody will have noticed him, even though it was so early. At this time of year, there are people out at all hours of the day and night.'

Jacobsson turned to Sohlman.

'Do we know anything about the weapon?'

'Only that it was probably a handgun, judging by the

bullet wounds and the empty casings that we found. We'll have to see what SCL comes up with.'

'This afternoon we'll be conducting several more important interviews,' Jacobsson went on. 'Thomas?'

Wittberg reported on the observations that had been made by the captain of the first ferry. While he was talking, Jacobsson noticed that Kihlgård was getting restless.

'Interesting,' he said when Wittberg was finished with his report. 'Is it lunchtime yet?'

For a change, head office reacted swiftly to Johan's demands. On Tuesday afternoon, as he and Pia were on their way back to their office, his mobile rang. Johan was startled when he recognized the voice. It was Madeleine Haga, a reporter for the national TV news. She and cameraman Peter Bylund had just arrived on Gotland and were staying at the Strand Hotel.

They agreed to meet at the editorial office.

Johan had known Madeleine for several years. Once, long ago, it had seemed as if something might develop between then, but the spark had fizzled out before any sort of relationship got started. Then he was sent to Gotland, and he met Emma. Since then, there had been no other woman in his life.

When Madeleine came into the Regional News office on Östra Hansegatan in Visby, he couldn't help taking notice. She had just returned from a holiday trip to Spain and was deeply tanned. A petite brunette wearing a denim skirt and a blouse, and with a cleavage that should have been considered too risqué for a reporter. Her big brown eyes were shining.

'Hi,' she said cheerfully.

He got up from his computer to give her a hug. She smelled faintly of lemon.

'Hi.'

The cameraman, Peter Bylund, appeared right behind her. Johan gave him a hug too.

'What a surprise to see you here again,' said Johan. 'How was Russia?'

Peter Bylund had worked with Johan for a summer several years earlier. The summer he'd met Emma. Peter had also been a bit infatuated with her.

'Good, thanks. Of course, Moscow is totally changed compared to ten years ago, when I was there last. It's a completely different city.'

'How long were you there this time?'

'It's been almost two years now. I can't believe it myself, but it's true.'

'You'll have to tell me more later, but it's damn good you're here, at any rate.'

'What about yourself? You and Emma? I heard that the two of you had a baby and everything.'

'Yes, we have a daughter, Elin. She's just turned one. She's the most amazing child in the world.'

'Jeez, that's something – you a father. I wouldn't have believed it.' Peter slapped him on the back.

Johan's face clouded over.

'Things aren't going very well, as a matter of fact; it's been pretty rocky, you might say.'

'OK, well, we don't need to talk about it now.'

Madeleine was looking at Johan with interest, though she didn't say a word. Peter patted his shoulder.

'So what's next on the agenda?'

Pia came back from the bathroom. She said hello to the two from Stockholm and sat down in front of her computer.

'We're in the process of uploading the material. Do you want to check it out?'

'Absolutely,' said Peter, whose face had lit up at the sight of Pia. He sat down next to her. Johan and Madeleine sat down on the other side.

'We won't have time to put together anything for today, but just let me know if you want me to do a short piece for the national news,' Madeleine offered.

Johan hesitated. It would actually be a big help; he was feeling super-stressed and would like nothing more than to get the report done as soon as possible. At the same time, he didn't like just turning over his material to another reporter. But he trusted Madeleine.

'Sure, go ahead.'

Grenfors would be pleased. Johan cast a glance at his newly arrived colleagues – he really liked both of them.

He was glad they were here.

HAMBURG, 15 JULY 1985

*F*ive more hours before the plane left for Sweden. They were up early to pack, and Vera suspected that her father hadn't slept a wink all night. By six o'clock she could hear him pottering about in the kitchen. Neatly lined up on her bed were piles of clothes ready to be packed.

'Keep in mind that you don't need to take a lot of clothes along. And nothing fancy,' called Oleg from the kitchen. 'We're going to be living outdoors – far away from civilization!'

Vera studied the piles: knickers, bras, bikinis, shorts, blouses, a few skirts and dresses, jeans and a heavy sweater.

That should be enough, she decided as she began stuffing items into her rucksack.

'What are you taking along?'

Tanya stuck her head into her big sister's room.

Her hair was pinned up in an untidy knot, her cheeks were flushed, and her eyes were shining. Tanya was at least as ecstatic as their father about this trip. She was nineteen and had never been out of Germany before.

'All of this.'

Vera gestured towards the bed. Tanya looked at the piles,

checked the contents of the rucksack and took out a couple of articles of clothing.

'That's all?'

'Yes, why?'

'But don't you think we'll have a chance to go out dancing a few times, you and I? At least in Stockholm or Visby?'

She gave her sister a poke in the side.

'I'd like to have some fun with those luscious Swedes. We can't miss out on the opportunity, since we're there anyway. They're supposed to be the cutest guys in the world, you know!'

'Do you really believe that?'

'My god, haven't you seen the pictures? And the Swedish girls are world-famous – so why shouldn't the men look just as beautiful?'

'I suppose you're right,' said Vera with a laugh as she opened her wardrobe. 'Of course we should take along something cute. And of course we'll go out. I could do with a little fun too.'

A week ago Gotthard had suddenly broken up with her. He'd met somebody else while he was on holiday in Portugal. And to make matters worse, it was a Swedish girl.

Unlike her younger sister, she never had any luck with boys. And she really didn't understand why. She and her sister were very much alike, except that they had different temperaments. Vera was more serious and pensive. She lacked her sister's spontaneity. Sometimes she wished she could be more like her little sister, more open, happier, more outgoing. Especially when she saw how Tanya stole all the attention, even from their parents. But that wasn't just because of her personality. Vera was well aware of the reason, but it still hurt. Tanya had been diagnosed with leukaemia when she was thirteen, and she'd been seriously ill for a long time. Their parents had been numb with shock and despair, and they had devoted all their time to Tanya. Vera had been forced to fend for herself as best she could. And she'd had to cope alone with her own sorrow and distress about her sister.

But everything had turned out well in the end. Tanya had undergone an intensive treatment and her body was now free of cancer. Slowly but surely she had returned to her old self, becoming even stronger and more energetic than she'd been before. Of course Vera was thrilled that Tanya had pulled through; at the same time, their parents' love and concern for her sister had increased even more after her illness.

Occasionally, when their father talked and laughed with Tanya while Vera was also in the room, he would cast a glance at his older daughter, as if he'd suddenly noticed her and was surprised that she was there too. Then he would sometimes look shamefaced, as if he'd been caught out. That was almost worse.

Strangely enough, Vera harboured no grudge towards her sister for this great imbalance that existed between them. Not any more. It had been worse when they were younger; back then she would secretly pinch her little sister and make nasty comments, just to get back at her a little. Now that they were both practically grown up, she had accepted the situation. At least she thought so. She refused to fight with Tanya, whether it had to do with the attention that she received from their parents or from men, so she might as well give up and be satisfied with who she was. She needed to stop comparing herself to Tanya. It just made her depressed.

Right now she looked at her sister, whose eagerness and enthusiasm for the trip was contagious. Vera truly loved Tanya; it wasn't her fault that things had ended up this way.

'The problem is, you're going to take all the guys,' she said with a sigh as Tanya showed her one top after another, each one more attractive than the last.

'No, I won't. You're super-cute! Come on, we'll pack some nicer things too. Forget about what Pappa says.'

'OK.'

Oleg was rushing about the flat, whistling and dancing as he packed, grabbing hold of Sabine and swinging her around so she laughed out loud. Vera had never seen her father so elated. Ever since they were kids he'd talked about Gotska Sandön, about how beautiful it was supposed to be, about all the unusual birds, the seals, the plants. And the fact that his great-grandfather had died when his ship went down off a beach called Franska Cove; he was buried there, and three cannons that had been salvaged from the vessel were still on the island. Since receiving permission to make the trip there, he'd hardly talked about anything else.

'The taxi's here!' shouted their mother from the kitchen.

They took one last look around the flat before they closed the door behind them.

Karin Jacobsson and Martin Kihlgård slipped out to the pizzeria around the corner for a quick dinner. They expected to be working all evening. Since they hadn't seen each other in quite a while, it was great to have some time to themselves. They'd worked together on a number of cases over the past few years, and they enjoyed each other's company.

While they waited for their food to be served, they discussed what motives might have compelled the murderer to kill Peter Bovide.

As he talked, Kihlgård munched on his salad, which was soaked with dressing and mixed with croutons.

'One possible motive, of course, is jealousy – some sort of love triangle. How faithful was Bovide? Maybe he was having an affair on the side.'

'The MO really indicates revenge,' said Jacobsson. 'Why else fire a whole clip of shots into his stomach when they were obviously unnecessary? He died from the first bullet, after all.'

'How do you know that?' muttered Kihlgård, continuing to chew.

'The ME phoned right before we left.'

'Is that right? What'd he say?'

'He was able to determine the time of the murder. Peter Bovide died at approximately six a.m., and it was the first shot that killed him. They found seven bullets in his stomach and one in his head. The slugs have already been sent over to SCL, and the lab has promised to put a rush on it. They've semi-promised me a report on the type of ammunition and hopefully the type of gun by tomorrow morning. The ME also told me that the entry wound indicates that the bullet was fired from an oblique angle above the victim. Which means that Bovide was probably sitting down or kneeling when the bullet struck his forehead.'

'Really?'

'Yes, unless the perp was up on a ladder when he fired the gun, but that's not very likely. When Bovide took the shots to the abdomen, he was lying down. So Sohlman's theory about the sequence of events was correct. First he was shot in the forehead, then he fell to the ground and finally the rest of the rounds were fired into his torso.'

Kihlgård looked thoughtful.

'But that's a little odd, don't you think? Why would he be sitting down? He was out running, right?'

'Maybe they started to talk and sat down on the beach. How would I know?' Jacobsson shrugged. 'I have a hard time imagining that he was killed by accident. Maybe they'd even made arrangements to meet.'

Their food arrived, and for a while they ate in silence.

'It certainly doesn't sound like it was a madman who killed somebody at random,' said Kihlgård pensively.

'But do you really think it was someone who was staying at the campsite?' asked Jacobsson, sounding doubtful. 'Wouldn't it be a little crazy to murder someone staying at the same campsite? Surely the killer must have realized that he would be interviewed and thoroughly scrutinized.'

'Sure, but if the murder wasn't premeditated or if it was the result of a fit of rage, then it's possible. Although it could also be somebody from that cottage community nearby. That's actually closer to the crime scene than the campsite. Or else it's someone from outside.'

'Right,' said Jacobsson. She was chewing absent-mindedly on the same slice of capricciosa pizza, taking tiny bites of it. Kihlgård had already finished most of his calzone.

'But I still think we have to assume that the murder was planned and carried out with a specific purpose in mind. The fact that the victim thought he was being shadowed, plus the anonymous phone calls, are important pieces of the puzzle,' said Kihlgård.

Jacobsson opened her mouth to say something, but her colleague waved his hand dismissively.

'OK, OK, I know that he was regarded as slightly depressed and vulnerable psychologically. But that doesn't rule out the possibility that somebody might have been tailing him, does it? So we need to ask ourselves: who was Peter Bovide? What was he spending his time on? What sort of people did he meet? How did he live?'

'Those covert threats, or whatever they were, might have had something to do with payments made under the table,' said Jacobsson. 'I mean, using illegal workers is such a widespread practice in the construction business. It's going to be damned interesting to see what the financial investigation of his company turns up. The worst part is that it takes such a long time.'

She shoved her plate away even though half of her pizza was still untouched.

'And then there's the fact that he was clearly a troublemaker as a youth,' said Kihlgård. 'I'm thinking about the charge of assault and battery. That sort of thing isn't usually an isolated event. The motive for the murder may lie in the past. Maybe Peter Bovide was mixed up in some big-time deals when he was younger, and then it all finally caught up with him. It's happened before.'

He eyed Jacobsson's plate greedily.

'Help yourself,' she said.

'It'd be a shame to throw out good food.'

He swiftly traded his empty plate for his colleague's.

Just as Jacobsson was about to oppose Kihlgård's theory, her mobile rang. It was Knutas.

'What, can't you resist phoning me?' she teased him. 'Don't you think I can handle the investigation on my own, or what? Just relax, Anders – you're on holiday.'

'Not any more.'

'What do you mean?'

'I just walked in the door of police headquarters. I came straight from the airport.'

'What?'

'I couldn't stay away. After I heard about the murder I couldn't relax, since I was so close to home. So I decided I might as well come back. My family is still in Denmark, but I caught the first plane home.'

Kihlgård saw Jacobsson's disappointed expression.

'I see,' she said.

'You don't sound especially happy about it,' said Knutas, a little annoyed.

'Sure I am. Of course I'm glad you're back. You know that.'

Emma had just raised her wine glass to her lips when she caught sight of Johan above all the heads in Donner's Bar. *How typical that he should be here too*, she thought, now that she had finally decided to go out, for a change.

She took several small sips, keeping her eyes fixed on him. He hadn't noticed her as he stood there chatting merrily with Pia Lilja and a man who looked familiar, although she couldn't place him. Closest to Johan stood a woman that Emma didn't recognize. Her appearance was disturbing, to say the least. She was everything that Emma was not: petite, dark-haired, mysterious, voluptuous. Like a soft, cuddly cat, she was laughing and affectionately nudging Johan, who presumably reciprocated in his usual playful way. His hair seemed abnormally long and curly, he was unshaven, and he looked pale among all the suntanned tourists. What's he been up to, anyway? Emma thought, annoyed. *Partying all night long and then sleeping through half the day? And why doesn't he have any colour in his face when he tans so easily?* She hadn't noticed it the day before when they met at Almedalen. At the time she was just thinking how cute he looked.

She studied him, feeling upset. The father of her youngest child stood over there, on the other side of the outdoor bar, holding a beer in one hand and a cigarette in the other, carefree and flirting, without giving a thought to her or Elin.

It was true that he'd phoned her several times on her mobile and left messages. She hadn't bothered to call back. Whenever she was uncertain how to handle a situation, her response was to flee. Emma was aware of this, but felt incapable of breaking the pattern.

Her relationship with Johan had come to a standstill, and she couldn't see any way out. He was going to be on Gotland all summer, working, and in her mind Emma had planned out how they could divide up taking care of Elin. That was as far as she dared think.

Now she needed to find a way to leave the restaurant without running into him. Just as she was wondering how to do this, he caught sight of her. She saw how startled he looked, and she quickly turned her head, pretending she hadn't seen him. It took ten seconds for him to appear at her side.

'Hi, Emma.'

A wave of heat filled her stomach when he said her name. She gazed into his dark-brown eyes, then looked away so as not to drown in his gaze. He made her feel weak, down to her very marrow.

'Hi,' she calmly replied.

'What are you doing here?'

'What are *you* doing here?'

'We just finished working, Pia and I, and Peter and Madeleine; they work for the national news division. The murder case on Fårö, you know.'

'Oh, that's right.' She nodded. *So that's who they were – colleagues from work.*

'How's Elin?'

'Fine, just fine.' She laughed awkwardly. 'Mamma and Pappa are babysitting her tonight.'

'OK.' Johan nodded and glanced over at the others.

Emma felt ill at ease.

'Shouldn't you be going back to join your colleagues?' she said, giving the last word a sarcastic emphasis.

The girlfriend she'd come with had disappeared in the crowd. Too bad she wasn't here with a guy.

Johan turned towards her again.

'You know, I rang you several times today. Why didn't you call me back?'

For a microsecond she relented, wanting to sink into his arms and shut out the whole world. Instead she said, 'I've been really busy. And by the way, I've got to go.'

She pretended to wave to somebody over by the door and strode off. Out of the corner of her eye she noticed Johan's expression, but when she cast a glance at the bar before she stepped out on to the street, he had rejoined the others and was chatting easily with the brunette. Emma felt a pang of bitterness. Without knowing why, she felt humiliated. She couldn't understand why she was reacting so strongly.

It felt as if her relationship with Johan had definitely come to an end. For good.

WEDNESDAY, 12 JULY

K nutas was welcomed with open arms the following morning when the entire investigative team gathered for a meeting. The only person he wondered about was Karin. He hoped that she wouldn't interpret his return as a sign that he didn't have confidence in her abilities. She hadn't been quite as warm as she usually was.

Coffee and cinnamon rolls from Konditori Siesta were on the table. Knutas cast a glance at Kihlgård, who had put two rolls on a plate in front of him. Of course he was the one who had replaced the fruit with pastries.

They had just started when Erik Sohlman came in, waving a piece of paper in his hand. His red hair was dishevelled, and his eyes were shining. Knutas recognized the expression; it was exactly the way Sohlman looked when he was watching a soccer match and the AIK team was winning.

'Hi, sorry I'm late, but I've been talking to SCL and the ME this morning. They've been unusually quick this time round.'

The air of anticipation in the room rose perceptibly,

and everyone looked at Sohlman with interest.

'We've received an answer from SCL regarding the type of ammunition that was used. It's Russian.'

'Russian?' repeated Knutas with surprise.

'You heard right. And it's such a special kind that the lab can even say what sort of gun the bullets came from. A Russian army pistol, a Tulski brand, and the model is called Korovin. It's a fully automatic gun in an odd calibre of 6.35 millimetres. It's quite old, manufactured in 1926.'

'Who would use an eighty-year-old Russian army pistol?' exclaimed Wittberg. 'That doesn't really sound like the work of a pro.'

'We need to check out everybody who has a gun permit on Gotland, in fact in all of Sweden,' said Knutas. 'Find out if anybody has a permit for that particular type of weapon. What does it look like? Do you have a photo, Erik?'

'No, but I'll find one ASAP. If I'm not mistaken, it's a very small gun, like a Browning.'

'We need to investigate what sort of Russian contacts Bovide had,' Knutas went on. 'Who could have imported an old Russian army gun, and above all: what sort of person would use this type of weapon to murder somebody?'

'The best-case scenario would be if we could find the gun, but the chance of that happening diminishes with each day that passes,' said Sohlman. 'The coast-guard divers are searching the waters today too, but that will be the end of it. And I don't think the gun is anywhere on shore, or else the police dogs would have found it.'

'What sort of part-time workers were hired by Bovide's company, aside from the full-time employees?' asked Wittberg. 'Do you know whether Bovide used illegal workers?'

'I've turned over that part of the investigation to the fraud division,' said Jacobsson. 'They're going over everything with a fine-tooth comb: financial statements, book-keeping practices, employees, what sort of projects the company was involved in – the works.'

'Every contractor probably uses the occasional illegal, and there are plenty of workers from the Baltic countries and from Poland in the construction business,' Wittberg went on. 'Maybe from Russia too.'

'Of course, but it doesn't necessarily mean that the perp has to be Russian, just because the gun came from there,' Jacobsson objected. 'There are plenty of Russian weapons in circulation on the black market.'

Knutas turned to Kihlgård, who had his mouth full. 'How's it going with mapping out Peter Bovide's life?'

Kihlgård carefully finished chewing before he replied.

'If we first look at his family, friends and circle of acquaintances, a large number of interviews have been done, and in summary I can say that so far nothing out of the ordinary has turned up. The neighbours didn't notice anything particular about the family, and the Bovides don't seem to have fought or argued. Not a single person could confirm that Peter Bovide thought he was being watched or that he'd ever received anonymous phone calls at the office. So far, that information has come only from his business partner, Johnny Ekwall.'

'What about the others who work at the company? The office secretary, Linda?' asked Jacobsson.

Kihlgård shook his head.

'Her answers were inconclusive. She says that somebody might have called, but she thought it was just a wrong number. She says she had no idea that Bovide felt he was being watched.' Kihlgård took a gulp of coffee and continued: 'According to their relatives, the Bovides were a perfect couple; they had a nice home, the children were well looked after and they always behaved politely. Everyone we talked to seemed genuinely shocked by the murder.'

'There's something else that comes to mind when I hear that a Russian gun was used, and that's the traffic related to the Russian coal transports in Slite harbour,' Wittberg interjected. 'I mean, the barges arrive several times a month, and everybody knows they're selling illegal booze over there.'

Jacobsson thought about the article she'd seen in the newspaper. The same idea had occurred to her.

Knutas agreed that Wittberg had a plausible argument. The coal barges were a problem. The police were well aware that the sale of illegal liquor was going on, but they didn't have the resources to check every shipment. They were able to make only random checks.

'That sounds reasonable,' said Kihlgård. 'We should follow up on that lead.'

'Does anybody know when the next transport is due to arrive?' asked Knutas. 'And on the Swedish side, who's responsible for the unloading?'

'The harbour master at the Cementa company,' said Wittberg. 'That's where the coal is headed. They use it as fuel in the furnaces.'

'OK,' said Knutas. 'I'll ring him after the meeting.'

'Wait a sec,' Kihlgård interjected. 'One of the neighbours mentioned something about Cementa.'

He quickly flicked through his notebook.

'Right. Here it is. An Arne Nilsson who lives next door to the Bovides said that Peter had a big fortieth birthday celebration not long ago. And quite a lot of booze was served. He said something about vodka . . . oh, that's right, he said that the vodka flowed and it wasn't the usual kind you can buy at the state liquor store. It was a stronger type that was imported directly from Russia. Apparently it was from one of the Russian barges that deliver coal to Cementa.'

'But plenty of people buy illegal booze,' Sohlman objected. 'Why should this have anything to do with the murder?'

'It's at least worth looking into,' said Knutas. 'I'll find out when the next shipment is due.'

When Johan woke up, he didn't know at first where he was. He peered at the ceiling, which had a yellowish tint he didn't recognize. Cautiously, he turned over; the bed was much softer and wider than his own. For a split second he thought he was lying in Emma's bedroom out in Roma. He felt a rush of euphoric joy shoot through his body until he realized that he hadn't spent the previous evening with her and the sounds outside the window were much louder and more diverse than in the peaceful residential neighbourhood in Roma. Then images from the previous day came flooding in. Oh shit. They'd gone to Donner's Bar and from there to the outdoor tavern Vinäger, where they'd run into a bunch of people from the local radio station. They'd partied all night and got very drunk. The night had ended outside the Saint Karin church ruins, with him and Madeleine getting together instead of going their separate ways. After that he'd accompanied her back to the hotel. No, he thought. *No, no.*

He turned on to his side and saw the cloud of brown hair sticking out of the covers.

Shit. They'd had sex. He'd slept with his work colleague. How low could he go? He wanted to forget the whole thing. As quietly as possible, he crept out of bed and went into the bathroom. He turned on the tap, but only halfway so the splash of the water wouldn't be audible. He looked at himself in the mirror: his face was a sallow colour, his eyes were bloodshot, with a weary and slightly melancholy expression. Who was this man he was looking at? He discovered several new wrinkles near his eyes and on his throat. A new furrow that hadn't been there before. His face had changed, aged. He had a bad taste in his mouth. The image of Emma's face appeared before him. How could he have been so stupid? He felt so sleazy, and the contempt he felt for himself was nauseating. He'd wait until he got home to take a shower. He had to leave, get out of here. He slipped back into the room and grabbed his clothes, terrified that Madeleine would wake up.

Without a sound he closed the door behind him.

The next coal transport wasn't due to arrive in Slite harbour until the following week. Knutas set the matter aside for the time being and decided instead to pay a visit to Peter Bovide's parents, even though they'd already been interviewed. He wanted to meet them in person.

It was great to leave police headquarters and set off alone. He chose to drive his own vehicle, an old Mercedes with no air conditioning, so he was feeling sweaty by the time he made it out to Slite. Katarina and Stig Bovide lived in a ground-floor flat in the middle of town. The blinds were closed, and from the outside it looked like no one was home.

Knutas rang the bell and then had to wait for a while. Eventually the door opened, and Knutas was taken aback when he saw the expression of the elderly woman standing there. Even though Katarina Bovide's face was both freckled and tanned, and in her long, bright dress she actually reminded him a bit of Lina, her grief and despair were painfully evident.

She merely nodded to him and led the way to the

living room, which under normal circumstances was no doubt quite pleasant, but right now it was only dimly lit. The curtains had been drawn so that very little light seeped in from the windows. It was as if Peter Bovide's parents wanted to close out the lovely summer day. As if they couldn't bear the beauty.

The next instant a man appeared in the doorway. He looked just as haggard and empty of all life as his wife. Stig Bovide was tall and thin with sparse light-brown hair and blue eyes. He wore a light-coloured shirt tucked into a pair of jeans. On his feet he had a pair of Birkenstock slippers. A heavy sense of grief hung in the air, and the temperature bordered on intolerably hot. Knutas was thirsty, but neither of them offered him anything to drink. He decided to try toughing it out.

'First, please accept my condolences, of course,' he began. 'As you may have heard, I'm in charge of the investigation. I was out of town, but I came back yesterday and I've taken over from Karin Jacobsson. She's my deputy superintendent.'

He cleared his throat, wondering why he was wasting words on such things.

'All right then. I have a few questions that I'd like to ask you.'

'We've already talked to the police,' said Stig Bovide. 'With somebody by the name of Kihlgård. He was here yesterday.'

'Yes, I know that. But since I've now taken over responsibility, I wanted to meet you in person. I hope you don't mind. Naturally we're doing everything in our power to catch the person who did this, and so it's important that I find out as much as possible about Peter. Could you start by telling me how you think he was doing?'

'How he was doing?' repeated Katarina Bovide tonelessly.

'I mean in general terms, both in his work and in his marriage.'

'Hmm, I don't really know,' Katarina said hesitantly. 'I suppose he was doing fine. He and Vendela had their problems, just like everybody else, but no worse than other parents of young children. What do you think?'

She turned to her husband. He didn't answer, just nodded.

'They had their hands full with William and Mikaela, of course, but we helped out as much as we could. Right now the children are staying with Peter's sister in Othem. We thought it was best at the moment, since she and her family live out in the country and keep animals. And the children will be able to play with their cousins, so that will give them something else to think about. But we go out every day to help out. Until Vendela is feeling better.'

'So you think Peter was happy?'

'I don't know if "happy" is the right word,' said Stig Bovide. 'He had his epilepsy to contend with, and that could be very difficult.'

Knutas frowned. 'You mean he suffered from epileptic fits?'

'Yes.'

'How often?'

'Not very often, maybe a few times a year. It was worse if he was under stress or feeling depressed.'

'Depressed? Was that common for him?'

Both parents fidgeted uneasily.

'Occasionally he felt a bit down,' said Katarina reluctantly. 'Whenever that happened, it was hard to talk to him. He would withdraw into himself.'

'He felt a great need to have time alone,' her husband added. 'I think that's why he loved running so much. He could be gone for hours. I know Vendela wasn't always very happy about that.'

'She thought he spent too much time away from her and the children,' explained Katarina. 'And that's not so strange, since he worked so much,' she said with a sigh.

'How often did he get depressed?'

'Maybe a couple of times a year.'

'Was he seeing a psychologist? Or was he on any kind of medication?'

'Yes, he took anti-depressants,' said Katarina.

Her husband looked at her in surprise.

'He did?'

'Yes, dear.' She put her hand on his arm. 'I didn't want to worry you. I'm sorry.'

Stig Bovide kept his eyes fixed on his wife. He pressed

his lips together but didn't say a word. Knutas changed the subject.

'We know that recently Peter felt as if he was being watched. Do you know anything about that?'

'No, we've really never heard anything about that.' Stig Bovide's voice had taken on a belligerent tone. 'Why did he think he was being watched? And who actually told you that?'

'I'm afraid I can't discuss that at the moment. Are you sure that Peter never mentioned anything about this?'

Stig Bovide leaped from his chair. 'Can't discuss it?' he shouted. 'What on earth do you mean by that? This is our son we're talking about. Our son who was murdered! We're his parents. Don't you understand that?' He pointed first at himself and then at his wife. 'We demand that you tell us everything about the investigation. And I mean everything!'

This sudden outburst caught Knutas off guard. Stig Bovide was now leaning over him, his face contorted with anger.

'You come barging into our home two days after our son was found murdered, asking a lot of questions that you demand we answer. And then you refuse to tell us what our boy was mixed up in. Are you out of your mind? Get out of here! Get out!'

He grabbed hold of Knutas's shirt collar.

'Calm down!' cried Katarina. 'What do you think you're doing?'

She managed to pull her husband away from Knutas, who quickly got to his feet.

'I think we should continue this interview at some other time,' muttered Knutas. 'I'm sorry if I've upset you, but we're not at liberty to discuss the investigation. Not even with family members. I'll be in touch. Goodbye. And again, please accept my condolences.'

Katarina Bovide was still holding on to her husband's arm as he glared fiercely at Knutas without saying another word. He was breathing hard and seemed to be having trouble regaining his composure. Knutas fled the stuffy room, grabbed his jacket and dashed out.

All the grief and despair in the flat seemed to follow him.

Johan was having a hard time concentrating at work. Pia asked him what was wrong, but he didn't feel like telling her what had happened. Not at the moment. Although she probably had her suspicions. Last night he and Madeleine had lingered on the street after the restaurant had closed, and she hadn't gone with her colleague, Peter, back to their hotel. *Who the fuck cares,* he thought. *Let Pia think whatever she likes.* He was neither married nor engaged. Emma had broken off their engagement, and since they hadn't been together in months, there was really no reason for him to feel guilty. She had pushed him away, yet he still felt miserable and didn't understand how he could have behaved so despicably. He needed to talk to Maddie as soon as she arrived at the office.

Grenfors, editor-in-chief of Regional News, rang from Stockholm. During the summertime he had to step in and actually get involved in the editing, which made no one happy, least of all himself. He discussed with Johan what had to be done for the day's report.

'I have a feeling that the police have no idea where to look,' said Johan. 'The murder seems to be a total mystery. On the surface at least, Peter Bovide appears to be a completely ordinary conscientious family man who loved his wife, worked hard and never drew much attention to himself.'

'Have you talked to his parents?'

'No,' said Johan sharply, annoyed by the question. 'Do you really think that's acceptable? It's only been two days since their son was found murdered. They must still be in a state of shock.'

'Give it a try, anyway,' Grenfors insisted. 'There's been nothing from them in the papers or on TV. We could be the first, and the national news—'

'Enough with the national news,' Johan interrupted him, tired of constantly sucking up to the national news big shots. 'If they want something from the parents, let them do the interview. Maddie can pester the parents – I won't.'

He'd hardly finished his sentence before Madeleine came into the office. She cast an inquisitive glance at Johan.

'I'll ring you later,' he snapped and put down the phone.

'Hi,' said Maddie. Her expression was both amused and not amused.

'Hi.'

For several seconds Johan considered what he should do, before deciding it was best to take the bull by the horns. He got up from his chair and was just about to ask Madeleine to step outside with him to have a talk when the phone rang. Pia picked it up. Judging by her expression and tone of voice, they could tell that she was listening to something important. She motioned for Johan to toss her a pen. Quickly she wrote down what the person on the other end of the line was saying. Pia looked so tense that Johan completely forgot what he'd been planning to say to Maddie. When the conversation was over, Pia slowly put down the phone.

'Hold on a minute. This tip might be a good one.'

Johan sat back down.

'That was a girl I know, Anna, who works at Sofia's Nails and Beauty here in town. A beauty salon. Anna is a manicurist, and she knows Vendela Bovide, in fact they're best friends. Vendela works in the same place, on Saturdays.'

'And?'

'Anna said that the two of them went out for dinner together just a week before the murder. Sort of a little farewell dinner before the summer holiday, because Vendela was going to be gone for a month.'

'OK,' said Johan impatiently.

He cast a quick glance at Madeleine, who had dropped on to the chair next to him.

'Vendela was nervous during the dinner because Peter had received some sort of threat. And now Anna doesn't know what to do. She's afraid Vendela might be in danger too.'

'She should start by talking to us,' suggested Johan.

'That's just what I was thinking.'

With Vendela Bovide's permission, the police had searched the family home and the company office, but they hadn't found anything of interest. The company computers had been confiscated and were being examined. On Wednesday afternoon, Wittberg and Jacobsson went to see the widow and interview her more extensively. She was now home from hospital, and they'd made an appointment to see her at three o'clock.

The Bovides' house was located north of town, on the road to Othem. A red-painted wooden house with white trim and a neatly raked gravel courtyard in front. On the lawn stood a blue trampoline; a short distance away was a playhouse, and a striped hammock hung between two apple trees. A low wooden fence surrounded the property. It looked freshly painted and the lawn had been recently mown.

They rang the bell and listened to the hollow clang.

They waited a while, then rang the bell again.

Jacobsson tried the door. It wasn't locked. She pushed it open and cautiously called out, 'Hello.' No answer.

They stepped into the front hall, which was hot and stuffy.

'I'll check upstairs, while you have a look around down here,' said Wittberg and then headed for the stairs.

The kitchen was off to the left; Jacobsson peeked inside. Light-coloured shutters on the windows, curtains with a floral pattern and windowsills crowded with flower pots. The flowers were wilting, as if they hadn't been watered in a while. Everything was shiny clean, but the house felt deserted. She went into the living room. The floor creaked under her feet. The room was quite large, with a hardwood floor, leather sofa, two armchairs, a TV and a bookshelf. Photographs of the two children adorned the walls.

One by one, Jacobsson picked up the framed photos that stood on a shelf. Traditional wedding pictures taken by Hemlin's photo studio in Visby, and a picture of Peter Bovide receiving a trophy. There was something about his expression and his crooked smile that Jacobsson didn't like. Especially the look in his eyes, which was strangely vacant.

'Find anything?'

Wittberg had come back downstairs and was giving her an inquisitive look.

'No. How about you?'

'Not really.'

Jacobsson cast a glance at the Mora grandfather clock in the room. It was 3.15.

'I wonder where she is. It seems strange to leave the door unlocked. Although I suppose they do that out here in the country.'

Wittberg gave a start. 'What was that?'

'What?'

'I thought I heard a car.'

They both stood still to listen. There was no doubt about it. They could hear a car engine outside.

Quickly, they slipped out through the patio door and made their way to the back of the house. They had no desire to get caught sneaking about inside. Jacobsson peered round the corner and saw Vendela being dropped off by somebody she recognized. It was Johnny Ekwall, her husband's business partner.

After the car had driven off, Jacobsson and Wittberg went round to the front and rang the bell.

It was a few moments before Vendela Bovide opened the door.

She stared in surprise at the two police officers.

'Hi,' said Jacobsson and then introduced Wittberg. 'We had agreed to meet today at three o'clock, but maybe you forgot?'

The widow's face flushed bright red.

'Was that today? I thought it was tomorrow.'

'I'm sorry for the misunderstanding,' said Jacobsson. 'Would this be a good time? It shouldn't take very long.'

Vendela Bovide hesitated.

'Where are the children?' asked Jacobsson, to break the stalemate.

'They're staying with Peter's sister in Othem. I'm actually staying there too right now, but I had to come by here to take care of a few things. I can't stand to sleep here yet.'

'May we?'

Jacobsson took a step forward.

'Yes, of course.'

Vendela sounded far from convinced that this would be a good idea, but she let them come in. She led the way to the living room.

'Have a seat. Would you like something to drink?'

'Yes, thanks,' said both officers in unison. It was hot, and they were thirsty.

Vendela came back in a few minutes with a pitcher of juice and glasses.

'Who was it that dropped you off outside?'

Vendela looked down as she filled their glasses.

'That was Johnny from the company. He's so nice and helpful.'

Jacobsson gave her a searching look.

'It turns out the gun that was used to kill your husband was Russian,' said Wittberg. 'So we're wondering whether your husband had any contact with Russians.'

'Russian?' Vendela's voice quavered slightly. 'The gun was Russian?'

'Yes. Did your husband have any contact with Russians or anyone from other Eastern European countries? A lot of them come here as guest workers, especially in the construction business.'

'Sure. He did have some part-time employees, from Poland at any rate. But I don't know about Russia. Peter handled all the company business. I didn't get involved. He took care of everything himself.'

'Did he ever talk about any of these guest workers?'

'No. He spent so much time at work, and we tried to avoid talking about the company here at home.'

'So you don't know anything about this?'

'No.'

'As we mentioned earlier, apparently, during the spring and early summer Peter felt that he was being watched. He also received some anonymous phone calls,' said Jacobsson. 'Are you sure you don't remember hearing anything?'

'Yes, I am. He never mentioned anything like that. I would have remembered it if he did.'

Jacobsson was convinced that Vendela Bovide was lying. She looked the widow in the eye and repeated the question one last time.

'So he never mentioned that he felt that someone was spying on him or following him?'

'No. But if that's really true, I'm sure he would have told me about it. We talked about everything.'

'Except for company business?'

'Yes.'

'How much time did he spend at the office?' asked Wittberg.

'I suppose you could say that he was there a lot. Like all small-business owners. He would leave the house early in the morning, but he came home for lunch if he was working in the office or at a construction site nearby. Then he usually got home around six or seven. Sometimes he worked in the evening. Mostly with the accounts; he put together bids and things like that.'

'What about at weekends?'

'He was usually home.'

'What sort of marriage did you have? What were your feelings for him?'

'I loved him. Now that he's dead, I don't feel like living any more. It's only because of the children that I'm trying to go on.'

She spoke the words in a voice that was dry and matter-of-fact, as if discussing some trivial matter. Yet when it came to Vendela's feelings for her husband, there was something in her voice that made both Wittberg and Jacobsson believe what she said.

The salon called Sofia's Nails and Beauty was located on a side street to Hästgatan, a bit off the main tourist path.

Roses clung to the rough façade, and lying on the worn stone steps outside the front entrance was an orange cat, basking in the sun. A bell jingled as Johan and Pia stepped inside, and the strong scent of a floral perfume overwhelmed them.

'It smells like bubble bath in here,' Pia whispered in Johan's ear.

Three sturdy wooden tables stood along the walls, covered with terry-cloth towels in pastel colours, and small pots and jars attractively arranged. Seated on either side of one of the tables were two young women. One was holding out her hands so the other woman could file and polish her nails. They were so immersed in their conversation that they didn't even turn round to see who had come in. From hidden speakers came the sound of gentle eastern Mediterranean music.

In the very back of the room they saw an old-fashioned cash register on a counter. Behind it sat

another woman with her head bowed as she wrote
something in a book. She glanced up as they
approached.

'Hi, Pia!'

The woman behind the counter wore a blue linen
dress, and her curly blond hair was pinned up in a bun.
She stood up to give Pia a hug and then shook hands
with Johan.

'Let's go over to the café next door so we can talk in
peace.'

As they sat down at a table in the café's garden, Anna
cast a nervous glance at Pia's camera.

'This isn't going to be on TV, is it? Because I don't
want any part of that.'

'No, don't worry,' said Johan soothingly. 'We won't
use anything that you'd rather not have included. We
always protect our sources. Nobody needs to know that
what we found out came from you.'

'Promise me that.'

'Sure. Of course we promise,' said Pia. 'You can trust
me.'

'So how was Peter Bovide being threatened?' asked
Johan.

'He had had anonymous phone calls, both at home
and at work. But that's not the worst thing. Just a few
days before Vendela and I went out to have our last
dinner together before the summer holiday, several
unpleasant types showed up at their house really late at
night.'

'What did they do?'

'They didn't go inside. They talked to Peter out in the front garden, apparently for quite a long time. Vendela said that when he came back into the house, he was very upset.'

'Did he tell her who they were?'

'No, but they spoke broken English. Vendela thought they might be from Finland or the Baltics.'

'Why did they threaten him?'

'He said that the company was having problems at one of the construction jobs they had taken on, but that everything was going to be fine. He hadn't received payment from the person who had contracted the job, and so he didn't have any money to pay the workers. And apparently it was a really big project.'

'Did Vendela have any idea what project it was? Or which building site?'

'I don't know. She didn't tell me.'

'Do the police know about this?'

'No. She didn't want to say anything because she's afraid everything would start to unravel.'

Anna leaned forward.

'I think it has to do with illegal workers,' she whispered.

'You still need to go to the police and tell them what you know. This could be a serious matter,' said Johan. 'And in our report tonight, we're going to mention the fact that Peter Bovide was being threatened. Although, as I said, we won't say where we got the information.'

'Good. Vendela doesn't know that Pia and I are friends, so I don't think she'll realize that I told you about this. But I actually don't care,' she said defiantly. 'I'll ring the police as soon as I get back to the salon. And to hell with what she thinks. The only reason I'm telling anybody about this at all is to protect her.'

She shrugged and tried to look like she didn't care, but it was obvious how worried she was.

'I'm sure everything will work out,' said Pia.

'It's just all so awful,' murmured Anna. 'I feel so bad about Peter. And so sorry for Vendela. And their kids.'

More questions began swarming through Johan's mind. Was it here, at this café table, that they had discovered the motive for Peter Bovide's murder? Was Vendela's life in danger too? How should he deal with the information?

This was much too serious to keep to himself.

After leaving Anna Nyberg and the beauty salon, Johan tried to ring both Grenfors and Knutas. Neither of them picked up.

'What do we do now?' he asked Pia.

'The only thing to do is to start working on our story. We need to use the information in tonight's report, but we have to have two independent sources. Unfortunately, it won't be enough to have Anna's account, even though I'm convinced she's telling the truth. Who else could confirm that Peter Bovide was being threatened?'

'Maybe someone at Slite Construction, but nobody is answering the phone there either,' said Johan with a sigh. 'The question is whether we should drive up there, even if nobody's in the office. In the meantime, I'll ring the union and find out if they know anything about that under-the-table job.'

'Do that. Then we'll drive to Slite.'

'OK.'

Johan got hold of the representative for the Union of Construction Workers on Gotland.

'I'm trying to find out some information about a company called Slite Construction.'

'Oh, right. He's the one who was shot to death on Fårö. Peter Bovide. Awful thing to happen.'

'I've heard that he was using illegal workers. Do you know anything about that?'

'Yes, we had our suspicions, as a matter of fact. He had a union at his job sites, but there have been rumours that he wasn't paying the proper wages. Those workers from Eastern Europe are willing to work cheap.'

'What do you mean?'

'They come here to Sweden and bring down the wages. Plus they take jobs away from our own members.'

'Yes, I see,' said Johan impatiently. 'Do you know which projects Bovide's company has been working on recently?'

'Sure. We've received job-site reports from a few guys who still work for them. I can check. Wait a sec.'

Johan heard him typing on a computer keyboard. It took a minute before he was back on the phone.

'The ones we know about are a residential project on Furillen, the remodelling of a restaurant in Åminne and a masonry job in Stenkyrkehuk. It's a limestone house that's being built right next to the old lighthouse up there. There's also been talk that he had a bunch of illegal guys from Poland or the Baltics or somewhere like that building summer cabins all over northern Gotland.'

'But how do you check up on that sort of thing? I mean, if you think they're using illegal workers?'

'It's extremely difficult. We can't keep track of every little construction site on the island; buildings are going up everywhere. The only way is if somebody rings us to say that they suspect illegal workers, but nobody ever bothers to do that.'

The representative heaved a big sigh. Johan checked his watch and made a quick decision.

'Do you know exactly where in Stenkyrkehuk this limestone house is being built?'

'It's probably less than thirty kilometres from here. Take highway 149 from Visby, heading north. Turn off at the shop in Hälge, past Vale, and you'll end up on a little gravel road that leads to the lighthouse. On the property beyond the lighthouse you'll see the building. They've cleared away a lot of trees and widened the road.'

'OK, thanks.'

After clicking off, Johan turned to Pia, who was driving.

'We're going to Stenkyrkehuk.'

The sound of pounding hammers could be heard from quite a distance away. They had followed the union rep's directions and found their way to the building site close to the old lighthouse. The house under construction was situated on a limestone cliff a hundred feet above the sea with a wonderful view of the shimmering waters of the Baltic. The walls were up and two bare-chested men were perched on the roof, hammering the roofing felt in place. The sun was high overhead, and their backs glistened with sweat. At one end of the house two more men were busy applying plaster to the gable.

'What a place,' said Pia, sighing with delight.

'Not bad.'

Johan looked around. A narrow, bumpy gravel road had been made, leading to the building site, which was surrounded by woods. A neighbour's house was close by, although it wasn't visible from the site. Only the old lighthouse, which was no longer in use, could be seen sticking up above the trees. The construction workers were busy with their tasks and hadn't noticed

Pia and Johan arrive. Music was blaring from a radio.

'Let's go over and have a talk with them,' said Johan.

But before he could make a move, a man came out of the construction shed that stood a short distance from the new building. He was very short and powerfully built, and he stared at them with suspicion.

'Hi,' said Johan. 'We're from Swedish TV, doing a story on the murder of Peter Bovide. Did you know him?'

'Know him? He was my partner. We ran the company together.'

Johan then realized that this man standing in front of him had to be Johnny Ekwall. He couldn't believe their luck.

'So you're Johnny? Could we have a talk with you?'

'Not if you're going to shoot video. I don't want to be on TV.'

'That's fine. I promise we won't.'

Johnny Ekwall cast a glance at the construction workers, who looked at the reporters with curiosity for a moment before returning to what they were doing. Then Johnny turned on his heel and went back inside the shed. He left the door open, which Johan took to be an invitation.

He and Pia followed. Inside the shed was a row of metal lockers, a bench and a stainless-steel sink with a dusty mirror hanging above it.

They passed through an opening into what seemed to be a kitchen. On a simple table next to the window was a plastic container of biscuits and several dirty coffee mugs. Along the wall stood a refrigerator and a shelf holding a microwave and a stained coffee-maker. In a corner, several mattresses had been propped against the wall. They all sat down at the table, and Johnny poured the coffee, shoving forward the biscuits. Johan decided to get right to the point.

'We've heard that Peter Bovide was being threatened. What do you know about that?'

'Where did you hear that?'

'I can't tell you. We have to protect our sources.'

'OK. Does that mean that if I tell you something, you won't tell anyone else?'

'We won't say that you were the one who gave us the information. If that's what you prefer.'

Johnny Ekwall took a gulp of the lukewarm coffee.

'Hmm . . . I don't know,' he said hesitantly. 'There's been a bit of trouble lately. Peter was the one who took care of paying the guys, but I think we're behind. With their wages, I mean. And a few workers have been unhappy, saying they should be paid more, things like that. But Peter always took care of these matters himself; he never discussed them with me.'

'Do you know if he was being threatened?'

'He told me several times that he thought he was being watched, that somebody was spying on him.'

'Is that right? Why did he think so?'

'I don't know. I think it was mostly a gut feeling he had.'

151

Johan leaned forward and lowered his voice.

'The thing is, we've heard from a very reliable source that he actually was being threatened, for real. He wasn't just imagining things. So, what do you know about it?'

Johnny Ekwall fidgeted nervously. His expression again turned suspicious.

'Where did you hear that?'

'As I said before, I'm afraid I can't tell you that. We're reporters, and we have to protect our sources. It's not the same thing as talking to the police.'

Ekwall regarded Johan for a moment in silence.

'Do you promise you won't tell that I was the one who told you? I don't want to get in any trouble.'

'We promise.'

'Well, Peter got some strange phone calls, mysterious types who rang up anonymously, but he never wanted to discuss it. He said they were just a couple of idiots, nothing to worry about. It had to do with financial matters, and he always wanted to keep that bit to himself.'

'Can you tell us anything else about these phone calls?'

'Somebody would ring and start making threats, saying that if Peter didn't pay the wages we owed . . . But that was only recently.'

'Why are you behind in paying the wages? Isn't the company doing well?'

'Yes, it is. But we have a big client who hasn't been paying us on time. And then we can't pay the wages, and we end up falling behind.'

'Who's been complaining?'

'Mostly the guys from Poland and the Baltics who've been working for us. They get paid less than those in the union; that's only natural. I suppose they've started comparing notes with the others.'

'Peter was apparently being threatened by several individuals who were thought to be from either Finland or the Baltics. They went to his house several weeks ago. Do you know anything about that?'

'Yes, he told me about them, and it made me nervous, but he said there was no reason to worry.'

'Do you know the nationality of the people who made the phone calls?'

'No, he didn't mention where they were from. And I didn't think to ask.'

'Do you have any Swedish workers on this job site?' asked Pia.

'No, not at this one.'

'How many employees does the company have altogether?'

'Three full-time construction workers, besides me and Peter. And Linda, our secretary. We bring in other employees as we need them.'

'What's your opinion about the murder? I mean, who do you think might have done it?'

'There's no doubt that it's made me think about those

threats and whether they might have something to do with the murder.'

'Are you worried for your own safety?'

'Not really, although of course the thought has crossed my mind.'

'What are you going to do about the company now?'

'I'll keep running it, along with Linda. We'll buy out Peter's share – provided Vendela agrees, of course. She's part-owner now. And if she does, Linda can handle the finances.'

'Will she be able to do that?'

'Sure. She studied economics in school. And she's taken a bunch of courses. One thing is certain – we're going to pay all those back wages so we can keep the employees happy. Although at the moment we can't do a damn thing because the police have got their mitts on our account books.'

'So you and Peter actually disagreed on how the company should be run?' asked Pia.

'Hell no, I don't think you can say that. Not really. We had a good partnership, Peter and I.'

FÅRÖSUND, 18 JULY 1985

Vera was seized by a feeling of unreality as the bus from Visby turned and then headed towards the Fårö ferry dock. The sea was spread out before them, with the island of Fårö across the channel. Car ferries shuttled back and forth between the two islands, and a long queue of cars was winding its way down to the harbour.

The boat to Gotska Sandön was expected on one side of the dock, where a crowd had already gathered. Before joining the group, Vera and her family dashed into the ICA supermarket to buy some last-minute provisions. There were no shops on the island, and they had to bring with them everything they wanted to eat and drink. Oleg ran enthusiastically up and down the aisles while the girls' mother, Sabine, walked around consulting her grocery list and ticking off what they needed to buy.

'Do you want anything else, girls?' Oleg asked. 'We won't have to carry everything, because somebody's going to pick up what we've bought, so it's OK if you want to buy a little extra. Go ahead and choose whatever you feel like eating.'

He reached for a package of chocolate cakes, and in the next instant exclaimed: 'Cheese and crackers would be *the perfect snack for tonight! We already have red wine. And didn't we pack some candles?'*

Down on the dock, more and more people had gathered to wait for the boat. Rucksacks, coolers and bags of food were stacked up in heaps. There were families with children, couples and birdwatchers. Real fanatics, thought Vera as she looked at their binoculars and other sophisticated outdoor gear. Many looked as if they were used to spending time in the woods and fields. Everyone was wearing heavy boots or had a pair fastened to their rucksack along with flasks and all sorts of other things.

An air of anticipation hovered over the crowd.

'Look! There it is!'

Oleg had his binoculars raised to his eyes to survey the sea, and he had just caught sight of the ferry. The next second, everyone could see the white boat approaching. It wasn't especially big. A young man came out on the foredeck to cast out a line. Slowly and steadily the captain manoeuvred the boat close to the dock. The passengers on board had formed a chain and began transferring all the bags off the boat. Rucksacks, suitcases and rolled-up tents were passed from hand to hand until they eventually ended up on shore, where two older, sinewy men then lined them all up on the dock. Oleg eagerly lent a hand.

When everything was ready and they were finally allowed on board, Vera and Tanya hurried to find seats on deck in the stern so they'd be able to soak up as much sun as possible during the two-hour crossing.

They leaned back comfortably as they watched the little

village of Fårösund fade into the distance on one side while Fårö disappeared on the other.

They were soon out on the open sea.

Vera listened to the thudding motor, the cries of the seagulls and the chatter of the other passengers. She was looking forward to their stay on the island.

Knutas was not pleased with the Regional News report on TV that evening. His face took on a resigned expression as he and Jacobsson sat in the staff room watching the news programme.

Johan Berg appeared to be standing at a construction site somewhere on Gotland, but it was impossible to tell exactly where he was. Then he began filing his story: 'This is one of the projects that Peter Bovide's company, Slite Construction, is working on. Behind me a classic limestone house is being built very close to the sea. Working at the site are some of the temporary employees hired by the company. And according to information obtained by Regional News, it's the workers from Poland and the Baltics who are dissatisfied with both their wages and the working conditions. Several independent sources have told Regional News that Bovide had received threats on more than one occasion over the past six months, and that these threats have been linked to his temporary workers. According to co-workers at the company, it was the murder victim who was responsible for paying the wages. No one else at Slite Construction has received similar threats. The police refuse to discuss how this lead in the investigation is being handled.'

Then a close-up of Lars Norrby appeared on the screen, with police headquarters in the background.

'Of course we're investigating several different leads in the case, but I can't say whether one is of greater interest than the others. We're taking a broad approach, without any preconceptions. We don't want to be locked into any one theory.'

'But what do you think about the information that threats had been directed against Peter Bovide?'

'That's not something I can comment on at the moment. As I said, we're working on a broad front. This is just one lead among many.'

Knutas switched off the TV angrily when the report was finished.

'How the hell did they get hold of that information?'

'I have no idea.'

'And that part about Bovide being threatened by construction workers from the Baltics who are unhappy about their wages – that's more than we've been able to find out! Why didn't Norrby say anything to us about it? That's a really interesting lead. I also wonder how much this is going to damage the investigation. Now the perp is probably going to take off running.'

'Sure, if he happens to be one of the construction workers. But we don't actually know that,' said Jacobsson acerbically. 'And I heard that Johan didn't talk to Norrby about all this until an hour ago. So Lars really hasn't had time to report to us. You forget that he's a single father with two sons to take care of. And this information isn't something that we can rush off and do something about tonight. Don't you agree?'

Ever since Knutas had cut short his holiday to come back to work, Jacobsson had been having trouble deciding how to deal with her boss. On the one hand, she was happy to see him again, but on the other, she would have liked to handle the investigation on her own. By coming back home, he had robbed her of that challenge. She wondered if he realized this.

'By the way, how's it going with the examination of the company's books? You're keeping tabs on that, right?' he asked urgently.

'It's not something that can be done overnight,' she replied. 'I'm sure that the fraud division is working overtime on it.'

Thomas Wittberg came into the room. They could tell from his expression that something had happened.

'Hi, I've got a damn good tip,' he said urgently. 'One of Vendela Bovide's friends who works at the same beauty salon has contacted us. She said that Peter Bovide had been threatened by some men who came to the house, and she thinks they were illegal workers from the Baltics. The last time was just a week before the murder.'

'How does she know about this?'

'Vendela told her.'

Jacobsson and Knutas exchanged glances.

'In the interview she repeatedly denied any such thing. We're going to need to bring her in again,' said Knutas.

He looked at Wittberg.

'Great that you turned up just at this moment. Now we know, at any rate, where the TV reporters got their information. We definitely need to have a talk with that woman.'

FRIDAY, 14 JULY

Thursday passed without anything else important coming to light that might move the investigation forward. Both Vendela Bovide and her friend Anna Nyberg had been interviewed, and the police were able to confirm that Peter Bovide had been threatened several times during the weeks prior to his death. His widow finally admitted that she knew about the threats, but she hadn't wanted to say anything because it involved the hiring of illegal workers.

Everybody having anything at all to do with Slite Construction was interviewed, but no one contributed any information that the police hadn't already known.

When the investigative team gathered for the Friday morning meeting, they were greeted by a beaming Kihlgård, who stood in the doorway to welcome them by singing the 'Marseillaise' at the top of his lungs.

Enthroned atop the light pine table in the middle of the room were two big chocolate cakes decorated with miniature French flags attached to toothpicks.

'What's this all about?' asked Wittberg. His eyes were bloodshot, and he was clearly suffering from a hangover. His blond hair stuck out in all directions and he was holding a bottle of Coca-Cola in one hand. For many years Wittberg had been the department's Don Juan, but a year ago he'd settled down and moved in with his girlfriend. Then early in the summer their relationship had fallen apart, as was clearly evident. Now he was back to his old partying ways.

'What are we celebrating?' asked Jacobsson.

Kihlgård sighed loudly as he gave his colleagues an insistent look.

'What sort of uneducated group is this, anyway? Don't you know what today is?'

No one in the room had a clue.

'It's a national holiday in France, damn it!' shouted Kihlgård enthusiastically. 'The fourteenth of July! Bastille Day, celebrating the French Revolution – haven't you ever heard of it?'

'Good lord,' said Jacobsson, laughing. 'We hardly even know why we celebrate Sweden's national holiday. I had no idea you were such a Francophile.'

'My dear, how could you not know? The food, the wine, the people, the weather – I love France. And these,' he said, pointing eagerly at the chocolate cakes, 'these are French chocolate cakes, homemade from a recipe I got from my French-born boyfriend, Laurent!'

A sudden silence descended over the room. Kihlgård had never mentioned before that he was gay or that he had a boyfriend. Knutas looked completely bewildered, and Wittberg's confused expression swiftly changed to amusement. Sohlman looked as if he'd seen a ghost. Jacobsson's expression remained neutral. She'd known about Kihlgård's sexual orientation for a long time. To her eyes, it seemed quite obvious.

It was interesting to see how her otherwise so astute colleagues could be completely blind when it came to someone's sexual preference. Some people in the department had even imagined that there was something going on between her and Kihlgård. Several times Knutas had displayed signs of jealousy. That had amused Jacobsson no end.

At the moment it was clear even to Kihlgård that he had just revealed something that his colleagues on Gotland hadn't known about, although it was common knowledge among his colleagues back at police headquarters in Stockholm.

'All right then,' he said to dispel the confusion that had arisen. 'Help yourselves. These cakes are fantastic!'

Kihlgård reached for a knife and began slicing the cakes. Everyone took a piece.

'So maybe we should get started with the meeting, if Monsieur Kihlgård doesn't mind?'

Knutas turned to give a wry smile to his colleague, who was already working on his second large piece of cake.

'Wittberg, I think you had some substantial news for us?'

'Yes, we've conducted another interview with Linda Johansson, who works at Slite Construction. She still claims not to know anything about the threats or about illegal workers. She's mostly in charge of the phones and the usual office tasks, and says she just does what she's told to do. When it comes to the company's finances, it was Peter who made the decisions, while she mostly took care of the paperwork. At least that's what she says. To be honest, she doesn't exactly seem like the brightest person.'

'What do we really know about her?' asked Jacobsson.

'She's from Slite, twenty-five years old. Married with two kids. Nothing out of the ordinary.'

'How long has she worked at the company?'

'Six months, apparently. They hired her and a couple of construction workers at the same time.'

'How credible is it that she had no inkling that the company was using illegal workers?' asked Jacobsson.

'If it's true that Peter Bovide took care of the finances, it could be that the others really had no idea about what was going on,' said Wittberg. 'Maybe they hired a few foreigners with work permits and the usual union agreement and then others who didn't have the proper documents.'

'We'll soon have a report from the fraud division on their investigation. It'll be interesting to see what they find out,' said Knutas. 'Moving on to a whole different matter – have you checked up on the passengers who were on the first ferry to Fårö?'

'Yes, and it turns out that all of them have an alibi for

the time of the murder. The couple from Göteborg drove straight over to their rented cabin, where they sat and drank their morning coffee with the female owner until eight o'clock, when she left for work. Upon arrival at Fårö the pregnant woman was apparently met by her husband, and they spent the whole morning together. And when the man with the horse trailer arrived home with the horse, he was greeted by his son. None of them noticed anything unusual.'

'OK, so that's that. How's it going with the interviews of people who spent the night in summer cabins on Fårö? Is the report ready?'

'Nothing noteworthy so far, but we haven't finished all the interviews yet. We still have to go looking for people who have left the area, you know.'

'Sure. I understand.'

SATURDAY, 15 JULY

Knutas woke up alone in the big double bed in his house on Bokströmsgatan, which was located just outside Visby's ring wall. The rays of the sun were shining right in his eyes. He always slept with the window open, in both summer and winter, but right now that wasn't helping matters much. It was hotter outside than in the house. He got up and went out on to the patio. The grass needed mowing, and the garden furniture was looking shabby; the white paint was chipping off, and he'd promised himself to do something about it this summer. But so far, nothing had come of his good intentions. He didn't even dare think about everything else that needed attention out at their summer house in Lickershamn.

Until the murder of Peter Bovide was solved, he probably wouldn't have time to go out there.

He took a shower and got dressed. In the kitchen he put on the coffee and then went to get the morning newspaper from the letterbox.

It was strange to be home alone; that hardly ever happened. Lina had two more weeks of her summer

167

holiday, so she and the kids had gone out to the summer house. Although they weren't really kids any more. In the autumn they would be starting college. Knutas couldn't understand how time had flown by so fast.

For the past six months Nisse, as his son now insisted on being called, had had a steady girlfriend, and their relationship seemed both sweet and grounded. Knutas had dreaded the conversation he realized he would be forced to have with his son. Of course, both he and Lina had previously talked to their children about the birds and the bees and how babies were made, but when Nisse began staying over at Gabriella's house, Knutas could see they were going to need to have a more serious talk. Even though he was reluctant to bring up the subject, the conversation had actually gone better than he'd anticipated. Nisse had promised to be careful and always use a condom, and afterwards he gave his father a hug. Knutas was both astonished and pleased by his son's reaction. It was as if the boy appreciated the concern behind his father's clumsy attempt at a man-to-man talk.

Unlike her twin brother, Petra hadn't yet focused her affections on any particular person, which, naturally, didn't make her parents feel any more secure. Knutas tried not to worry too much. Fortunately, Lina and Petra were very close, and Lina talked about everything with her in the same open and easy way as always.

He made himself a sandwich for breakfast and sat

down at the kitchen table with a cup of coffee and the *Gotlands Allehanda*. It was still only six thirty, since Knutas was an early riser. He didn't need much sleep, and he appreciated both the late-night hours and the early morning.

The murder was no longer a front-page story as nothing new had surfaced over the past few days. He suddenly pictured Karin's face. He thought about how the investigation had been run while he was away. He couldn't see that any outright mistakes had been made, but Karin was new at taking charge, and this was the first homicide investigation she'd had to initiate. He was extremely aware of how crucial the preliminary stage was in this type of investigation; everything had to be done right from the very beginning. The time aspect was often decisive in terms of whether the killer would be caught or not. By now almost a week had passed, and they were getting nowhere. The perp already had a big head start, and if nothing new happened soon, there was a risk that he might get away. It was unlikely that he was still on the island.

Knutas leafed distractedly through the newspaper and downed the last of his coffee. He was ready to leave for the office and go through all the material in peace and quiet.

He didn't have far to go to work, just a fifteen-minute walk, but after only a few yards he was soaked with sweat. Even though it was still so early in the day, it was already very hot. He rang Lina, but she didn't answer.

She and the kids were probably still asleep. Sometimes he forgot that not everybody was a morning person like he was.

Knutas was deeply immersed in the ME's report when Jacobsson stuck her head round the door.

'Good morning. How's it going?'

'Morning – good, thanks,' he replied. 'How about you?'

'So so. I didn't sleep well last night.'

'No?'

'I just kept going over everything in my mind about the investigation.'

Jacobsson sighed as she ran her fingers through her short dark hair, and then dropped on to the visitor's chair in Knutas's office.

'Have you made it all the way through yet?' she asked, casting a glance at the papers piled up on his desk.

'Yup, I'm just about finished.'

Knutas took his pipe out of the desk drawer and begin filling it with tobacco.

'So what do you think? Have I made a total mess of things?' Jacobsson gave him a crooked smile. She had on a white linen summer dress with polka dots.

'I can't believe you're wearing a dress. You hardly ever do.'

'I just felt like it today, since it's so hot – OK? And why are you focusing on what I'm wearing when I'm trying to discuss the investigation? Talk about changing the subject . . .'

'That wasn't what I intended to do.'

'But seriously – do you think I made any major mistakes during the first twenty-four hours, while you were away?'

'Absolutely not. On the contrary. It looks like you handled everything in an exemplary manner.'

'Does that surprise you?'

'No. I know that you're perfectly capable of leading a murder investigation on your own.'

'Then why did you rush back here?'

Her question made Knutas uncomfortable. He fidgeted with his unlit pipe and then starting plucking at the tobacco in it.

'I'm sorry, Karin. Did that upset you? If so, that certainly wasn't my intention. How stupid of me. I should have called you first.'

'My dear Anders, of course you don't have to ask my permission to interrupt your holiday. But I'd like to know why you did it.'

Red blotches had appeared on her throat. A sure sign that she was upset.

'It had nothing to do with you or your capabilities. I just couldn't stay away. It's such an unusual murder investigation.'

Karin sighed and looked at her boss with resignation. 'Are you ever going to be able to give this job up?'

'Yes, sure, of course I'll be able to one day. You know I will. It just might take some time.'

'I dread the day you retire. You'll be ringing up

headquarters every other day and trying to meddle.'

'Hey, slow down a bit. I'm not even fifty-three yet.'

'Sorry,' she said with a grin. 'It's actually great to have you back. If only you'll let me handle some of the work on my own.'

'Of course I will.'

The last thing Anders wanted was to have a falling-out with Karin.

'Getting back to the investigation, I went to see Peter Bovide's parents yesterday.'

'Oh, that's right. How did it go?'

'Good. They gave me a lot of valuable information.'

He quickly told her about Bovide's epilepsy and depression.

'If he was taking anti-depressants, he must have had a doctor who prescribed them.'

'That's right. His name is Torsten Ahlberg, but he's out of town at the moment, on holiday in Italy. He'll be back next week. I'll go and talk to him myself.'

'How were his parents, by the way?'

'The father seemed really out of control. In the end he got so riled up that he kicked me out.'

'Wow. What exactly did he do?'

Knutas waved his hand dismissively.

'It was nothing really. A typical reaction from some-one who's in shock.'

The phone began ringing in Jacobsson's office. Before she left the room, she put her hand on Knutas's shoulder and said in a low voice, 'I really am glad you're back, Anders. At the same time, it makes me furious.'

Knutas got up and went to stand at the window. He looked out at the idyllic summer scene, or at least as much of it as was visible on either side of the big customer car park at Östercentrum outside the Co-op Forum.

His thoughts were focused on Peter Bovide's construction company. He hadn't personally been out to the victim's place of business, or to his house either. Others had handled that part of the investigation. Maybe a visit would be productive, give him some new ideas. It was unlikely that anyone would be working on a Saturday, but he could at least take a peek at the office. Knutas looked at his watch. Nine fifteen. Would it be all right to ring a woman who had just lost her husband so early? Probably. She had young children, after all. Vendela Bovide should be up by now. He punched in the phone number. It rang and rang, and he was just thinking about giving up when someone picked up. At first he heard only silence, then a boy's high-pitched voice.

'Hello?'

'Yes, hello, this is Anders Knutas from the police. Who am I talking to?'

'William.'

'Is your mother there?'

'No. Mamma can't talk right now. She's sleeping.'

'Sleeping? Are you the only one awake?'

'No. Mikaela is here too. We're hungry. But Mamma just keeps sleeping. She won't wake up.'

'Has she moved at all?'

'No. She's not moving. And her face looks really strange.'

Knutas immediately punched in the emergency number, 112.

'Send an ambulance over there fast. A woman is lying unconscious, and her two young children are home alone with her.'

After ordering a vehicle from the city police force, which was used to responding swiftly, he slammed down the phone, grabbed his service revolver and called for Jacobsson. Two minutes later they were in a car on their way toward Slite, sirens wailing. *If only we can get there in time*, thought Knutas as they drove north-east. *If only she's not dead.*

'What's going on?' muttered Jacobsson through clenched teeth. 'What's happening with this family?'

'If Vendela Bovide is still alive, maybe we'll have an answer to that question very soon.'

Jacobsson said a silent prayer that Vendela would still be alive. She rang Peter Bovide's parents and asked them to drive over to the house. The children needed to be taken care of by someone they trusted.

When they turned on to the drive in front of the

Bovide family home, police cars and an ambulance were already there. The door was wide open, and they rushed inside. Shocked, they came to an abrupt halt. The whole house had been turned upside down. Drawers had been pulled out, cupboards stood open, papers, dishes and pillows had been tossed to the floor. In the bedroom, two medics were lifting Vendela on to a gurney. The children were sitting on a sofa in the living room, staring wide-eyed at all the police officers. They had a packet of biscuits between them. The TV was on, showing a cartoon programme.

'We didn't make the mess,' said William.

'No, of course you didn't,' said Knutas. He stood in the doorway between the bedroom and living room, looking with dismay at Vendela. Her face was bruised, and one eye was badly swollen. She seemed to be in a deep sleep.

The investigative team met on Saturday afternoon to discuss the assault on Vendela Bovide. Knutas had called the meeting, and he started as soon as everyone was seated around the table. He briefly explained what had happened.

'Vendela Bovide was assaulted, subjected to kicks and punches, both to her face and the rest of her body. She has bruises and contusions, but the injuries appear to be superficial. According to the doctors, her life is not in danger, and she has no internal injuries other than a broken rib. She was probably given some sort of sedative or other drug, since she was sleeping so soundly. They had a tough time at the hospital getting her to wake up. Somebody obviously searched the house, maybe looking for money – who knows? The place was in utter chaos when we arrived. Right now, the techs are gathering evidence.'

'When do the doctors think the assault occurred?' asked Wittberg.

'Presumably late last night or in the early morning hours. It's a miracle that the kids didn't wake up, but they do sleep at the other end of the house. This morning they found their mother in bed, but she didn't respond when they tried to wake her. They knew their grandparents were supposed to come over later, so they decided to watch TV and wait. It was pure luck that I happened to ring so early.'

'When was that?'

'Just after nine o'clock.'

'What the hell does this mean?' Kihlgård tossed out the question.

'As we all know, threats and assaults are not uncommon in the construction business,' said Knutas. 'Especially if illegal workers are involved.'

'Russians,' retorted Kihlgård. 'The gun was Russian.'

'I know. Although that doesn't necessarily mean that Bovide was killed by a Russian. Anybody could have bought a Russian gun.'

'Maybe the murder of Peter Bovide was not well planned, after all,' interjected Jacobsson. 'Suppose that he owed money to some illegal workers, and for some reason he wasn't paying them. It's possible that they hadn't planned to kill him; maybe they just wanted to scare him. But something went wrong, and one of them may have lost control and shot him without thinking. And later, after killing him, they come and demand money from his widow instead. The question is why they didn't approach his business partner, Johnny Ekwall. That would have been easier.'

'You may think so, but if we're to believe what he

said, he had nothing to do with the company finances or paying out wages,' interjected Wittberg. 'They probably assumed that Bovide had a safe or something like that at home. Many CEOs do, especially abroad.'

'We need to talk to Vendela Bovide as soon as possible,' said Knutas. 'I'm hoping she'll have a lot to tell us.'

Both Knutas and Jacobsson flinched at the sight of Vendela Bovide when they arrived at Visby hospital an hour later. She was barely recognizable. Her face was swollen and badly bruised, her upper lip deformed. They had to make a real effort to act normally.

Vendela lay in the bed with her eyes closed and her hands resting limply on top of the covers.

'Hi, Vendela. We're here again, from the police,' said Jacobsson softly. 'It's me, Karin Jacobsson. I came to see you before. And this is Detective Superintendent Anders Knutas. He's in charge of the investigation.'

No reaction. The woman in the bed didn't move, and her eyes remained closed.

'Do you feel up to talking to us, just for a little while? We need to find out who did this to you.'

Slowly she turned towards the two officers and opened her eyes, squinting up at them.

'Could you draw the curtains?'

'Of course.'

Jacobsson got up and did as the patient asked. The light dimmed in the room. She helped Vendela to sit up in bed. The woman groaned a bit and grimaced with pain.

'Can you tell us what happened?'

Vendela licked her lips as if she were parched. Jacobsson picked up the glass of water from the night stand and handed it to the woman. She took several sips before she began to talk.

'It was early in the morning and someone rang the doorbell. When I opened the door, two men were standing outside. At first I thought it was a robbery, but they told me that Peter owed them money and, now that he was dead, I had to pay his debts.'

Bovide's widow paused to gather her strength. She kept her eyes shut as she talked, and her breathing was strained, as if every breath hurt. Jacobsson listened attentively.

'I asked them how much Peter owed them, and they said 300,000 kronor. I told them the truth, that I didn't have that much money and had no idea how to get it.'

'Then what happened?'

'They didn't believe me. They started threatening me, saying that if I didn't pay up, I was going to get hurt.'

'So what did you do?'

'I tried to make them understand that we didn't have any money in the house, that all our money was in the bank.'

'How did they react?'

'You can see for yourselves.'

Vendela shuddered, as if to shake off the memory.

'What did they look like?'

'One was really tall and thin, about six feet, blond with a pierced tongue. The other was shorter, maybe five ten, and heavier, more muscular and with dark hair.'

'How old?'

'Twenty or twenty-five. Both of them.'

'What were they wearing?'

'Jeans and T-shirts. One had on black shoes; I think the other man was wearing trainers. One had tattoos all over his arms. And they weren't Swedish. They spoke broken English.'

'Have you ever seen them before?'

'I think so.'

'When was that?'

'They came to the house one night and talked to Peter. That was just a few days before we drove up to Fårö.'

'What did they say?'

'I don't know. They stayed outside, in the front garden. Peter was upset when he came back in. It was something about the fact that they were working illegally for him and they wanted money that he didn't have.'

'You said that they spoke broken English. Do you know where they were from?'

'I think they spoke Finnish or some Baltic language.'

They didn't find out much more from their interview with Vendela Bovide. They asked her to look at a collection of photos of known criminals, but she didn't recognize any of them. The investigative team spent the rest of Saturday working on the assault on the widow and how this might be connected to her husband's murder. By knocking on doors in the neighbourhood they found a witness who had seen a car with Estonian plates drive past in the morning; the tip was considered of major interest.

Yet by late afternoon Knutas felt as if he'd run out of steam. He was sitting in his office, sucking on his unlit pipe, as thoughts raced through his mind like a roller coaster. He pondered the unusual MO. What could that tell him? On the one hand, it testified to a cold-blooded murderer devoid of any emotions who had shot his victim at close range without batting an eye. On the other hand, the reckless shooting of the victim in the stomach indicated that the perp had lost control, a murderer overcome by emotion. If they followed that line of thought, then they could rule out a hired gunman. The perp had probably known the victim and had some type of emotional bond with him. The fact that Peter Bovide had been shot in the forehead reinforced this hypothesis.

Knutas couldn't make everything fit together. There was nothing more he could do, so he decided he might as well go home. Lina and the kids were still out at the summer house. He was looking forward to sitting alone in the garden with a cold beer. Maybe then everything would seem clearer.

When he arrived back home Lina phoned. She sounded happy.

'We've spent the whole day at the beach. It's so beautiful out here. The water is 73 degrees. Right now Nisse is turning over the salmon steaks. He's the grillmaster since you're not here,' she said with a laugh. 'I'm sipping a glass of cold white wine. You should be here, sweetheart. Can't you get away?'

Knutas told her about the assault on Vendela Bovide.

'How awful. Imagine somebody breaking into a woman's house when she's all alone, and with children there too. They must be real brutes to do something like that. Do you think they're the ones who killed her husband?'

'They're suspects, of course. But they've disappeared, and by this time they could be back in their own country.'

'Do you know where they're from?'

'We think they might be Estonian.'

'It doesn't exactly sound like they're professionals. Shouldn't they have used fake licence plates on their car?'

'Yeah, you'd think so. There are so many contradictions in this investigation.'

'So have you contacted the Estonian police?'

'Sure, of course. We're hoping to track down these guys quickly.'

'OK, sweetie, I can hear that you've got your hands full.'

Knutas suddenly realized how much he missed Lina. But he didn't say anything. He could hear Nisse shouting in the background.

'I've got to go and help Nisse with the salmon. Shall we talk again early tomorrow morning?'

'Sure. Say hi to the kids.'

'I will.'

He managed to drink two beers before the phone rang again. It was Karin.

'Hi, Knutie. How are things going?'

In the background Knutas could hear people talking and laughing, and glasses clinking. It was obvious that she was in a restaurant. The only person who ever called Knutas 'Knutie' was Kihlgård, and Jacobsson was well aware how much he hated that nickname.

'Are you drunk?' he asked. 'Isn't it a bit early for that?'

Jacobsson seemed to pay no attention to her boss's critical tone.

'Thomas and I are sitting here in Packhuskällaren. We've had dinner and quite a lot of wine, actually,' she said, giggling. 'Plus a few drinks. We thought we needed it. We're wondering if you'd like to come and join us, since you're on your own. Isn't your family still out at the summer house?'

'Yes, they are. But I was just planning to cook myself some dinner.'

'Come over here instead and have some wine with us. We never see you except at work.'

'Come on over, damn it,' he heard Wittberg shout. Knutas debated with himself for a moment.
'OK. I'll be right there.'

Knutas decided to cycle to the restaurant. The mood in town was completely different from the mood inside his head. Tourists dressed in their summer best were strolling through the cobblestone streets inside the ring wall, on their way to or from restaurants and bars. Later, the nightclubs would be packed. The heat had held on for the past two weeks, and plenty of people had a good suntan. He glanced at his own arm below the short sleeve of his tennis shirt. Abnormally pale for this time of year. He hadn't had a chance to spend any time out in the open air. Ever since his summer holiday had been interrupted, there had been no time for either sunbathing or swimming.

There was a festive atmosphere in town, and everyone looked so happy and cheerful that he started feeling better himself. And he couldn't help looking forward to seeing Karin Jacobsson in an intoxicated state. He couldn't remember ever having seen that before, even though they'd attended dozens of parties together. Karin was the sort of person who never lost control. Maybe it was her strong sense of integrity that made her reluctant to let loose. And since she was so petite, it wouldn't take much alcohol to get her drunk.

Karin and Thomas were sitting outside at a corner table, and both of them waved enthusiastically when they saw him approach.

'Hi! How great that you decided to join us!'

Karin gave him a big smile, showing the gap between her front teeth. She made room for him on the bench next to her. *How can she be so suntanned?* thought Knutas. He hadn't noticed before. He ordered beer and a steak.

While they waited for the food to arrive, Jacobsson lit a cigarette.

'You've started smoking again?' asked Knutas. 'So what's the reason? Are you celebrating something, or is there some sort of problem?'

'What do you think?' She gave him a friendly poke in the side. 'I only smoke when I'm out partying.'

'Right. That's what they all say.'

'Good lord, you sound like an old married couple,' said Wittberg with a laugh.

Knutas looked at Jacobsson. To his amusement, he noticed that she was blushing.

'Well, I guess we almost are,' he said. 'We've been working together for a hell of a lot of years.'

'Maybe too long.'

'Not on your life. I hope we'll always work together. We're a dream team.'

They drank a toast to that. Knutas relaxed, realizing

he hadn't had so much fun in a long time. This was probably exactly what he needed. Wittberg was in top form. He was a real charmer and very popular with the ladies, and not just because of his surfer looks. Wittberg was one of the funniest people Knutas had ever met. He told one joke after another, making Knutas and Jacobsson howl with laughter.

A couple of hours later, it was time for a last round. The restaurant was about to close.

'But we can go over to my place,' said Jacobsson.

Knutas hesitated. He was starting to feel quite drunk, and tomorrow was a work day, even though it was Sunday.

'Come on. Just one drink, since we're having such a good time. Good lord, how often do we go out and have fun? We just work, work, work.'

'OK. But just one drink.'

It was only one a.m., and no one was waiting for him at home.

They left the restaurant and headed towards Mellangatan. Knutas walked alongside his bike. When they had almost reached Jacobsson's place, Wittberg stopped short.

'Listen here, I'm going to have to renege on the invitation. The booze has suddenly taken effect, and I'm feeling really drunk. I think it's best if I go home to bed.'

'But why? Are you sure?' said Jacobsson. 'Don't you want to come over?'

'No, I'm sure. I'll see you tomorrow.'

Jacobsson looked at Knutas. He felt confused. What should he do now?

'Would you like to come over for a little while at least?'

'All right,' he muttered, feeling as embarrassed as a gawky schoolboy. But this was just Karin, his long-time colleague.

They trudged up the four flights of stairs. Outside her door, he held his breath so as not to reveal how out of shape he was. Lately he hadn't been getting as much exercise as usual.

Knutas had been to Jacobsson's flat before, but that was a long time ago, when she once gave a small party for her colleagues.

He'd forgotten how attractive her place was. Wide wooden floorboards, a high ceiling, plasterwork on the ceiling, and country-style furniture mixed with modern pieces. Cosy and tasteful. And there was nothing wrong with the view, either, although at the moment the sea was barely visible in the dark.

'Good morning!' shouted Vincent enthusiastically when the lights were switched on. Knutas cautiously poked his finger through the bars of the cage where the cockatoo was enthroned in the middle of the living room.

'I didn't know you still had the bird,' Knutas called to Jacobsson, who was out in the kitchen.

'Yes, well, I don't think I could live without him.'

She came in holding a bottle of champagne and two glasses.

'That looks expensive.'

'Oh, it's been in the fridge for a while. We might as well finish it off. I love champagne. What kind of music would you like to listen to?'

'Have you got anything by the Weeping Willows?'

'Of course.' She raised her eyebrows appreciatively. 'I thought you were going to say Simon and Garfunkel, or something else from the Stone Age.'

Everybody at police headquarters was always teasing Knutas about driving around in his old Mercedes, weeping over 'Bridge Over Troubled Water'.

Jacobsson sat down in an armchair, while Knutas, with his long legs, chose the sofa. She lit a few candles standing on the coffee table and filled their glasses with ice-cold champagne.

'God, that's good,' said Knutas. 'Really delicious.'

'Isn't it? People should drink champagne more often.'

Both of them fell silent.

'So how have things been going for you?' Knutas asked awkwardly after a moment.

'What? How are things going? Good, fine, damned good, actually.'

'Great.'

He took a sip of his champagne. Why did she always have to be so secretive? Especially since he told her practically everything about himself. She was the one person at work he could really talk to, and she knew almost everything about him and Lina. Except for the recent lull in their relationship, which he hadn't yet mentioned.

On the other hand, he knew very little about Karin. She was almost forty, and he thought she was very attractive, but year after year she had remained single. He never heard about any boyfriends, at any rate. Occasionally he'd asked her personal questions, but she'd made it clear that she didn't want to talk about herself. Consequently, he'd stopped asking about her private life. Yet she was more than willing to talk about ordinary, trivial matters, such as soccer, which played an important role in her life, and her friends and other activities. But never about how she was feeling or her problems, and definitely not about her love life.

The conversation lagged, as if the fact that the two of them found themselves alone in Karin's flat in the middle of the night was affecting them more than they had planned when she initially suggested that they go to her place.

'Would you like something to eat?'

'Sure. Thanks.'

She got up and went out to the kitchen. *How petite she is, and dainty*, he thought. Nothing like Lina. She came right back with a bowl of pretzels.

'This is all I could find. Hope it's OK.'

She sat down on the sofa next to him. Knutas felt his mouth go dry. He took another sip of champagne. They started up the conversation again, but he could hardly concentrate on what they were saying. The situation felt so odd. He cleared his throat and glanced at his watch.

'Well, I think it's about time for me to get going.'

He could have bitten his tongue. How could he sound so stilted? Like an old fogey. Annoyed with himself, he stood up. Maybe a little too quickly.

'Right. Of course,' said Jacobsson, brushing back a lock of hair from her forehead. She followed him out to the hall. At the door he leaned forward to give her a hug. Again it occurred to him how petite she was. Before he knew what was happening, she kissed him on the mouth. A quick, warm kiss. And yet.

'Bye,' she said, opening the door for him.

'Bye. See you tomorrow.'

'Or today, you mean.'

She smiled. There was that gap between her teeth again.

Emma was awakened by her own scream. The night mare had ended with her falling into a deep abyss.

She sat up with a jolt, breathing hard and staring into the darkness. The bed was as big and hot as a desert. For a moment she sat there without moving, hardly able to think and overcome by a loneliness that seemed without end.

Not a sound came from Elin's cot. Suddenly Emma had the feeling that something was wrong. She leaped out of bed and went over to look at her daughter. There she lay, clad only in a nappy and white knickers. She had kicked off the thin blanket in the heat.

Emma sank back down on to the bed. She stared vacantly at the ceiling, realizing she was longing for Johan to be with her. Before now, her body had certainly missed him, but her mind had always said no. Had the nightmare made her weak? Couldn't she think clearly any more?

She decided to phone him right then. It was a little past three in the morning, but maybe he was still awake. He could get a cab and come over. Within an hour he could actually be lying next to her in bed. The thought was so enticing that she got up and dashed out to the hall, picked up the phone and punched in his number before she could change her mind. With her heart pounding, she listened to the ring tone on the other end of the line. One, two, three. Maybe he was asleep after all. Then she heard someone pick up. The next second, a woman's voice spoke.

'Hi, this is Maddie, on Johan's mobile.'

Emma could tell that it was very quiet in the background. At first she was disconcerted and didn't know what to do. She had been totally unprepared to hear a woman answer the phone. Who the hell was Maddie? Then she remembered – Madeleine Haga, the reporter for the national news who worked at *Aktuellt* and *Rapport*. They must be working together in the editorial office. Maybe something new had happened in the murder case. Emma was so relieved she felt dizzy.

'Hi, this is Emma Winarve. Could I speak to Johan?'

A brief pause before the woman answered.

'He's in the shower at the moment. Can I ask him to call you?'

Emma didn't reply. She had already hung up.

SUNDAY, 16 JULY

The investigation into the murder of Peter Bovide plodded on; the longed-for breakthrough hadn't occurred. The perpetrator was still on the loose.

The fraud division's examination of the finances of Slite Construction showed that Peter Bovide had taken on far more jobs than could be handled by his employees. This reinforced the suspicion that he had been using illegal workers. Currently the company had several projects under way: the biggest included a new house on Furillen, another in Stenkyrkehuk and the remodelling of a restaurant at Åminne campsite.

On Sunday, Knutas decided to go out and have a look at all three sites, if he had the time. He hoped to find a worker who was willing to talk. Since he wasn't in any hurry and didn't want to attract attention, he took his own car, the old Mercedes. The vehicle should really have been junked long ago, but Knutas couldn't bear to part with it, no matter how much Lina urged him to do so. In the end, she had simply gone out and bought her own car. He had been surprised to find the brand-new Toyota parked in their garage when he came home from work one evening, but he couldn't really blame her. There was a limit; even Knutas could understand that.

The lovely weather was still hanging on, much to the delight of the tourists. The sun seemed to have parked itself over Gotland for the foreseeable future, and the beaches were crowded with sunbathers.

In no time, Knutas was out of the city, and he was still able to appreciate the idyllic Gotland countryside as he drove through it. Well-nourished livestock grazed in the pastures of the farms he passed, and the road was lined with bright red poppies and blue chicory. Now and then he caught a glimpse of the sea along the way. Billowing fields of grain and chalk-white churches. He loved this island that he called home, and he couldn't imagine moving anywhere else. Knutas had lived on Gotland all his life. He was lucky that Lina had agreed to move here; if he was perfectly honest with himself, he doubted he would have done the same for her.

On his way to Slite he rang the hospital to find out how Vendela Bovide was doing. The doctor thought she would need to stay a few more days. The broken rib was giving her a lot of pain, but otherwise her injuries were largely superficial. The men who had beaten her had apparently meant only to scare her. It made Knutas sick to recall how she had looked when they found her. He had never understood how men could be capable of beating up women.

He decided to start with the house on Furillen. He

didn't really think that anyone would be there on a Sunday, but you never knew.

Furillen was a rough-hewn and isolated island encompassing five hundred hectares, located at the tip of Gotland's north-eastern coast. It had a diverse landscape, combining dense forest with sandy and stone-covered beaches, hills, boulders, sea-stacks and moors. In the past there had been a large limestone quarry on the island, and the vestiges from those times were still visible in the form of old factory buildings.

The factory had been transformed into a hotel and restaurant by several enthusiasts from Göteborg. The defence ministry also had a few buildings at its disposal, but otherwise Furillen was mostly uninhabited. A long bridge went from Gotland out to the island. From looking at the map, Knutas had determined that the construction site was right across from the old factory. He drove along the gravel road, dusty with limestone, past the factory buildings. Not a soul in sight.

When he came to the top of the hill behind the hotel, he had a splendid view of the sea, and of Kyllaj, the last outpost on Gotland, in the distance. A lonely village on the shore of Valleviken that had previously subsisted on seafaring and the stone quarry but was now occupied almost solely by tourists.

He found the job site without any trouble. On an open plot of land with a view of the water and the nearby islets stood a newly built house that looked almost finished. An expensive, fancy two-storey house with panoramic windows facing south. A two-car garage stood next to the house, and a curved stone staircase with pillars on either side framed the front entrance. The whole place had a nouveau riche air about it, as if the owner wanted to show that he could afford to be ostentatious. Knutas parked outside. No one was around. At the back, he saw a huge patio made of wood, built on several levels, with a swimming pool and an unobstructed view of the sea.

A fishing boat was on its way towards Kyllaj, followed by a flock of shrieking gulls which kept diving at the deck. Knutas perched on a saw horse near the construction site and filled his pipe. Then he lit it and began puffing away. Images of Peter Bovide's lacerated body and of his injured wife filled Knutas's thoughts. *Was this what it was all about? The fact that Bovide owed money to some illegal workers?* It had to involve more than 300,000 kronor, at any rate. But to murder the person who owed the money seemed completely idiotic. And then assaulting his widow afterwards didn't seem to indicate any sort of careful planning. *Maybe it's about something else entirely*, thought Knutas as he studied the house.

He got up to peer through the windows, admiring the stone fireplace, the floor paved with pebbles, a tiled bathroom and an ultra-modern kitchen with all the appliances in place. Mosaic, tile and brick everywhere.

The silence was suddenly shattered by the sound of an approaching engine.

Knutas walked over to the very edge of the plateau and looked down the slope. On the road below he saw a large delivery van which turned in at the hotel and then continued past, on its way up towards the building site.

Suddenly Knutas felt uneasy. He had come out here to talk to the workers, but at the same time it was possible that one of them might be the killer. He was here all alone, without his service revolver, and he wouldn't have a chance if the situation turned hostile. He cursed himself for not asking someone to come with him. The smartest thing to do now would be to hide and then wait to see who or what appeared on the scene. He looked around. Did he have time to move the car out of sight? He yanked open the door and put the key in the ignition. The road continued on past the property.

He'd just managed to drive around the curve before the front of the delivery van appeared in his rearview mirror. When he had driven safely out of sight, he turned off the engine and rolled down the window to listen to what was happening. The van doors slammed, and he could hear voices speaking a foreign language. It sounded like Finnish, except softer. Maybe it was Estonian. A witness had seen a car with Estonian plates outside Vendela Bovide's house. Had her attackers arrived? Knutas's nerves were on high alert.

Cautiously, he opened the car door and got out. He kept to the edge of the woods as he made his way back and then stopped behind some trees and bushes where he had a good view.

Two young men came out of the house carrying something that looked like a washing machine. A third man was waiting next to the van and helped them load it inside. Then they went back into the house and returned with a full-size stainless-steel refrigerator. *Good God*, thought Knutas. *They're going to empty the house of all the appliances.* Nervously, he fumbled in his pocket for his mobile and punched in Jacobsson's number. He swore when he heard her voicemail start up. He tried Wittberg. The same result. What bad luck. Was everybody unavailable just because it was Sunday? The day of the week shouldn't matter, since the whole investigative team was still supposed to be working. He punched in the number for the criminal division. Kihlgård answered in his usual hearty manner, although it was obvious that he was eating something and his mouth was full.

'Kihlgård.'

'Hi, it's me, Knutas.'

'Hi, Knutie.'

'I'm out at one of the job sites that Peter Bovide's company is working on. They've built a luxury home on Furillen, and right now there's a gang out here taking away all the appliances.'

'Why are you whispering?'

'Because I'm standing only a few yards away.'

'OK. Are you alone?'

'Yes, unfortunately. And I don't have my gun with me, so I don't dare intervene.'

'No, don't do that, for God's sake. Who exactly is out there?'

'Three young guys with earrings and tattoos. I think they might be Finns, or possibly from the Baltics.'

'Where did you say this house is?'

'It's on Furillen, right across from the old factory that's now a hotel.'

'Furillen – what sort of place is that?'

'An island, damn it,' Knutas hissed. 'I'm not planning to draw you a road map. Talk to the others, but you've got to get out here, and be bloody quick about it.'

'Sure. Stay where you are, and we'll leave right away.'

'Do that, but use unmarked cars and no sirens. And ring me when you're driving across the bridge to the island. You have to wait for my go-ahead before you can drive past the hotel, because they'll be able to see you from there. The building site is right across the road.'

'OK. We're leaving now. Did you say how many there are? And do you think they're armed?'

'Shit!'

'What is it, Knutie?'

'Someone's coming. I'll ring you later.'

Knutas cut Kihlgård off. One of the men was heading straight for his hiding place. With his heart in his mouth, Knutas waited to see if he was going to be discovered. The lanky man had a shaved head, and his bare chest was covered with tattoos. A knife was sticking out of the back pocket of his shorts.

Knutas kept his eyes tensely fixed on the young man. If he moved a muscle, his hiding place would be found.

He cast a glance at the others. They were still bringing things out of the house.

The next second, Knutas realized what was about to happen. The man reached inside his trousers, and was obviously about to take a piss, only a couple of yards away. Knutas bowed his head and stared at the ground, silently praying that he wouldn't be seen.

Then his mobile rang.

Even though Johan had felt so awful about sleeping with Madeleine Haga, he had ended up in bed with her again. On Saturday night, the whole group had gone to Munkkällaren restaurant. There he had run into several other journalist colleagues who were on the island, and the evening had ended with a little post-party gathering at Johan's one-bedroom flat. Madeleine stayed after the others had left. When he opened his eyes the next morning, he had felt even worse than the first time, if that was possible, and all he wanted to do was get out of his flat. He suggested having breakfast at a café on Stora Torget.

They drank lattes, ate croissants and read the morning papers. The conversation was halting and revolved around innocent topics such as the lack of fresh information and how they should go about following up on the story.

'If nothing new happens today, I'll be forced to go back home,' said Madeleine with a sigh. 'And just when I'm having such a good time here on Gotland.'

She gave Johan a coy look as she rubbed his shin with her sandal.

Johan didn't know how to respond. He smiled awkwardly and pulled out his mobile to check to see if Knutas had tried to call. Johan had rung the superintendent several times during the weekend, but without result. Normally, Knutas called him back.

As Johan looked at the incoming calls on his mobile, he was surprised to see Emma's number. She'd rung him at 3.14 in the morning. And someone had picked up, but it wasn't him. He glanced at Madeleine, who was intently reading the paper. He noticed that she had croissant crumbs at the corner of her mouth.

'Did you happen to answer my mobile?'

No reply. She kept on reading as if she hadn't heard him.

'Hey, Maddie.' Johan leaned forward and raised his voice. 'Did you happen to answer a call that came in on my mobile?'

She looked up.

'What? Oh, right. It rang early this morning while you were in the shower. I forgot to mention it. You were so hot when you came out of the bathroom that I had other things on my mind.'

A crumb fell from her lips and landed in her coffee cup without her noticing.

'Who was it?'

'It was Emma. I'm sorry, Johan,' she said politely. 'I just forgot.'

'What did she say?'

'She wanted to talk to you. I told her that you were in the shower, and then she hung up.'

Johan jumped to his feet.

'Why didn't you say anything? It could have been important – maybe Elin's sick, or something like that.'

'You don't have to get so upset,' she said sullenly. 'I can't help it if she hung up on me.'

Without another word, Johan left the table. He was furious. What the hell was Emma going to think? The truth, of course. That he'd been to bed with another woman. He punched in Emma's number as he stomped off towards Adelsgatan. At the same time, he glanced at his watch. It was eleven fifteen and the sun was shining. No answer on her mobile either. She was probably at the beach with Elin. They both loved going there. Suddenly he felt on the verge of tears. How could he have been such an idiot?

He quickly made up his mind and ran the whole way to the Swedish TV building. That's where his car was parked.

He jumped in and drove away from Visby, taking the road out to Roma.

Knutas pressed his body against the wall of the house, straining to make sure that his panting wouldn't be heard.

He'd flung his mobile as far away as possible when the tattooed man had been surprised by the ring tone. It was lucky for Knutas that the guy was already in the middle of taking a leak; that gave him a head start.

The man yelled to his companions, and the three of them immediately spread out to search the woods. Knutas, who was hiding behind a tree, decided the best thing to do would be to head back towards the house. He'd managed to sound the alarm, and his colleagues were on their way. It was just a matter of keeping out of sight until they arrived.

He hesitated only a second before he emerged from the woods and ran as fast as he could across the yard. He kept close to the house as he crept further away, the whole time keeping his eyes fixed on the woods. The gravel crunched under his feet. Just a little further. His mouth was dry, and he was trying to slow down his breathing.

He caught sight of a patio door that stood ajar. Swiftly, he slipped inside the living room and then dashed up the stairs in a few bounds to reach the next floor. There he suddenly found himself standing in what looked like a studio, with a high ceiling and an enormous circular window facing the sea. All of a sudden he heard the front door open downstairs. Shit. They were back already.

He didn't dare move. Frozen in place, he listened to at least two men moving around below. They exchanged a few words in their incomprehensible language. At any moment they might decide to come upstairs. Did the floor creak? His stomach turned over as he lifted one foot with the greatest caution. For several seconds he held it up in the air before he dared set it down again. Keeping his weight evenly distributed, Knutas soundlessly moved towards what looked like the door to a bedroom. He had noticed earlier that it had a balcony, so maybe it would be possible to climb down from there.

Doors opened and slammed below as they searched for him. He wondered how much time had passed since he'd spoken to Kihlgård on the phone. Ten minutes? Fifteen? It would take a while before the police reached the isolated island. He was on his own.

Suddenly he heard someone coming up the stairs. The door to the bedroom was open slightly; two more steps and he was inside. He could hardly believe his eyes when he saw that he had found a good place to hide and that the room also had a big wardrobe fastened to one wall, with sliding frosted-glass doors. He stepped inside and slid the door shut, hoping that no one would hear him, then waited tensely. A strong smell of paint filled his nostrils. It was stuffy inside the wardrobe, and the heat was almost unbearable. He took short, shallow breaths in order to save on oxygen.

Only a few seconds later he heard quick footsteps approaching. Someone was inside the room now; a man's voice muttered something, and then there was the sound of the door to the balcony being opened. Footsteps tramped on the wooden deck, shouts to someone who was apparently outside the house, further away.

Thoughts of Lina and the kids flew through Knutas's mind. A flash of fear raced through his body. Was he a hair's breadth from death?

That was all Knutas had time to think before the door to the wardrobe slid abruptly open.

The street was silent and deserted. It was so hot that the air shimmered. An elderly woman was slowly heading along the road, taking her dog for a walk. Otherwise nothing moved in the idyllic residential area. Johan parked his car outside the house. The garden was resplendent, but the grass was much too high. Last summer he had been the one who mowed the lawn. That was when Elin was a newborn, and he was the happiest man in the world. It felt like so long ago. Like a whole different life.

He quickly walked up the front path. The patio furniture was out, and the hammock was in place, but it didn't look as if anyone had used it in a while. The house looked empty even though the pram stood on the porch. Perhaps she wasn't home after all? Maybe she hadn't taken the pram when they went to the beach.

He rang the bell and listened to it echoing inside. Waited nervously and tried to peer through the kitchen window, but he didn't see anyone.

He rang the bell again. Now he heard the sound of

shuffling footsteps. Slowly, someone turned the dead-bolt inside. A fly was making its way up the door jamb. He stared at the painted sign: 'Home of Emma, Filip, Sara and Elin.'

One name is missing, he thought.

Finally Emma opened the door.

'Hi,' he said.

How small she looked, as if she'd shrunk in the wash. She made no motion to let him come in.

'Where's Elin?'

He glanced uneasily at the hall behind her.

'She's asleep.'

'Can I come in?'

'No.'

She folded her arms.

'Please let me come in. I've driven all the way here from town just to see you.'

'Why? What possible reason could you have for coming to see me?'

'What's the matter?' he asked hesitantly.

'"What's the matter?"' she repeated. 'There's nothing in particular going on with me – the question is, what's going on with you? You've got a new girlfriend, right? So what do you and I have to do with each other any more? Nothing.'

'Take it easy.'

He tried to step inside, but Emma blocked his way. She stared at him with a cold expression, and her voice changed into a snarl.

'You're not welcome to set foot in this house ever again! Do you hear me? And from now on, you can pick Elin up at the day-care centre or at some other neutral location, because you're not welcome here. I don't want to have anything more to do with you!'

Anger flashed through Johan's mind. Everything that he'd had to endure descended on him all at once.

'Damn it all,' he snapped as he stepped forward, forcing her to retreat into the hall. 'Calm down. Is it really so strange that I'd sleep with somebody else? You've pushed me away, treated me like I have the plague. And why did you do that, Emma? Why? Because a mentally ill man kidnapped our daughter? Was I the one who took her away? Did I have anything to do with what happened? No, but apparently you think I was to blame for the whole thing! And why do you think that? Oh right, it's because I was just doing my fucking job! Do you really think, in your wildest imagination, that I would do anything that might harm Elin? Or you, for that matter?'

Looking frightened, Emma backed her way into the kitchen, unprepared for the strength of his reaction. She'd never seen Johan so angry.

'Well, let me tell you one thing, Emma. I'm sick and tired of longing for you, tired of hoping that everything will turn out all right. I've had enough. For three years I've done everything in my power to bring us together, but what good has it done? I can't do it any more. So just go ahead and sit here in this house feeling sorry for yourself.'

Emma couldn't look at him any more. She sank down on to a chair and turned away. She held her hands over her ears and closed her eyes tight in order to shut him out. She intended to sit there like that until he finished what he was saying and left. The only thing she wanted was for him to disappear. For some strange reason, she felt perfectly calm inside. It was as if all her thoughts had now been confirmed. That it was over between them, it was definitely over. Once and for all. When Johan finally left, slamming the door behind him, she was still sitting in the same position.

And she stayed like that for a very long time.

The young man stared at him in astonishment.

'Who are you?' he asked in English.

'Wait, wait. I'm a police officer,' said Knutas, stumbling over his words.

The man standing in front of him suddenly looked nervous.

'Police?'

He grabbed Knutas by the arm and hauled him out of the wardrobe, calling to his companions.

The next moment, Knutas was surrounded by all three. With trembling hands he pulled out his police ID.

The man with the most tattoos, who seemed to be the leader, studied the ID, then turned it over and looked at the back. He cast a glance at the other two and muttered something incomprehensible.

'Can I sit down?' asked Knutas. His legs were shaking.

'Yes. Come with us.'

They escorted him down the stairs and out to the back of the house to some patio furniture.

'What are you doing here?' asked the leader.

'Just checking on things,' said Knutas. 'Purely routine.'

'On a Sunday?'

All three men regarded him dubiously. Close up, they didn't seem particularly hostile. Two of them were standing on either side of Knutas, holding on to his arms. They immediately started up a lively discussion in their own language.

'Where are you from?' Knutas ventured.

The leader glared at him without replying, and the discussion grew more heated. Suddenly they were in a big hurry. They yanked Knutas to his feet and made him hold out his arms while the leader frisked his pockets. Wallet, car keys, pipe tobacco – he took everything. Then he yelled something to the others, who hustled Knutas back inside the house. He tried to pull himself out of their grasp and resisted as best he could, but he found it impossible to get away. He was terrified at the thought of what lay in store for him.

'What are you doing?' he yelled, in English. 'Let me go! I'm a police officer.'

With resolute expressions, they dragged him towards the front door.

'What the hell do you think you're doing?' Now Knutas had switched to Swedish. 'I'm a police officer, damn it!'

Were they going to kidnap him? Kill him? Cut his throat, or shoot him and throw his body off the cliff? Or maybe lock him in the boot of his own car so he'd die of suffocation?

Knutas thought his last hour was near when the leader opened the door to a clothes cupboard in the hall and signalled to his companions to throw him inside.

'We are very sorry!' Knutas heard him say before the door slammed shut with a bang.

Forty minutes later, Martin Kihlgård and Thomas Wittberg roared up the drive, closely followed by several more police vehicles. There was no one to be seen. The front door of the house stood open.

From inside they could hear a dull pounding. Wittberg was the first to run in. The sound was coming from a room in the hall. A board had been nailed across the door.

He found a crowbar on the ground outside the house and with some effort finally got the door open.

'What the hell?' he panted when he peered inside.

They had found Knutas.

Johan sat with his head in his hands, staring down at the dust-covered gravel. He was much too upset to drive, so he'd started walking along the road from Emma's house and continued on towards the football pitch. It was deserted. He sat down on a bench and smoked one cigarette after another until his throat was burning. He had no idea how long he'd been sitting there when he noticed a woman with a pram coming closer. His stomach turned over when he saw who it was. There was Emma, with Elin, his daughter. He wanted to rush over and yank the handle of the pram out of her hands, but he restrained himself.

Then she turned her head and glanced in his direction. For several seconds he wondered whether she would come over to him or just keep going, pretending not to have seen him. Out of the corner of his eye, he saw her approach. He froze.

'Oh, look, here's Pappa,' she cooed in a cheerful voice, holding Elin out towards Johan.

Johan raised his head, and all of a sudden his little daughter was so close he could smell the scent of her.

Those little brown eyes, that heart-shaped little face, the dimple on her chin. His dimple.

He made an effort to smile at her as he held out his hands. The next moment he was holding her warm, chubby little body close to him. That's when he fell apart. Johan hugged his daughter tight and wept so that his shoulders shook.

At a loss, Emma sat down next to him without saying a word.

Knutas was taken to the hospital. He wasn't injured, but Kihlgård still insisted that he go, if nothing else to talk with somebody about what had just happened. Knutas submitted to a medical examination and then recounted the entire course of events to a kindly doctor in the psychiatric emergency unit he happened to know quite well. Lina and the kids came back from the summer house, and Lina urged him to take it easy and stay home for the rest of the day, but Knutas refused. By two o'clock that afternoon, he was back at police headquarters.

The entire team was on the job, as the investigation had now picked up steam. There was no time to lose.

Knutas had barely sat down at his desk before Jacobsson stuck her head in the door.

'Hi. How are you doing?'

She came over to give him a quick hug.

'What a thing to happen. I'm glad it turned out well.'

Knutas smiled wanly.

'I heard you got locked inside a clothes cupboard, but then what happened?'

'They went back to emptying the house of everything that wasn't nailed down. I'd probably been sitting there for half an hour when I heard the van drive off. I wasn't really worried, since I'd already managed to contact Kihlgård. And it wasn't more than ten or fifteen minutes later that they showed up.'

'Could you tell what language those guys were speaking?'

'I'm not much of a linguist, as you know, but I think it was one of the Baltic languages, probably Estonian.'

'Do you think they were the same guys who beat up Vendela Bovide?'

'It seems highly likely.'

'Have you gone through the book of mug shots?'

'Yup. That was the first thing I did when I got back from the hospital. I've already been debriefed and looked at photos of plenty of ex-cons. Nothing, unfortunately.'

'How well does Vendela's description of the men match what you saw?'

'It seems likely that two of them were the guys who beat her up. But there was also a third guy out on Furillen.'

'So now everything seems to indicate that the murder of Peter Bovide did have something to do with his illegal workers.'

'It seems so,' Knutas agreed. 'At the same time, I don't think they were the killer type.'

'What do you mean?'

'At first I was scared, of course, thinking they might be the ones who shot Bovide. For a few seconds I really thought it was going to be the end of me. But then what happened? They locked me in a clothes cupboard, and even apologized for doing it.'

'What?'

'The last thing I heard them say was "We're sorry!" Can you believe it?' Knutas gave her a wry smile.

'That doesn't exactly sound like a cold-blooded murderer.'

'No, it doesn't.'

'But if the murder isn't connected with the illegal workers, what the heck is this all about?'

'That's the very question I've been asking myself over and over again.'

223

MONDAY, 17 JULY

Knutas woke up in his bed at home on Bokströmsgatan and found himself staring at Lina's freckled back. She was taking deep, calm breaths. Cautiously, he kissed her shoulder, and she grunted softly.

They'd had a marvellous time. He and Lina had sat out on the porch in the warm summer evening, sipping cold white wine and talking the way they used to. They discussed what had happened out on Furillen. When he spoke the words aloud, it was as if he finally realized what a serious episode he'd been through.

They talked about how lucky he'd been, since the whole drama had ended well, even though the three men had escaped with all the appliances and everything else. Knutas was reminded of what he and Lina actually had together. What did it matter if their sex life was going through a lull when he thought about the camaraderie and intimacy they shared? They had fun together, laughed a lot and he loved her bold outlook. It was so easy living with Lina.

He needed to make more of an effort, do more to

rekindle their love. It really wouldn't require such major changes to improve things. He'd already made a start the previous evening by making sure they went to bed long before they were too tired to do anything but fall asleep.

When Knutas arrived at the investigative meeting an hour later, he noticed a particularly charged mood in the room. Even though he was a few minutes early, everyone else was already there, and they all seemed remarkably focused. Knutas started off the meeting.

'So the primary suspects are these three men from Estonia, according to information we received from Peter Bovide's partner, Johnny Ekwall. Since they're undocumented workers, the construction company only has a mobile number for one of them, whose name is Andres. We're now using that number to search for him in Estonia. I also jotted down the licence-plate number of the van before they found me, and fortunately they didn't find the little scrap of paper when they searched my pockets. The car is registered to someone named Ants Otsa. We've enlisted the help of the Estonian police, and the hunt is on for all three men, now suspected of murdering Peter Bovide. We have a statement from a witness who said that three Baltic men and a large white van were seen on the boat to Nynäshamn yesterday around lunchtime, and if that's true, then they could be back in Estonia by now.'

'What do we know about these guys?' asked Wittberg.

'I've talked to Interpol,' said Kihlgård. 'Ants Otsa is on

the police books in Estonia for possession of narcotics and as an accessory to armed robbery several years ago. The other two are unknowns; we don't even have their last names.'

'How long have they been working for Slite Construction?'

'About six months, according to Johnny Ekwall,' replied Knutas.

'Does Ekwall have any idea what's behind their actions?' asked Jacobsson.

'He continues to claim that he knows very little, that he was just doing his job, and that he didn't get involved in how the company was otherwise being run. According to him, it was a subcontractor who had responsibility for the house project on Furillen, but we haven't yet located the person in charge. Of course, Ekwall had his suspicions that things weren't being done entirely on the up and up, but he reasoned that as long as the company was doing well and he received his salary, he shouldn't get involved.'

'Typical male reaction,' snorted Jacobsson. 'Just stick your head in the sand and refuse to see what's going on around you, and then you can't be held responsible.'

'At any rate, he had a hard time explaining how the company could have taken on so much more work than its employees could handle. I think that as soon as the examination of the company's finances is complete, we'll be able to charge both him and possibly the secretary, Linda Johansson, with tax evasion,' Knutas went on. 'She couldn't have been unaware of what was going on, even if she too did probably try to stick her head in the sand. Provided that tactic isn't exclusive to men.'

'Has anyone talked to her husband?' asked Kihlgård.

'Yes, but from what I understand, we didn't learn anything useful,' said Jacobsson. 'I don't have the transcript here, but we can take another look at the interview.'

'Good.' Knutas drummed his fingertips impatiently on the table. 'Anything else? How's it going with the search for a safe?'

'We've been over the house and the office again with a fine-tooth comb,' said Sohlman. 'There's no sign at all of a safe or any money stashed away.'

'The fraud division is continuing their investigation, although the wheels turn slowly,' said Knutas. 'But at least they've gone through the bank accounts of the company, as well as Bovide's personal accounts. When it comes to the company, it's obvious that he was making extensive use of illegal workers, at least during the past two years. He was clearly taking big risks, committing the firm to major projects and laying out a lot of money. But as a corporation, the company is separate from his private finances, and there we've been unable to find anything out of the ordinary – either too much or too little money. According to his wife, everything adds up.'

'The question is whether she's being honest,' said Knutas pensively. 'And whether the business partner, Johnny Ekwall, is telling the truth. Let's bring both of them in again.'

The phone rang as soon as Knutas was back in his office.

A husky male voice spoke on the other end of the line.

'Hi, it's Torsten Ahlberg from Visby hospital. You wanted to talk to me?'

'Yes, thanks for getting back to me.'

Knutas quickly outlined the details in the Bovide homicide case.

'He was a regular patient of mine, and I had prescribed anti-depressants for him. That's true.'

'Why? What sort of problem did he have?'

'He suffered from panic attacks and needed help in quelling the symptoms, in order to avoid the real abyss, so to speak. But I'm afraid I can't tell you what the underlying problem was.'

'Was it related to his epilepsy?'

'Not directly, but he started having epileptic fits about the same time as the panic attacks began. That was years ago.'

'When did he first come to see you?'

'I have a very clear memory of that,' said the doctor. 'After I heard about the murder, naturally I started thinking about my contact with Peter Bovide. I thought that was what you wanted to ask me about, so I've already taken out his casebook. I have all the information here. Under normal circumstances, the contents would be confidential, but it's a different matter now that a homicide investigation is involved – and besides, the patient is dead.'

'I'd like to know as much as you can tell me about Bovide.'

'He came here in the early hours of 1 August 1985, at 3.15 a.m., to be precise,' the doctor read from the file. 'He was suffering from violent convulsions. We gave him the appropriate medicines and detoxified him. His blood alcohol level was .16 when he arrived.'

'From what I understand, that was his first epileptic fit, and it brought on a severe depression.'

'Hmm . . . that's not exactly how I'd describe the situation. Peter Bovide did begin therapy after that event, and then he started seeing an authorized therapist. The psychologist and I kept in contact the whole time, since I was the doctor handling his case from a purely medical perspective, and we both saw a connection between the epilepsy and the depression.'

'In what way?'

'It's not easy to say. But both started at the same time.'

'On that day, 1 August?'

'No, he'd actually had his first epileptic fit a week earlier.'

'Really? In what context?'

'Unfortunately, I don't know. He didn't want to say. On that occasion he was admitted to Nynäshamn hospital.'

'Nynäshamn? What was he doing there?'

'He may have been on his way either to or from Gotland. It was in the middle of the summer, after all. He must have been on holiday.'

'Sure, you're probably right. Well, don't hesitate to ring again if you think of anything else.'

Knutas thanked the doctor for his information.

Late Monday night, Knutas received the message he was hoping for. The Estonian police reported that the owner of the white van, Ants Otsa, had been arrested, along with his two companions, at his home in central Tallinn. All three had openly admitted to the police that they'd been working illegally in Sweden for a company on Gotland called Slite Construction. The contact between the Swedish and Estonian police had functioned beyond all expectations. The extradition process, which was normally difficult to handle, had been carried out with astonishing ease. On Tuesday the men would be flown to Stockholm, and from there to Gotland.

Knutas leaned back in his chair. He was pleased to know that the men who had most likely beaten Vendela Bovide and also threatened him and locked him in a cupboard had now been caught. And maybe all three, or at least one of them, had murdered Peter Bovide.

TUESDAY, 18 JULY

Right after lunch on Tuesday, the three Estonians arrived at police headquarters, along with officers from the Estonian police force. An interpreter was summoned to help out if needed.

Knutas was not allowed to participate since he was a plaintiff in the incident that had occurred on Furillen. He caught a glimpse of the men as they were escorted to the interrogation room, and he recognized them at once. A wave of revulsion ran through his body. Maybe he'd been more affected by the experience than he thought.

The men were identified as Ants Otsa, Andres Sula and Evald Kreem. They were interviewed separately.

Jacobsson and Wittberg started with Ants Otsa, the owner of the van.

They took seats in one of the interrogation rooms on the ground floor of police headquarters. The arrested man sat on one side of the table, and Jacobsson sat across from him. As a witness to the interview, Wittberg sat in a chair a short distance away. Otsa was no more than twenty-three years old, and he seemed nervous.

His English was good enough that they didn't need an interpreter.

'We had nothing to do with killing Peter. Nothing. You have to realize that,' he insisted over and over again, even before the interview had begun.

'OK, OK,' Jacobsson admonished him. 'Take it easy. Let's take one thing at a time.'

She switched on the tape recorder, asked the usual introductory questions and then leaned back in her chair to study the young man's face; he was clearly panic-stricken. He was blond, with a pale complexion, and his tongue was pierced. A pinch of snuff made his upper lip bulge on one side. His eyes were a watery light blue.

'What have you been doing here on Gotland?'

'I work in construction.'

'Illegally?'

'What do you mean?'

'Do you have a work permit?'

'No.'

'How long have you been working here?'

'About six months.'

'Is Slite Construction the only company you've worked for?'

'Yes.'

'Tell us about the building project on Furillen.'

'What?'

'For instance, how many of you worked there?'

Otsa looked away.

'I don't really know. Three or four.'

'OK. Why did you remove all the appliances from the house?'

The young man fidgeted uneasily.

'Because we hadn't been paid. We'd been working day and night for two months without getting an öre.'

'Why hadn't you been paid?'

'Peter said he'd pay us, but he never did.'

'But you got your wages in the beginning?'

'Yes, back then he came out every two weeks and gave us the wages we'd agreed on. Later on, he started making excuses.'

'Do you know why?'

'He said he was waiting for money from someone else who was late in paying, and that we'd get paid soon, but we never did.'

'Was Peter always the one who paid you?'

'Yes.'

'How did he give you the money?'

'He came out to the building site.'

'Were you paid in cash?'

'Yes.'

'How much?'

'Eighty kronor an hour.'

'But you haven't been paid anything recently?'

'No. We worked on several jobs for him, and we haven't received any wages for the past two months.'

'OK, let's go back to that Sunday on Furillen. Why did you lock up Superintendent Knutas?'

'We felt bad that we had to do that. But when we saw that he was a police officer, we got scared. We needed to go back home to our families. We have wives and children to support. We took the things from the house as payment for back wages.'

'What about the beating?' said Jacobsson. 'What do you know about the assault on Vendela Bovide, Peter's wife?'

Otsa looked like he'd been expecting the question.

'It wasn't something we'd planned. We were desperate, because we hadn't been paid, and now Peter was dead. And that other guy, Johnny, said that he had nothing to do with the money. So the only one who could pay our wages was Peter's wife. We'd heard that they had a safe at home. We didn't intend to hit her, but Evald lost control.'

'Evald? You mean he was the only one who hit her? While you two stood and watched? Or maybe you were comforting her two little children while he beat her?'

Jacobsson was infuriated by the man's evasive answers.

Otsa lowered his eyes. 'No. We didn't think about the fact that she had little kids in the house. I'm sorry, but we were desperate. We didn't know what to do.'

Jacobsson and Wittberg exchanged glances.

'Do you own a gun?'

'A gun? No.' The man sitting across the table shook his head.

'Do any of your friends own a gun?'

'I don't know.'

'Where were you on the morning of 10 July, around six o'clock?'

'I don't know,' said Otsa, and for the first time his voice shook.

'Take your time and think about it,' Jacobsson urged him.

'On 10 July, that early in the morning? I was sleeping in the construction shack out on Furillen. That's where we were staying. Well, I was probably up by then. We usually started work at seven.'

'Is there anyone who can confirm your statement?'

'Sure, my friends who are here with me. All three of us were out there.'

'Are they the only ones?'

'Yes, we were the only ones sleeping there.'

'So there's nobody else who can vouch for the truth of what you're telling us?'

'No.'

'In other words, you don't have an alibi for the time of the murder?'

Ants Otsa didn't reply. He just stared straight ahead with a vacant expression.

GOTSKA SANDÖN, 21 JULY 1985

As the two sisters walked around Kyrkudden on Gotska Sandön and saw the waters of Franska Bukten ahead of them, they felt like explorers who had just come ashore on a deserted island.

There was no sign of any human habitation as far as the eye could see. The shoreline stretched out for several kilometres, making a soft curve of fine-grained sand all the way out to Tärnudden on the other side. Even though it was still before noon, the heat was already intense; the sun glittered on the water, and the only living creatures to be seen were a few black-backed seagulls strutting about on the beach. Some distance from shore and higher up was a belt of short-shafted reeds, and beyond them began a lowland pine forest. It would be hard to get much farther away from civilization.

They stopped for a moment to catch their breath. Their rucksacks were heavy, and their feet hurt after walking for three hours along the uneven shore, which alternated between sand and stones. They had left behind their camp-site on the other side of the island, where people could pitch their tents or rent one of the few cabins available to tourists.

Oleg had been walking around in an elated state ever since they had come ashore on the island several days earlier. Gotska Sandön was more beautiful and more amazing than any of them could have imagined. They had seen the place where Oleg's great-grandfather had drowned when the Russian ship, the Vsadnik, had sunk in a storm on an August night in 1864. They had visited the cemetery and admired the Russian cannons that were still on the beach called Franska Bukten. It was the girls' favourite beach, and they had been given permission to spend the night there under open skies. Pitching a tent was not allowed.

They started making camp by laying out their sleeping bags in the middle of the beach and setting up a windbreak, even though there was only a light breeze. The weather forecast promised beautiful summer weather for the next few days, and almost no wind at all. One of their rucksacks was functioning as an insulated bag containing their dinner, which consisted of roast beef and potato salad.

After they'd set up camp, they took off their clothes and ran naked into the sea. The water was invigorating and crystal clear.

They spent the whole day swimming, reading and playing beach tennis. Every once in a while someone would walk past, but they could see from far away if anyone was coming, so they had plenty of time to put their clothes back on. Towards evening, they sat on the sand looking at the water. They had smuggled along a bottle of wine, which they shared.

'Cheers,' said Tanya, raising her paper cup. 'Oh, how cosy

it is here. I wish we could stay here all day tomorrow too.'

Vera tapped her cup against Tanya's.

'Me too. I don't think I've ever been in a more gorgeous place.'

'Or more isolated. It's like a dream. Somehow unreal. I could stay here my whole life.'

They gazed out at the sea. Just at that moment, a sailboat rounded the point.

THURSDAY, 20 JULY

Johan strolled through the streets of Visby. It was early evening, and many of the shops were still open, while the tables in the restaurants were filling up. Down by Stora Torget he went into a bar and sat down to drink a cold beer. Sometimes he really did enjoy being alone, with no one making demands on him; he didn't need to think about anyone but himself. His thoughts wandered from Emma to Elin to his job.

He finished off his beer and got up to continue on his way through town. The lead that he and Pia had uncovered regarding threats and illegal workers, which had at first seemed so hot, had already gone cold. They simply hadn't made any headway. It had been leaked to the media that the police were looking for a Russian in connection with the murder. Johan had no idea how the information had got out, but it wasn't really so strange. Such things happened sooner or later. The head office in Stockholm was no longer particularly interested in the murder; other news had taken priority. It was now ten days since Bovide had been killed, and that was an eternity in the news business. As the murderer hadn't struck again, the tourists had calmed down and everything had gone back to normal. The campsites were just as full as usual. And it looked as if, this summer, the temperatures would reach record highs, which of course was good for tourism. Many people who came to Gotland decided to do so at the last minute, especially young people. These days it was hard to find a single empty space on the most popular beaches after eleven in the morning.

Both Johan and Pia had made a search for the Russian citizens who lived on Gotland and tried to ferret out what sort of Russian contacts Peter Bovide might have had. The problem was that Grenfors, back in Stockholm, kept interrupting them with new stories that had to be covered, all of them more or less meaningless. This very morning they'd ended up in a major argument when the editor wanted Johan and Pia to drive out to the countryside near Gerum and interview a father whose son had died the previous day from drinking illegal booze. The son had gone to a party and was offered some sort of industrial alcohol. Afterwards he came home and went to bed, never to wake up again. Now his father wanted to talk to the media to issue a warning to others. Johan had tried to make Grenfors understand that, naturally, the father was in shock and incapable of comprehending what consequences there might be if he appeared on TV. It was obvious that all the newspapers and other media would come running, and his home would be besieged by reporters. For Grenfors, it was enough that somebody was willing to speak publicly – he didn't think his responsibility extended any further. Johan didn't agree. Over the years they'd had countless clashes over what was ethically or morally defensible for journalists.

Pia had sided with Grenfors and said that of course they should interview the father, since he seemed so adamant about wanting to talk to the media. Everybody else would be reporting the story, she insisted.

Johan lit a cigarette and had hardly managed to take a few puffs before he passed Strandgärdet, outside the ring wall to the north. Judging by the music coming from the loudspeakers, he should have realized what was going on. The Friskis and Svettis gym was holding its daily session outdoors on the big lawn. A hundred people were doing exercises in unison under the open sky. The evening sun shone over the energetic crowd, and Johan felt like a truly bad person as he walked past. He considered putting out his cigarette but decided against it.

He started thinking again about the father who had lost his son; the boy had just turned seventeen. The Russian coal transports that came into the harbour at Slite popped into his mind. They sold illegal booze there. He'd almost forgotten about that lead. And now they knew that Peter Bovide had been shot with a Russian gun. Quickly he punched in Pia's number on his mobile. She answered immediately.

'Are you still pissed off?'

'No, not at all. I know that I'm right, and you'll feel the same way after you've worked in this business long enough,' he teased her.

'Super. Why'd you ring?'

'Do you remember when the next coal transport is due at Slite? Bovide was killed with a Russian gun, and those ships come from Russia. And they also sell illegal booze. That's a story we've never reported before. We can kill two birds with one stone, so to speak, and hopefully find out more about the murder.'

'Do you know whether the police are following up on that lead? I haven't seen or read anything about it.'

'Me neither, but I'm sure they're checking it out. It should be of great interest to them.'

'Have you talked to Knutas?'

'No, I was thinking of phoning him, but do you know when the next boat is due?'

'No idea, but I can find out. I have a friend who works at the harbour.'

'Of course you do.'

Johan began walking home through the botanical garden. All of a sudden, he felt much more cheerful. Pia rang back.

'We're in luck. Those boats arrive only a couple of times a month, but the next one is expected here tomorrow.'

'Fantastic. Now all we need to do is convince Grenfors to let us work on the story.'

He ended the call and rang Max Grenfors in Stockholm. The editor agreed at once.

'Good thinking. If the transports have nothing to do with the murder, it's still a story that's worth reporting. And we've never covered this angle before. Russian coal transports, illegal booze – sounds really exciting. But shouldn't we do the story undercover?'

Johan felt like laughing. Grenfors loved to use police terms. Especially in English.

'OK, we'll take along a little camera that we can hide under our clothes. I don't think we're going to get any major scoop if we show up down at the harbour carrying a big TV camera.'

'Good. And then we just have to hope that something related to the murder will come out. It's been confirmed that Peter Bovide bought booze down there, right?'

'Yes, we've had that information confirmed by several sources,' said Johan. 'So you can count on having some sort of story, at any rate.'

'Fine. Good luck tomorrow night. And be careful.'

'Your concern is very touching.'

FRIDAY, 21 JULY

Knutas had lain awake most of the night, brooding over the investigation. At five in the morning, he gave up and got out of bed. The swimming pool opened at six thirty, and it had been a long time since he'd had a chance to get some exercise. He made himself some coffee and ate a couple of sandwiches before he woke Lina.

Solberga swimming pool was only a ten-minute walk from his house, and on the way to police headquarters. In the water he was weightless and free; his thoughts became clearer as he swam one lap after another at the same monotonous tempo. He practically had the whole pool to himself, except for a couple of elderly, plump women wearing swimming caps who swam at a snail's pace and talked non-stop, as if they were at a coffee morning. He chose the lane furthest away from them, hoping that no other early-morning swimmers in need of exercise would show up. As he ploughed his way through the water, he went over the case in his mind.

Three days had passed since the Estonian

construction workers had been brought to police headquarters in Visby, but unfortunately their arrest had not
signified the breakthrough the police had been hoping
for. The interviews had led nowhere. All three men gave
the same account of events, except when it came to the
assault on Vendela Bovide. Then they each accused
the others. The court proceedings for the issue of a
detention order had been held the previous day, and all
three had been arraigned, charged with working
illegally, assaulting Vendela Bovide, burgling the house
on Furillen and depriving Anders Knutas of his liberty.
It remained to be seen whether they were involved in
the murder of Peter Bovide. No matter what, the
sentence was bound to be harsh.

Knutas's feeling that the murder had to do with
something other than illegal workers had grown
stronger. From the very beginning, he'd actually been
sceptical that any of the three Estonian construction
workers would turn out to be the perpetrator the police
were looking for, especially after his own encounter
with them on Furillen. Their behaviour didn't
mesh with the image of a brutal killer. On the other
hand, they had definitely assaulted Vendela Bovide.
Maybe they'd been more cautious with Knutas because
they knew he was a police officer.

One lead that the police were now following, and
which had made him wrack his brain all night, concerned the Russian coal transports that regularly docked
at Slite harbour. They'd been waiting for the arrival of

the next boat, and now it was finally going to happen. Over the past week the investigative team had been working on how to make its move, which would take place late this evening. Knutas was hoping that things would become much clearer after talking to the crew on board.

He stood in the shower for a long time, letting the water course over him. Then he studied his body in the mirror. It was impossible to tell that, so far, the summer had been one of the hottest in years. The slight tan that he'd acquired in Denmark was nearly gone. When he looked at himself in profile and sucked in his stomach, he looked OK; it was another matter when he viewed himself from the front. He needed to be exercising more regularly, which was made apparent by the flab that had started forming around his waist whenever he was too lazy to go swimming. Knutas was actually very athletic, but the indoor hockey season was over, and he hadn't yet found time to play golf.

When he came out on to the street again, he was blinded by the sunlight. The heatwave was continuing, which explained why the swimming pool was almost empty, since most people naturally preferred to go to the beach. The algae blooms that often struck Gotland at the height of the summer had not yet appeared. In the evenings, all the outdoor restaurants lining Visby's streets were packed. He and Lina were supposed to go out to dinner tonight and then enjoy a classical concert in the ruins of Saint Nicolai church. He'd finally made an effort, and ordered the tickets and reserved a table. Lina was so surprised and happy that he felt guilty.

After the morning meeting he and Jacobsson got in the car to drive up to Slite. They'd made an appointment with the harbour master who was responsible for the coal transports, who was going to show them around before the police raid, planned for that evening.

As soon as they parked the car near the front entrance of Cementa in Slite, a stout man came forward to greet them. He wore a blue overall and a cap. He gave them a friendly smile and introduced himself as harbour master Roger Nilsson.

They followed him in their car down to the harbour and then went into the office, where they all sat down to drink coffee.

Knutas got right to the point.

'We know that illegal alcohol is being sold in connection with the coal transports, and we've also had it confirmed that Peter Bovide occasionally made purchases down here. What do you know about this?'

The harbour master fidgeted nervously.

'That's a big concern of ours. We depend on receiving coal from Russia, but at the same time, it brings other problems. The sale of illegal alcohol seems constantly on the increase. As soon as a boat docks, all sorts of people come down to the harbour to buy vodka. We've also noticed that more and more young people have started making purchases from the boats. We've contacted the police numerous times and asked them to do something about it, but so far it hasn't done any good. Every once in a while the police come down here to check things out, but that's about it. I can't understand what they are waiting for. How many teenagers have to drink themselves to death before they take action?'

The harbour master shook his head. Jacobsson shifted uneasily in her chair. She had no desire to enter into a debate about how the police force made use of its limited resources.

'Unfortunately, we can't do anything about the matter at the moment,' she said, 'but I can have a talk with our county police chief later on. How are the sales conducted?'

'People have figured out when the boats are due, and the schedule is made known through word of mouth. It's not as if we announce it in the newspapers or put up a sign on some bulletin board. People start gathering as soon as the boat docks, and then they fall into conversation with the crew members, who also come ashore. We can't very well forbid them from moving about freely in Slite. They usually go to the restaurants and pizzerias and to the local pub. That's where they meet their customers, if they don't at the harbour. We've also had problems with certain people who go on board the boats, so it's been hard to keep track of what goes on.'

That caught Jacobsson's attention.

'People go on board? Why?'

'The Russian crew members normally stay here for two days, and they come here so often that it's not unusual for them to make friends with residents in the area.'

'And some find lovers here too, perhaps?'

'I'm sure that happens.'

'Have you noticed any signs of prostitution?' asked Jacobsson.

'No, we haven't seen any of that.'

'Narcotics?'

'We're not sure, but of course it can't be ruled out. Although I think we would have noticed if that sort of trafficking was occurring on a large scale. But we think the sale of illegal alcohol is serious enough.'

'Did you know that Peter Bovide had been here to buy booze?'

'No, not until people started talking about him after the murder.'

'Do you know whether he had any contact with the Russian crew members?'

'I don't know if he did.'

'Is there anyone else who works here who might have known him?'

'It's very possible, but I can't think of anyone in particular.'

'But he was from Slite, and people must be talking about the murder,' Jacobsson insisted. 'Do you seriously mean to say that you haven't heard about anyone who knew Peter Bovide?'

'No, like I said, I haven't.'

Harbour master Roger Nilsson was obviously annoyed.

Knutas changed tack.

'How often do the boats come here?'

'Previously it was every other week, but as of 1 August, they're arriving twice as often. The demand for cement is increasing all the time, and since we're not yet making full use of the factory's capacity, we've been able to increase production, and that means we need more fuel to stoke the furnaces. That's how the lime-stone is melted down and transformed.'

'And what's your opinion of this development, in your position as harbour master?'

'It's double-sided. On the one hand, it's a positive thing, of course, that the demand for cement is on the rise and that we can increase production. On the other hand, we can probably expect more problems in connection with the sale of illegal alcohol.'

When they said goodbye to the harbour master, thoughts were whirling through Knutas's head. Who was to say that drug deals weren't taking place in connection with the boat transports? Was it possible that Peter Bovide was a drug addict? Maybe ampheta-mines. Was that the reason he could run ten kilometres or so each day, keep his company going, take care of his young children and get up early every morning? He'd suffered from regular bouts of depression and he was epileptic. That sort of thing could lead to drug abuse. It was also possible that he could have been dealing drugs without taking any himself. Did he owe some ugly customers money? The MO seemed to indicate this might be a possibility. The murder was committed with a Russian gun, and the victim was shot at very close range, which testified to a brutal ruthlessness. Maybe the perp was a professional hitman.

Yet there were two circumstances that didn't fit the picture: the fact that the perp chose to shoot Bovide in the head first and then several times in the stomach; and the fact that the gun was so old. What hitman or hard-boiled drug lord would use a gun that was eighty years old?

Knutas couldn't make the facts add up.

Emma was lying on the sofa in the living room, watching an action film on TV. It was supposed to be exciting, but she didn't have the energy to get involved.

Images flickered past on the TV screen: a car chase, gunshots, men running after each other through a big crowd – classic scenes. But superimposed over everything she saw vestiges of herself and Johan, like damaged fragments of a dream that had never come true. Unwanted, troublesome thoughts hounded her, and she kept shifting around on the sofa cushions. It was impossible to find a comfortable position.

She was alone in the house, left to her own thoughts. Their fight the previous Sunday and the ensuing silence from Johan had truly shaken her. At first she was angry because he'd yelled at her, but then came the shame when she realized that he was right. Even though she was upset because he'd slept with another woman, she could partially understand why it had happened.

She pictured his face and how miserable he'd looked as he sat there on that bench. She had felt so awkward, just waiting there like an idiot until he stopped sobbing. Then he handed Elin back to her, got up and left. The distance between them was so obvious. What if he never wanted to let her in again? There was a risk that the door had now been shut for good.

When her parents offered to take care of Elin for a few days, Emma had gratefully accepted. She needed to be alone to think things through.

Again she asked herself what was actually preventing her from being with Johan. She had pushed him away for a very specific reason. How could she have done otherwise, when he had put their child's life in jeopardy? But she hadn't received any support for her actions – not from her parents or any of her friends. Everybody thought she was being too hard on him, even her ex-husband Olle. His attitude towards Johan had become significantly friendlier ever since he'd met Marianne, who was the new woman in his life. Many things in their relationship, previously so inflammatory, had now become easier, including their shared custody of the children, Sara and Filip. Right now the kids were spending two weeks with Olle and Marianne on Crete.

The kids liked Johan, and he, in turn, had clearly demonstrated his affection for them. His job was really no obstacle either; he could work as a freelancer from Gotland or find a job with one of the local newspapers or radio stations.

She sat up on the sofa and turned off the TV. Why

was she so resistant to creating a future with Johan? Was she afraid of true love? Did she think, deep in her heart, that she didn't deserve it?

All of a sudden she had a clear insight into what was going on. She was the one, not anyone else, who kept blocking their relationship, and if she didn't stop soon, she was going to lose Johan for good.

She was suddenly in a big hurry. Now she knew what she had to do; she just hoped it wasn't too late.

The boat could be seen from a great distance away. A barge-like vessel was silhouetted against the horizon. It was eight p.m., and the sun, which was on its way down, had coloured the sky red. Johan and Pia were sitting on a hilltop, gazing out at the sea. They had brought along grilled chicken and several beers so it would look as if they were just an ordinary couple enjoying an evening picnic. They ate their food in silence. Pia had binoculars with her, and now and then she would raise them to her eyes.

'Now it's turning in this direction.'

Johan took the binoculars from her. He saw that she was right; the boat had changed course and was slowly turning towards land. Earlier, they had gone down to the harbour to reconnoitre. Everything had seemed very quiet, like the calm before a storm. Pia had made an appointment with her friend who worked at the harbour to meet them at nine o'clock. He was a long-shoreman, and officially they were just friends who were getting together and at the same time planned to buy some booze from the boat. Pia's friend, whose name was Viktor, had told them that a bunch of people always turned up on the dock whenever the boats arrived. So they could blend right in.

Johan gave only monosyllabic replies to Pia's attempts to carry on a conversation. He was thinking about Emma, and he had no desire to chat.

'What are you thinking about? You seem really far away,' said Pia, opening the cool-box. 'Would you like another beer?'

'Sure. Thanks.' He took a big gulp of the cold beer, then lit a cigarette.

'You've really started smoking a lot. Why is that?' Pia grabbed the pack and shook out a cigarette for herself.

'You should talk, especially when you happen to use snuff too. But it's the same old issue: Emma.'

'I can't understand why the two of you can't get along. What do you think you're doing, anyway? Even a blind chicken can see that you're made for each other.'

'Yes, but it's so complicated.'

'Well, don't make it even worse. If you ask me, I think it's just plain human for Emma to panic after that kidnapping episode, but what surprises me is that you fail to understand it.'

Johan sat up. 'What do you mean? What is it I don't understand?'

'How tough it's been for Emma, practically since the first day she met you. It seems perfectly reasonable that she wouldn't want to have anything to do with you after the kidnapping; from her point of view, you were the one who put Elin in danger. But now she's become stuck in that attitude, and so it's just easier for her to shut you out completely. After everything else, her divorce, and then the fact that you can never seem to get your life together – I mean, you seem unable to decide whether to stay on the mainland or live on Gotland. And in the meantime, she's here and has to take full responsibility and try to work things out with her other children, with Olle, and with you and Elin. How hard have you tried to understand her position? You act so damned empathetic and ethical when you're on the job, always taking consideration of one thing or another, but how much compassion do you really have when it comes right down to it? When it has to do with your own personal life and the people who are closest to you?'

Pia ended her harangue by taking several big gulps of beer.

Johan had a perplexed expression on his face as he sat and stared at her.

'Why haven't you said any of this before?'

'I've tried, in small doses, but you never pay any attention.'

Johan couldn't think of a single thing to say. Pia's mobile rang before he could collect himself.

'That was Viktor,' she said after ending the conversation. 'It's time.'

They drove down to the harbour and parked a safe distance away from the huge iron gates that marked the entry to the actual harbour area.

Pia was fitted out with a camera and microphone inside her thin shirt, invisible under her jacket. The ship was just about to dock. It had arrived an hour ahead of schedule. Johan wondered what sort of cargo it was carrying besides the fuel. The harbour master, with whom he'd had a talk earlier in the day, had said that the fuel was unloaded via pipes that were hooked up to the boat, leading straight into big silos inside the factory. The operation took several hours. Then the cargo was replaced with cement. The boat would remain docked for a day or two each time.

Johan lit a cigarette and felt his pulse quicken.

More people came down to the dock. Longshoremen, the harbour master, and others, who were presumably waiting to buy booze. Like Pia and himself, they pretended they were there simply to watch.

When the boat docked, a hatch opened immediately

and several rugged-looking men emerged. Pia poked Johan in the side.

'Coarse-looking types,' she hissed. 'By the way, I'm shooting. I'm going to take off and have a look around.'

She gave him a wink. Between two buttons on her jacket he caught a glimpse of the camera lens.

The men from the boat jumped ashore. One lit a cigarette and glanced around expectantly. Another clearly knew some of the people who were standing on the dock, and he went over to give them a warm hug. They chatted and joked. Things started happening around the ship, and the harbour master began issuing orders. The unloading commenced at once, as an engine roared. Johan guessed that the transfer of the coal had already started.

He had disguised himself behind a pair of sunglasses and had pulled a cap down over his face as he didn't want to take the chance of being recognized. He was frequently on television, even though he was a reporter and not a TV newsreader.

He glanced around and saw some men looking at the ship with anticipation. There wasn't much for him to do at the moment, so he sat down on a barrel and lit another cigarette. Two guys were standing near the gangway, looking as if they were conducting business. One of them pulled bottles of booze out of a box, while the other collected the money. Notes changed hands as the transactions were carried out quite openly. Johan hoped that Pia was getting it all on film; he looked around to see where she was.

The next second he saw her standing next to Viktor, who was buying some booze from the man at the gangway.

When the purchase was completed, she nonchalantly went on board.

Johan couldn't make up his mind. Should he follow her?

He didn't have to ponder his decision for long. The next second, police sirens began wailing, and four cars came to a screeching halt on the dock. Within a few minutes, a dozen officers had gone on board the boat while others rounded up the people on the wharf. Knutas didn't seem to be among the officers, but Johan caught a glimpse of Karin Jacobsson in the crowd.

It didn't take long before people began coming out. Pia was escorted by two solid-looking policemen who resolutely hustled her down the gangway. Then Johan discovered Knutas, his face bright red, striding towards Pia.

'What in the world are you doing here?' he shouted. 'What the hell do you think you're doing?'

She didn't hesitate to answer.

'We have every right to cover any story we like, and to whatever extent we deem worthwhile. Or are you saying that we should ring the police and ask permission every time we're going to put together a report?'

'Damn it all, you could ruin the whole investigation. Get her out of here,' he ordered his colleagues.

A moment later, Knutas caught sight of Johan.

'You're here too? Why can't you stay out of police business?'

Ever since Johan's report from the construction site in Stenkyrkehuk had been shown on TV, Knutas had been noticeably annoyed and curt with him. Now he was furious.

'It's damned hard to do our job when we keep having reporters swarming at our heels. How are we supposed to conduct an investigation with you hanging around all the time? Do you think this is going to benefit the investigation in some way?'

Johan felt his hackles rise.

'What the hell are you talking about? This is a public place, and we're just doing our job. Like you are.'

'Get out of here,' roared Knutas. 'Before I decide to arrest you.'

'What for? Disturbing the peace? Or endangering somebody? I call this a fucking threat against journalists.'

The officers who were holding Pia now let her go, and she came over to Johan and took his arm.

'Come on,' she said quietly. 'Let's get out of here. We've got what we came for.'

Reluctantly, Johan complied. He was shaking his head at Knutas and muttering something inaudible.

'Lucky for you I didn't hear what you just said,' snapped Knutas. 'You'd bloody well better watch your step.'

SUNDAY, 23 JULY

Knutas had tipped back his worn oak desk chair as he sat on the leather cushion, shiny with age. The appearance of the chair offered a stark contrast to the rest of the furnishings in his office. Police head-quarters had been remodelled a couple of years earlier, and it was all Scandinavian design, with white walls; the old things had been replaced with plain, simple furniture made of light birch. But Knutas had refused to give up his favourite chair. It stimulated his thought processes, as did the pipe which he was now filling with the greatest attention. He rarely lit the pipe, but just fiddling with the aromatic tobacco helped him think.

He'd come back to headquarters, even though it was Sunday evening, because he wanted to go over the interviews that had been conducted over the weekend with the crew of the Russian coal transport. The results of the police raid had been meagre, at least from his perspective. They had confiscated hundreds of litres of Russian vodka, and a number of individuals had been arrested, suspected of illegal sales, but nothing new had surfaced that might propel the homicide investigation forward.

The search for the murder weapon was continuing without interruption. Everyone who lived on Gotland and had a licence for a gun had been checked, but nowhere had they been able to locate the Korovin gun that had been used for the killing. The police knew full well that a good many illegal weapons could be found in Swedish homes. But every few years a gun amnesty was conducted in the country for several months, when anyone could turn in their weapons to the police anonymously and without risking any sort of punishment. The last time this was done, they had collected 17,000 guns in three months.

Knutas leaned his head in his hands. There was something fundamentally wrong with this whole investigation, but he just couldn't work out what it could be.

GOTSKA SANDÖN, 22 JULY 1985

*T*he merciless rays of the sun woke Vera as she lay tangled up like a snake in the sleeping bag. It was a moment before she was fully conscious, but the first sensation was a dull nausea in her stomach.

She blinked at the light and heard voices further down the beach. With an effort, she pulled herself into a sitting position and lifted away a corner of the windbreak. Ten or fifteen people were walking past. They were in late middle age, with rucksacks, sunhats and sensible shoes. She heard scattered laughter interspersed with their chatter. Without a care in the world, they continued on, although one person did cast a glance in her direction, but quickly looked away. They paid her no attention.

The sleeping bag next to hers was empty. She was wearing her watch, which told her it was eleven fifteen. Good God, how could she have slept so long? She peered out again. Tanya was nowhere in sight. Maybe she'd gone for a walk or a swim. But then Vera began thinking more clearly, and memories from the previous evening returned. Those boys from Stockholm. They'd had fun grilling food, swimming and drinking a lot of beer and booze. One of them had a *guitar; she'd almost had a crush on him when he played. Then she'd suddenly felt sick and couldn't sit up any longer; everything began spinning around. She had to go and lie down for a while. She told them she needed to pee and walked away. She threw up in the bushes and then crawled into her sleeping bag behind the windbreak. She'd intended to stay only until she felt better, but she must have fallen asleep.*

Again she pushed aside a corner of the windbreak to peer out at the water. The boat was gone. She sank back to the ground. Her throat was parched, and she was hot and thirsty. She staggered to her feet, found a bottle of water and drank some of it. Her head was spinning and she was sick with worry. Where was her little sister? What if something had happened to her?

'Tanya!' she shouted, as loudly as she could.

She walked from one end of the deserted beach to the other without finding her sister. Then she went into the woods to look for her. The longer she searched, the more worried she became. The idyllic beach suddenly felt menacing and inhospitable.

By two o'clock, she had given up searching and packed up as much as she could carry. For safety's sake, she left behind the windbreak, some food and water, and Tanya's rucksack. She wrote a note explaining that she'd gone back to the campsite.

Before she left the beach, she turned around one last time, straining to see as far as she could.

But nothing moved.

MONDAY, 24 JULY

The heat in the limestone quarry was almost unbearable.

Morgan Larsson wiped the sweat from his forehead and left the barracks-like office in the western section of the pit, next to the car-wash for the tractor-trailers.

Underneath the broiling sun, the temperature slowly but relentlessly rose to more than 85 degrees, even though it was not yet noon. He got into his pick-up and drove along the road towards the biggest limestone quarry, Fila Hajdar, five kilometres away.

He was going to set things up for the blasting to be done that day.

It was scheduled for eleven thirty. That was the best time, because that was when the shift change took place and most of the workers were on lunch break in the factory's big cafeteria at the other end of the property.

The road, 200 feet wide, was dusty and white with limestone. The road had to be wide in order to make room for all the vehicles travelling between the factory and the two quarries. The tractor-trailers drove back and forth all day long carrying stone to the big crusher inside the factory, where it was transformed into cement. If they didn't water the road to keep down the dust, a gigantic dust cloud would be perpetually visible over Gotland.

The vehicles drove the road every day, year round, from six in the morning until ten at night. The only time they took a break was during the daily blasting.

On either side of the road was a lowland forest. Dwarf pines and juniper shrubs looked as if they were fighting for their lives in the arid surroundings. They were covered with white dust, as if someone had sprinkled the entire forest with powdered sugar, producing a ghostlike and sinister impression.

Morgan Larsson waved a greeting to the driver of a fully loaded truck on its way back from the quarry.

He felt the familiar tingling in his stomach that always occurred right before the blasting, when forty thousand tons of stone were broken apart in an instant. Even though he'd participated in so many blastings, he never stopped being fascinated by the sight when enormous chunks of the hillside collapsed, making the huge crater open up even more. There was something irrevocable about the whole spectacle. The rock gave way, cracked open, never to exist again.

When Morgan Larsson reached the quarry, he drove up the slope until he came to the top. He stopped a safe distance from the edge, opened the door of his pick-up and got out. Sweat was running down his back, soaking his armpits and groin. He took the edge off his thirst by finishing off a whole bottle of water in one draught.

His two colleagues, who would help supervise the blasting, were due to arrive in a few minutes. He couldn't see them from where he was standing, but they had contact via radio. Strict safety measures were enforced so that no one would be in the blast area or even nearby when it occurred. A tremendous explosive force was released when tons of stone were broken away from the edges and roared down into the gigantic pit, which lay below where he stood.

There was a risk that stones would fly through the air. Last year, a fellow worker had died when a rock struck him on the head.

Morgan took up position as close to the edge as he dared and ran his eyes over the rim surrounding the quarry. It was 1,000 yards long and 650 yards wide. The surrounding walls were 200 feet high. It was one of the largest stone quarries in Sweden, and he was proud to be working here. He'd been an explosives expert for almost twenty years, and he enjoyed his job. It was also a big responsibility, making sure that the holes packed with two or three hundred kilos of explosives had each been bored in the right place and at a precise depth.

About 65 feet from the precipice stood a round wooden shed; that was where he took shelter during the actual blasting. Inside was a cable, which he would soon attach to the detonator that was now in his pocket.

He glanced at his watch: ten more minutes. He saw a

flash of light from the other side of the quarry. The car with his two colleagues had arrived. They took up positions on either side of the pit, 1,000 yards apart, as they checked that nobody else was in the vicinity. He switched on his radio.

'Hello, Morgan here. Everything OK?'

'Sure, it looks deserted,' he heard Kjell say.

'Five more minutes.'

'Fine. Want to have lunch afterwards?'

'Absolutely. See you then.'

He stuffed the radio in his breast pocket, turned round and walked over to the many deep holes that had been bored in rows along the edge of the quarry. He bent down and checked to see that everything was as it should be.

When he straightened up again, he thought he saw someone moving down below in the pit. What the hell? Such an unexpected development was worrisome, to say the least. Only authorized personnel were allowed here. Especially since only a few minutes remained before the blasting. He rushed over to the pit and shouted. His colleagues were much too far away for him to attract their attention. He fumbled for his radio and managed to switch it on just as he reached the pit opening. Strangely enough, it was completely deserted. He looked up towards the edge of the woods. Nothing. Was it some sort of optical illusion? Maybe it was the heat playing tricks on him. It was almost time to detonate. He glanced up at the sky. Not a cloud in sight, and the sun was like a blazing lamp shining in his face. His mouth was completely dry, and his tongue stuck to his palate. A crackling sound came from his radio.

'Is everything ready, Morgan?'

'Yup. I thought I saw somebody, but I must have been imagining things. You haven't seen anything strange, have you?'

'No, the quarry is empty. But I can check again with my binoculars, just to be sure. We've still got a few minutes.'

'OK, thanks.'

He peered through the observation slit in the shed while he waited. The sweat was pouring off him. He felt upset and wasn't filled with the usual anticipation; all he wanted was to get this over with so he could leave and have something to eat.

'Hey, Morgan. I don't see anything unusual. Everything seems quiet.'

'Good. Let's go, then.'

When he glanced up again, he gave a start. He hadn't noticed how it happened, but a stranger was standing across from him, just outside the opening of the shed. He looked into the cold eyes of the intruder. All of a sudden, the muzzle of a gun was pointing at him.

'What's all this about?' he stammered.

The walls of the cramped shed seemed to close in on him.

The radio in Morgan Larsson's pocket began crackling.

'Come in, Morgan . . . Are you there? Morgan . . . Morgan?'

'Turn it off,' said the stranger. 'Otherwise I'll shoot you.'

With trembling fingers, Morgan switched off the radio. Silence.

All sorts of thoughts were whirling around in his confused brain. He should have detonated the explosives by now. He was always very precise, down to the second. He wondered how long it would take for his two colleagues to react when they discovered his radio was turned off and the explosion hadn't taken place.

The image of Peter Bovide's face flickered past. He'd been shot to death two weeks earlier. Was it his turn now? That was all he had time to think before the intruder handed him the cable that was supposed to be attached to the detonator and signalled for him to proceed.

He fumbled in his pocket for the detonator, which was no bigger than a pack of cigarettes. Then he attached the cable and pressed the button. The sound was deafening. The low, scraggly forest, covered with white powder, shook from the blast. An enormous cloud of dust rose up from the crater below. The little shed was enveloped in a haze of dust from the explosion.

The dust stung his eyes, filled his mouth, got under his clothes. He closed his eyes tight to avoid the worst of it and because he had no idea what was going to happen next. The thundering of the huge boulders still filled the air as they broke apart and then plummeted to the bottom of the pit with a deafening crash.

When the first shot was fired, the sound was drowned out by the din of the explosion.

Foreman Kjell Johansson slowly lowered his hand, which was holding the silent radio. At least Morgan had carried out the blasting, although after a delay of several minutes. He was never late, but no doubt he'd be able to explain. It was odd that he wasn't answering his radio. Had he put it down somewhere? That seemed very unlikely. They always stayed on site for five or ten minutes after the explosion, just for safety's sake. Sometimes rocks broke loose quite a distance away from the detonation.

Something wasn't right. Kjell Johansson raised the binoculars to study the other side of the quarry and find out what his colleague was doing.

At first he didn't see anything. The blasting hut looked deserted, and Morgan's pick-up was still parked in the same place. He began surveying the area and couldn't believe his eyes when he spotted a dark figure, which definitely wasn't Morgan Larsson, emerge from the shed and disappear into the woods. Kjell Johansson tried his radio again, his eyes still peering through the binoculars.

'Morgan, damn it all. Morgan, what's going on?'

Still no answer.

Kjell Johansson called to his colleague on the other side of the pit.

'Something's wrong. Morgan's not answering, and somebody was here, inside the shed. I just saw him come out. We have to go over there. Right now.'

When the two men drove up to the opposite side of the quarry, they instantly realized that something serious had happened. Morgan Larsson's communications radio lay on the ground, smashed to bits.

When they approached the shed that was the explosives expert's domain, they suddenly slowed their pace.

Both men recoiled at what they saw. Morgan Larsson was lying on the floor, his body twisted at an odd angle. Their eyes went first to his abdomen. It was riddled with bloody bullet holes; in the heat, flies and other insects had already begun to swarm over the wounds.

Knutas, Jacobsson and Wittberg were all riding in the same vehicle, on their way up to Slite. The big factory buildings dominated the town, located on the north-east side of Gotland. The limestone quarry was gigantic, with its huge crater off to one side of the road.

Knutas pulled to a stop at the entrance to the factory.

The Cementa harbour master then joined them to show the way to the quarry where the body had been found.

'Can you tell us what you know so far?' asked Knutas as they drove through the wrought-iron gates to the factory area.

'Sure. Morgan was in charge of the blasting here, and he had two workmates with him, although they were on the other side of the quarry to him, almost a kilometre apart.'

'How did they stay in contact?' asked Jacobsson.

'By radio. The two other men were supposed to make sure that nobody came near the site while the blasting was going on. It creates a tremendous force, you know, when thousands of tons of rock are broken up. Right before the detonation, Morgan said that he thought he could see someone near his shed, but then he decided it was only his imagination. The explosion went off, but it was late, so his colleagues tried to get hold of him by radio. He didn't answer. One of them used his binoculars and saw somebody running away from the area, heading for the woods.'

'What's the name of that man, and where can I find him?'

'Kjell Johansson. He's probably still sitting in the office with the workmate who was there, Arne Pettersson. They were the ones who found the body.'

'Ask them to stay there so we can talk to them before they leave. It's very important.'

The harbour master called the office on his radio and gave instructions for both witnesses to remain in the office.

'We're almost there,' he said then.

First they drove past the factory with the enormous silos, the conveyor belts that transported gravel for additional processing and the rotary kilns in which the limestone was heated.

They drove towards the larger stone quarry where the murder had taken place. The car jolted over the gravel road, which ran like a flat, wide furrow between the towering walls.

'How well did you know Morgan Larsson?' asked Knutas.

'Quite well. He's worked here for twenty years, almost as long as I have.'

'How difficult is it for unauthorized personnel to get into the area?'

'It's really not very difficult. We can't block off the whole factory property, or even the area around the limestone quarry. Across from it there's a big stretch of forest called Fila Hajdar, which is where the quarry gets its name.'

'So if somebody was up above here, they could get away without any problem? Even in a car?'

'Of course. There are all sorts of small tracks going through the forest.'

Knutas cursed silently. The car continued up a slope next to the entrance to the quarry itself, and they parked outside the explosive expert's shed.

'That's where he is. Inside there,' said the harbour master.

The circular wooden shed was no more than 16 square feet. They stopped outside so as not to destroy any potential evidence. Morgan Larsson lay on the floor, turned on his side, his face up.

Knutas saw immediately that he'd been shot both in the head and in the abdomen. Just like Peter Bovide. There could be no doubt that they were dealing with a murderer who had now killed twice.

He glanced at Jacobsson. All colour had left her face.

'Bloody hell. What a lunatic,' muttered Wittberg.

Jacobsson didn't say a word. Knutas looked at his colleagues.

'OK, it looks like there's no question that it's the same perpetrator. The wound in the forehead looks identical to the one that killed Peter Bovide.'

Two more police vehicles came up the hill. Erik Sohlman jumped out of the first one.

'What's happened?'

Before anyone could answer, Sohlman stepped over to the body. He stopped short and stared with dismay at the dead man's face.

'Morgan . . . Morgan, what the hell?'

Jacobsson went over to Sohlman and put her hand on his shoulder.

'What's wrong? Did you know him?'

'It's Morgan,' murmured Sohlman. 'Morgan Larsson.'

Several barracks at the smaller quarry housed offices and staff rooms. That was where Kjell Johansson, the foreman who'd been present when the murder was committed, was now waiting. He was in his fifties; he looked pale and upset. Most likely, he was in a state of shock.

'Could you tell us what happened?' Knutas began.

'We drove over to the quarry, as usual, about fifteen minutes before the scheduled detonation. Morgan was already there; he was always early.'

'Did you notice anything in particular on the way there?'

'No, nothing.'

'So what happened when you arrived?'

'My colleague and I each went to our usual positions, meaning on the other side of the pit from where Morgan was. We talked to each other on the radio, as always, but then Morgan said he thought he'd seen somebody moving around near the shed where he waits during the blasting.'

'Where was he when he said that?'

'He was checking the charges. That's what he always did.'

'What exactly did he see?'

'He didn't say, just that he noticed something moving. He asked me to check it out. I scanned the area with my binoculars but didn't see anything.'

'Then what happened?'

'I don't really know. It was eleven thirty, and Morgan always detonated the explosion on the dot. It was a little game of his, to detonate at precisely the scheduled time. But this time, several minutes passed and nothing happened. I tried to call Morgan, but he didn't answer. Then came the explosion.'

Kjell Johansson fell silent as he looked down at his calloused hands.

'What can you tell us about the person you saw?'

'I only caught a glimpse of him, but he was wearing a lot of clothes, considering the heat. I think he had on dark trousers and a dark, baggy shirt.'

With a solemn expression, Knutas stared at the man seated across the table.

'What you're telling us is extremely important. You've actually seen the killer with your own eyes. Try to remember as much as possible about how he looked. Even the smallest detail is important.'

'Take your time,' Jacobsson added. 'Think carefully.'

'I only saw him for a few seconds, and from far away. He came out of Morgan's shed right after the explosion. He moved in a rather strange way, sort of awkwardly. Maybe he had a slight limp. He was shorter than Morgan, who I think was about six feet tall. The other person was at least four inches shorter. I'm positive about that.'

'That means that the person you saw was about 5 foot 8?'

'Yeah, I think so.'

'Anything else?'

'No. It all happened so fast.'

'What were they doing?'

'I think they were talking to each other. Since Morgan didn't answer his radio, I kept my binoculars trained on the shed. When the explosion was detonated, the whole shed disappeared in a cloud of dust, but then the person came out and headed for the woods.'

'Then what?'

'Nothing after that. I was worried about Morgan, so we drove right over there.'

'And by then the other person was gone?'

'Yes.'

'Do you know whether Morgan knew Peter Bovide, the carpenter who was shot to death a couple of weeks ago?' asked Jacobsson.

Kjell Johansson's face clouded over.

'I don't think so, but I noticed that he acted kind of strange whenever anyone else at work started talking about the murder on Fårö.'

'Strange in what way?'

'Well, everybody was talking about it, of course. Peter

Bovide lived in Slite, after all, and his company has done a lot of work for the factory; for instance, they remodelled the barracks. Morgan was the only one who never commented on the murder. At first, I didn't think anything about it, but after a few days I noticed that he would get real quiet and move away every time the murder came up in conversation. And so I asked him whether he knew Bovide.'

Jacobsson leaned forward.

'And?'

'He denied it and asked me why I thought he might. He looked really worried, as if the mere question made him nervous.'

'What did you say?'

'Nothing, really. I could tell that it was a sensitive subject, for some reason, so I dropped it. And now Morgan has been killed too. Damn it to hell.'

Johansson sounded despondent.

'Is there anything else you can tell us about Morgan?' asked Knutas. 'Anything you reacted to or thought was strange? Any new person he may have met?'

The foreman rubbed his eyes and looked up at both officers.

'Actually, there is one thing.'

'What is it?'

'He seemed really insistent about going out to Gotska Sandön.'

'Gotska Sandön?'

'Yes. He was there this past weekend. He used to go

out there occasionally, even though he wasn't exactly the nature type. In fact, he detested anything having to do with hikes through the woods or other outdoor activities. Whenever we had any sort of excursions here at work, he never participated. Morgan preferred to sit inside and drink beer while he watched sports on TV. That was how he relaxed. But he did go out to Gotska Sandön. Last weekend, he booked a trip out there, and even though we were really short-handed here at work because several people called in sick, he wouldn't postpone his trip. I know that the boss offered him various incentives to try and persuade him to stay and work, but he refused. He needed to go out there right away, and he couldn't delay it a week.'

'What was he going to do on Gotska Sandön?' asked Jacobsson.

'I have no idea. I only know that sometimes he went out there. He's been there several times before.'

'Did he go alone?'

'Yes, I think so. He was a real loner. Didn't have any family or girlfriend. He lived alone, and I think he did almost everything by himself.'

'When exactly did he go out there?'

'He left on Friday and came home last night.'

'So that was the last thing he did? Visit Gotska Sandön? And he'd been there before?'

'Yes, a least a few times.'

'Do you know where exactly he went?'

'I have no idea. I've never thought much about those

trips before, but this time it was obvious that nothing could make him change his travel plans, so there must have been something really special about that trip. I asked him what could be so damn important to make him leave his workmates in the lurch, and then he got real mad and started shouting that it was none of my business. I was really surprised that he overreacted like that.'

'We need to look into this,' Knutas decided. 'Right away.'

He cast a glance at Jacobsson.

'OK, don't worry, I'll do it. I can leave now.'

Johan decided to sleep late, even though it was Monday. He didn't know whether he even had the energy to go to work. The problem with Emma had thrown him completely. A whole week had passed since their fight, and he hadn't been able to make himself get in contact with her again. Madeleine had gone back to Stockholm the day after that unhappy Sunday, and that was just as well. He'd been busy at work all week long, trying not to think about Emma at all. He needed a break from her and all their problems. He'd taken time off work and gone up to where Emma's parents lived on Fårö to pick up Elin to spend the whole day with her. It had been both wonderful and painful, because he didn't get to see his daughter very often.

Now Johan was worn out and feeling low. He rang Pia to tell her that he'd be at home if anything special happened. He didn't give a damn what Grenfors might think about it. He went back to bed for an hour before he finally got up out of sheer boredom.

He took a shower and made some coffee. With his hair wet and a towel wrapped around his waist, he went out into the hall to get the morning papers, and there he discovered an envelope lying on the mat. He recognized the handwriting.

All it said on the front was 'To Johan'.

She must have come over and delivered it personally, which meant it was important. He had to pour himself a cup of coffee and light up a cigarette before he could open the envelope. He didn't usually smoke indoors, but what the hell. A thousand thoughts flew through his head as he tore open the envelope with fumbling fingers.

He licked his lips nervously before he read the message.

When Pia rang he was still sitting with the card in his hand, incapable of moving. He was too busy trying to collect his thoughts.

He could tell from her voice that something was happening.

'A man was shot to death out at the stone quarry in Slite. It happened only about half an hour ago. I'll pick you up. Go over to Söderport, and I'll be there in five minutes.'

Johan stood up. Only something of this magnitude could have torn him away from studying Emma's note. He pulled on a pair of shorts and a T-shirt and ran down towards Söderport, his hair still wet.

Ten minutes later they were on their way to Slite. Johan spent a major part of the drive talking on his

289

mobile. First with the police, who refused to say anything except that a man had been found dead at the
quarry in Slite. Then he talked to Grenfors, who could
hardly believe that another murder had been committed on Gotland.

The area near the entrance to the quarry and factory
had been cordoned off.

'Damn it, we won't be able to get in at all, we're
screwed,' said Pia with a sigh.

They stood there staring like two fools. Suddenly
Pia's face lit up.

'I know somebody who works here. I'll try to get hold
of him,' she said.

The area where the murder had been committed was
gigantic and it would be impossible to force their way
in. Plus the factory employees were keeping their
distance from the entrance, so there was no one to
corner for an interview.

When Pia finished her phone call, she gave Johan a
look of triumph.

'I've found out what to do.'

A short time later, they reached the top of the stone
quarry. Pia turned off from the main road and took a
small track through the forest. The car jolted along.
They could see limestone everywhere. The ground was
white, and the bushes and trees that had managed to
survive in what seemed like such an inhospitable
environment were covered with a fine layer of
dust.

'It feels unreal,' said Johan. 'What a ghostly atmosphere.'

The track got narrower until Johan began to wonder whether they should venture any further.

'What if we can't turn round?'

'We'll just have to take that chance,' said Pia, staring straight ahead. Branches and boughs kept striking the windscreen, and they had to plough their way through dense underbrush. Gradually, a clearing opened up, and that was where they parked.

Pia brought her camera with her as they followed an even smaller path into the woods. A moment later, they reached the quarry. It yawned before them like some sort of giant cauldron.

'Good god,' exclaimed Pia. 'Have you ever seen anything like this before?'

'No, never.'

The view was both fascinating and terrifying.

'How typical that we forgot to bring along anything to drink. My throat feels as dust-coated as the ground.'

They ventured closer to the edge and saw several police vehicles with people moving around them. They quickly backed up into the woods so as not to be seen.

'What's that over there?' asked Pia, pointing to the other side of the quarry.

'I have no idea.' Johan squinted into the glare of the sun. 'It looks like a little hut.'

Pia set up her tripod and began recording. She took

a panoramic shot of the quarry and then pointed the lens at the hut.

'What now?' she asked.

'What do you see?'

Pia raised her hand to shush him. She stood there for such a long time, shooting without moving the camera, that Johan began to feel uncomfortable in the heat. And he couldn't see what had caught her eye, since it was too far away. When she finally finished, she simply looked at him, giving him an odd smile.

'I think I'll have a job with *Rapport* by autumn. Just so you know.'

Jacobsson was out of luck. The police helicopter was in use, and the coast guard happened to be conducting extensive exercises elsewhere. To interrupt what they were doing in order to go out to Fårösund to pick up Jacobsson would take longer than her just catching the regular ferry out to Gotska Sandön. The next boat departed at two thirty. Before she left the quarry, someone at police headquarters had enough foresight to fax over personal information on Morgan Larsson, along with a copy of his passport photo.

When Knutas returned to police headquarters, the place was a whirlwind of activity. His colleagues were running from one office to another, exchanging information. Kihlgård came over to talk to Knutas.

'What on earth is going on? This so-called summer paradise is turning out to be another Sicily!'

The allusion may have been something of a stretch, but Knutas understood what he meant, since he still had the events of the previous year, when decapitated horses had played a role, fresh in his mind. He chose not to reply. Instead he took his colleague by the arm and steered him towards the meeting room.

'Meeting – of the investigative team – right now!' he shouted as they moved quickly down the corridor. In spite of all the noise and commotion, his words seemed to penetrate through the walls, because a minute later everyone had gathered.

The only person missing, aside from Karin Jacobsson, was Erik Sohlman, who was still out at the crime scene.

'At 11.52 a.m., a call came in to the officer on duty, reporting that a man had been found shot to death in a wooden building at the biggest stone quarry in Slite, known as Fila Hajdar and located on the western edge of town,' Knutas began. 'He was found by two individuals who were there with him to supervise the blasting. He was lying on the shed floor, shot in the forehead. And that's not all. He'd also taken a large number of shots to the stomach. Exactly like Peter Bovide.'

'What's the victim's name?' asked the prosecuter, Smittenberg.

'The man's name is Morgan Larsson. He's forty-one years old, unmarried, no children. He worked as an explosives expert at the factory, where he'd been employed for twenty years. He lived in a flat in central Slite. That's all we know so far. Except for the fact that he was a classmate of Erik's.'

'Oh. So they knew each other? How well?' asked Kihlgård.

'Not very well, from what I can gather. At any rate, Erik is still out there. And by the way, when we were at the scene, we heard that Morgan Larsson had visited Gotska Sandön over the weekend. So that was the last thing he did before he was murdered. Karin caught the next ferry out to the island. All right, then. We've cordoned off a large area around the quarry. The forest above it is being searched by police dogs, and roadblocks have been set up all around Slite. All indications are that we're dealing with the same killer. The empty casings that were found at the crime scene match those from the first murder, and according to Sohlman, they appear to have come from the same gun, meaning a Russian army pistol from the 1920s.'

'Who the hell would use such an old gun?' asked Kihlgård. 'It's practically an antique.'

'It doesn't sound like a professional, but it does seem to fit the MO,' said Wittberg. 'And by the way, this means we can forget about the Estonians as murder suspects, since they're sitting in jail.'

'Let's take a look at the facts,' said Knutas abruptly. 'We do have a witness. One of the foremen who was present at the blasting saw the perpetrator with his own eyes. Granted, from quite a distance, since he was on the other side of the quarry and looking through binoculars, but still. He says the perp was wearing dark clothing. He was about 5 foot 8 and apparently had a slight limp.'

'5 foot 8,' said Wittberg. 'Then it's no surprise that he wears only size 7½ shoes.'

'It's a good description, and let's just hope it helps us catch him soon,' Knutas went on. 'We've put out an all-points bulletin, also on the radio. In the meantime, we need to find out what links there might be between Morgan Larsson and Peter Bovide. Did they know each other? Did they have the same circle of friends?'

'Does Morgan Larsson have a police record?' asked the prosecutor.

'No,' replied Knutas. 'We've already checked on that.'

The door opened, and Erik Sohlman came in.

'How's it going?' asked Kihlgård sympathetically, patting Sohlman's arm as he sat down next to him.

'I'm fine,' said Sohlman. 'Just fine.' He turned to look at the others. It was obvious that the situation had upset him. 'We're positive that it's the same perp who killed Peter Bovide. Morgan took one bullet to the forehead and seven to the abdomen – exactly like before.'

'What sort of technical evidence have you found?' asked Knutas.

'Footprints that are identical to the ones found on the beach at Norsta Auren. Also size 7½, and the same type of shoe, an ordinary, cheap brand of trainer you can buy just about anywhere. The bloodstains on the ground show that Morgan was shot where he was found. Most likely first in the head, then in the abdomen. Several casings were lying on the floor, and they match those we found in connection with Peter Bovide's murder. Of course, they'll be sent over to the

SCL, but I can tell you right now that the same gun was probably used.'

'How sure are you about that?' asked Wittberg.

'Quite sure, since the gun is so unique. A Russian army pistol from 1926, a special-calibre Korovin. And once again, the perp emptied the clip.'

'How well did you know Morgan Larsson?' asked Kihlgård.

'Not very well, actually. We were classmates in primary school, and we lived fairly close to each other in Slite. But we were never close friends.'

'He was unmarried with no children and, according to his workmates, had no girlfriend. Do you know if he was dating anyone?'

'I don't think so. He lived in a flat in Slite. Alone, as far as I know.'

'Do you have any idea whether he had contacts in the construction industry, or whether he knew Peter Bovide?'

Erik Sohlman shrugged.

'No clue.'

'We'll start by mapping out any links to Peter Bovide,' Knutas decided. 'Right now, finding a connection between the two victims has to take priority. Plus, finding out what Morgan Larsson was doing on Gotska Sandön, and why he was in such a hurry to go there.'

Johan was inclined to believe that Pia was right when she predicted what her future would be. The images from the stone quarry were sharp and revealing. A good photographer also had to be lucky, and in this case good fortune had definitely been on Pia's side. Just as she'd started shooting, the body was carried out of the little hut, which they later learned was the shed where the explosives expert always stood when the blasting took place. Pia had also filmed Knutas, Jacobsson and crime-scene tech Sohlman as they inspected the site.

They'd found out the victim's identity by talking to Pia's good friend who worked at Cementa. Everybody knew who he was: Morgan – the explosives guy. Forty-one years old and a bachelor. The killer had chosen to strike at the precise moment of the detonation.

'Maybe he wanted to make use of the explosion to drown out the sound of the gunshots,' Johan suggested as they sat in the office, splicing and editing the images.

'Wouldn't it be simpler just to use a silencer on the gun?' said Pia. 'By the way, what's going on with you? Seems like you're in an especially good mood today. It's not just because we've got ourselves a scoop on this story, is it?'

'That should be enough. But here's another scoop for you.'

'What is it?'

Johan stood up to fetch an envelope, which he handed to Pia.

'Take a look.'

'But isn't this a personal letter?' asked Pia hesitantly when she saw that it said 'To Johan' on the envelope.

'Yes, but it's OK. I want you to read it.'

Pia opened the envelope and frowned.

A card fell out with a picture of a potato patch on the front. Underneath were only a few handwritten words: 'Yes, I will. Again.'

'I don't get it. From somebody who grows potatoes?'

'A bit more than that, Pia.'

'Huh?' Pia gave her colleague a quizzical look. 'What do you mean?'

Then she noticed the ring on his left hand.

'What? Don't tell me you're engaged again? You and Emma? Oh, Johan, that's great! Congratulations!'

'Thanks,' said Johan, laughing. 'Thanks.'

The wharf at Fårösund was crowded with people wearing shorts and sensible shoes and carrying rucksacks, heading out on nature expeditions to the island of Gotska Sandön. When Jacobsson boarded the boat, she noticed the captain looking pleased as he waved and motioned for her to come into the wheelhouse. She couldn't remember having seen him before, but apparently he recognized her.

'I know you're from the police because I've seen you on TV,' he explained when she came in and shook hands with him. He introduced himself as Stefan Norrström.

The first thing that struck Karin was that she and the captain were actually rather similar. He was about her height and age. He also had dark hair, and when he smiled, she saw the gap between his middle teeth. The one difference was that he was short and stocky while she was fine-boned.

Stefan Norrström turned out to be easy to talk to, and he gave a lively account of Gotska Sandön during the two-hour crossing. He told vivid stories about how ships often sank in the fierce storms that raged over the island, about accidents and the hardships of the lighthouse-keepers. In the past, several lighthouses had been manned, but in the 1970s they were automated. Four rangers still worked at the national park year round, and during the tourist season, which was from May to September, there were campsite supervisors available to help visitors. In the winter the island was mostly deserted. Its lonely location in the middle of the sea meant that Gotska Sandön was subject to harsh weather conditions, which made it difficult for anyone to live there permanently.

While the captain talked, Jacobsson admired the view. They had left Fårö and Gotland behind and were making their way through open waters. Nothing but sun-glinting water as far as the eye could see.

'It won't be long now,' said the captain after little more than an hour, and Jacobsson caught a glimpse of a solitary strip of land in the middle of the sea. It grew into a green ribbon without any discernible hills or significant elevation. As they got closer, she could make out the sandy beach that emerged from a long, light-coloured border around the remote island. She was surprised to see so much forested land.

Jacobsson had never set foot on Gotska Sandön before, and she'd always imagined it to be nothing more than a flat, sandy strip of land. As they approached, her image of the place changed.

The boat rounded the last promontory before

reaching the area where they would go ashore, and Stefan Norrström handed her his binoculars.

'Take a look. Out there is Bredsand promontory. See the birds? There are eider ducks, goosanders, black-throated divers, and of course black-backed gulls, common terns and herring gulls.'

Jacobsson raised the binoculars to her eyes. It took a moment before she found the correct focus, but when she did, she was astounded.

She was looking at thousands and thousands of seabirds flying around each other at different elevations and sailing back and forth over the promontory. It was an impressive sight.

'You have to go out there and watch at sunset. It's really something worth seeing. And it's not far from the camp-site, just a five-minute walk. The beach is so white and wide you'll think you're in Bali or somewhere like that.'

'How often do you get to leave the boat and spend time on the island?'

'Rarely. This boat shuttles between Nynäshamn, Gotska Sandön and Fårösund. But I once worked as an assistant to the head ranger. That's why I know my way around the island.'

Jacobsson took out the photo of Morgan Larsson.

'Do you recognize this man? His name is Morgan Larsson, and he used to come out to Gotska Sandön every once in a while.'

Stefan Norrström took the picture and studied it carefully.

'No, I've never seen him before. And the name doesn't sound familiar. But I see so many people. It's impossible to remember them all.'

GOTSKA SANDÖN, 22 JULY 1985

*B*y the time Vera reached the campsite, she was physically
*and emotionally drained. The hike back had been ten
times harder than when they had taken the same route on
the previous day. She prayed to God that her sister had
returned to the campsite on her own, or gone there by boat
with the boys they'd met. Her mother and father were sitting
outside the cabin drinking coffee when she arrived. Judging
by their expressions, she could tell that Tanya hadn't come
back yet.*

*'Why are you alone? Where's Tanya?' shouted Oleg before
even saying hello.*

*Both her parents stood up from the table and came to meet
her. Their faces expressed surprise and concern. In spite
of the circumstances, Vera couldn't help feeling a twinge of
irritation. Her sister was always number one in their minds
and the focus of all their attention. She'd been walking for
almost four hours, worn out and sick with worry. She'd
finished off the drinking water long ago, as she'd left
behind half of what they'd taken with them. She was soaked
with sweat, parched and completely done in, but neither of
her parents made any move to help her with her gear or*

304

offer her anything to drink. Vera clenched her teeth. Then she came right out and told them exactly what had happened. She would never forget the look on her father's face when she finished her story. He'd turned pale under the suntan, and his lips were pressed tight into a narrow line.

'Are you telling me that you got so drunk you just went to bed? You left her alone with two total strangers?'

'Yes, but . . .' Vera tried to reply but fell silent when she saw her father's ominous expression.

'How could you? You're the older sister and should take responsibility. Tanya doesn't know how to look out for herself. You just fell asleep, and now she's gone missing – presumably with two boys we don't even know!'

He was standing only inches away from her, and his saliva sprayed her in the face. Vera just stood there, the sweat pouring from her armpits and the heavy rucksack a leaden weight on her back. She felt dizzy and faint; her head began to spin.

'Calm down,' she heard her mother say. 'It's not Vera's fault that Tanya is missing. We need to go looking for her. She probably just got lost.'

They looked for Tanya all evening, with help from other visitors, the ranger and the rest of the employees. Their shouts echoed all over the island, but the search proved futile. When it began to get dark, they alerted the police. The next day, a patrol was due to come over to the island, and a helicopter was going to start searching as soon as it was light.

A search was also initiated for the boat with the two young men, but Vera had only a vague idea of what sort of boat it was. Nor did she recall their names, although she thought they came from Stockholm.

After the meeting of the investigative team, Knutas rang Peter Bovide's parents. Katarina Bovide answered the phone.

'Hello, this is Superintendent Knutas here, from the Visby police. I'm very sorry to disturb you again, but I was wondering whether Peter knew somebody named Morgan Larsson.'

There was silence on the phone.

'That's not the man who was found dead, is it? I just heard on the radio that somebody out at the stone quarry . . .'

'Yes, I'm afraid so. Naturally, we haven't yet made his identity public, but his name is Morgan Larsson. And he was shot in exactly the same way as Peter.'

Knutas heard Katarina Bovide take a deep breath.

'But that's horrible! Why Morgan? And Peter? I don't understand. They were such nice boys.'

'I'm afraid it's true. Did they know each other?'

'Yes, they were best friends when they were younger. But not later on. They haven't been in contact for years.'

'Do you know why?'

'I suppose that's just what happens. People grow apart.'

'But you said they used to be good friends?'

'Morgan was a year older than Peter, so they were never classmates in school. But when Morgan was thirteen, something terribly tragic happened. His parents died in a car crash. He was an only child, so he moved in with his grandparents, who lived only a stone's throw from Slite. Morgan wasn't doing well after everything he'd been through, but Peter knew lots of kids in the neighbourhood, and the two boys quickly became friends, so Morgan also became part of the whole group, you might say. Later, they were as thick as thieves for years. They travelled together on Interrail cards, and things like that. But eventually their friendship came to an end. I don't know why.'

'And you never asked Peter about it?'

'I'm sure I did, but I don't actually remember what he told me. By that time Peter had been living on his own for a long time, and Morgan too. Both of them lived in Visby. That's how it goes with friends; they come and go. You can't take it for granted that you'll have the same friends your whole life. It's just like everything else.'

Katarina Bovide's voice quavered, and Knutas could hear that she was close to breaking point. He thanked her for her help and said goodbye.

The boat docked on the north-east side of the promontory, near the lighthouse, only a few minutes' walk from the campsite. The weather was perfect, sunny and without a breath of wind. The temperature was 77 degrees. Karin almost forgot that she was here because of a homicide investigation. The huge beach stretched out before her, kilometre after kilometre, as far as the eye could see, until the shoreline disappeared in the distance behind the next promontory. She couldn't remember ever seeing a wider beach, and the sand was fine-grained and practically white.

It was four thirty in the afternoon, and she was thinking of taking a dip before she started interviewing the park personnel on the island about Morgan Larsson. At the moment they were busy with all the new arrivals. Bags were flung on to a cart, which tractors then came to haul away. That was the only type of vehicle that could make it through the loose sand. The visitors were directed to walk along the wooden planks that had been placed on the sand, stretching for over 300 yards up to the campsite.

First they passed Fyrbyn, a cluster of red-painted wooden houses with white trim and splendid gardens. They belonged to the local folklore society. Members of the society and the head ranger lived in the houses during the summer and on a few weekends during the rest of the year.

Karin Jacobsson drew a deep breath into her lungs. The air was fresher than any place she'd ever been. From the woods came the scent of pine needles with a touch of moss, and mixed with sea air.

In the middle of the open square, which was surrounded by the cottages, stood a small museum that also housed a library and archives. That was where the rangers had their office. The ranger currently on duty was on his way back from the other side of the island, and it would take about an hour before he returned.

The path continued up to the campsite where the tourists would be staying. Tents and small cabins were arranged around an open clearing. In the centre were the public buildings, with laundry and kitchen facilities as well as showers. A short distance away were the toilets, which were actually outhouses, set up in a long row. The only thing to drink on the island was well water; all the food and anything else to drink had to be transported over. No kiosks, no shops, nothing. That was another sort of experience, in addition to everything else exotic about the island.

Jacobsson realized that she'd be forced to spend the night, since she'd arrived so late in the afternoon, so she asked for help in finding a cabin, food and clothing.

She was soon installed in her cabin, where she changed into a swimsuit, and then walked past the campsite towards the west side of the island. She wondered where Morgan Larsson had stayed and whether he'd been alone. She hoped that the people who worked on the island would remember the visitors who had stayed here, at least for the past few days.

The path to the beach wound its way through a wooded section. She couldn't recall ever having experienced such silence. She stopped to listen. No car engines or voices, not even a rustling from the trees. And no sounds from the sea. Karin was filled with a sense of calm and almost forgot about the tragic events that had brought her here. The beach was at least 50 yards wide, and the sand glittered in the afternoon sun. A few sailboats were anchored a short distance away, and here and there she could see several sunbathers on the shore, but not many.

Yet people travel halfway around the world to find beaches that aren't even half as beautiful, thought Karin. She dropped her towel on the sand and ran into the water.

As soon as Johan returned to the editorial office, and in spite of being in a rush to file his report about the new murder, he rang up the pastor. The Fårö church was free for a wedding one Saturday in August at four in the afternoon. Someone had cancelled. Was that a bad omen? He pushed the thought aside.

Ever since he'd first seen the church, he'd wanted to get married there. To Emma. This time they were going to do it.

That evening he drove out to Roma. As he walked up the gravel path to Emma's house, he was in good spirits. He'd bought twenty red roses, which he was holding behind his back, along with a bottle of champagne.

He rang the bell and listened to the chiming inside. No one was visible in the kitchen window. If only she was at home. He hadn't wanted to ring ahead to say he was coming over. He wanted to surprise her, just as she had surprised him with her card.

Then the door opened, and there she stood. Wearing a grey hoodie and sweatpants, her hair wet. She looked exactly the same as when they had first met. He would never forget that day. He and the photographer Peter Bylund had come to the house in Roma to interview Emma, who was best friends with a woman who had been brutally murdered with an axe on the beach. The two men had both left feeling slightly infatuated with Emma.

He felt quite moved when he saw her. She almost seemed unreal.

'Hi.' She looked pleased.

'Emma,' was all he said.

He pulled her soft, lean body into his arms and buried his face in her long, wet hair. Then he stepped back and looked deep into her eyes.

'I'll leave at once if you can't answer my question.'

'OK,' she said, sounding puzzled, although she didn't look at all nervous. Just full of anticipation.

'Will you marry me on 19 August in Fårö church, in the presence of our families, relatives, friends and all the children? And I'm talking about a big church wedding with a huge party afterwards.'

Emma replied without hesitation.

'Yes, Johan. I will.'

He put down the bouquet of roses and champagne bottle and lifted her up in his arms. How light she was. She'd lost a lot of weight since the spring. He carried her upstairs, put her down on the bed. Pulled off her sweatpants and the grey hoodie as he caressed her silky skin. Then he held her head in his hands and kissed her soft lips. His mouth pressed against hers. The kiss went on and on. She unbuttoned his shirt and straddled him.

How long it had been – an eternity since they'd last made love. The kiss didn't stop. She never wanted to let go. And neither did he.

Jacobsson entered the museum building, where she was to meet with head ranger Mattias Bergström. He was in his thirties, with a beard and ice-blue eyes. On the phone she had explained why she wanted to see him. He suggested they should sit in his office, where they could talk undisturbed. The office was small and crowded with shelves; books and papers were everywhere. They sat down on either side of his cluttered desk, and he gave her a cup of coffee, though without offering milk or sugar.

'So it has to do with the murder of that man at the stone quarry in Slite,' he said. It was more of a statement than a question.

'Yes, exactly. Apparently he was over here at the week-end. The next day, he was fatally shot while he was at work. We want to find out whether he met anyone here, or whether something happened that might have caused the murder.'

'How horrible. I talked to him just yesterday. He'd been to the island on numerous occasions.'

'I see. Did he come out here alone, or was someone with him?'

'I think he was alone, actually.'

'Do you have any idea when he was here the first time?'

'Sure, I can check.' Bergström got up and opened a filing cabinet.

'We keep a handwritten list of everybody who has stayed here, and the dates. I guess we're a little old-fashioned that way.'

He carefully flicked through the file.

'Now let me see . . . L . . . for Larsson. We keep a file on everybody, arranged by last names, nothing else. We need only the last name to see when each visitor has been here, how long they stayed, and where; also whether they came alone or with somebody else.'

'Yes, I see.' Jacobsson could feel her impatience growing.

'Larsson, yes, here it is,' he said, sounding pleased when he finally found the name. 'Morgan. The first time he was here was 1990. He's been back quite a few times since then.'

'How many times?'

Bergström counted them up.

'Five. Approximately every third year. And always on the same date.'

Jacobsson raised her eyebrows and leaned forward.

'The same date, you said? When?'

'He came over on 21 July and left on the twenty-third. Every single time.'

'Strange. That could hardly be a coincidence. Do you know why he chose those dates?'

'No, I have no idea. And now we'll never know. Unfortunately, it's too late to ask him.'

'Has a man named Peter Bovide ever spent the night here?'

The head ranger picked up a different file and looked for the name.

'We have an Anette Bovide, and Stig and Katarina Bovide, but no Peter.'

'When were they here?'

'Anette came here with her husband, Anders Eriksson, in June, three years ago. And Stig and Katarina have made two visits to the island. The first time was in August 1991, and the second last year, in May.'

'Do you have a list of the other people who were here at the same time as Morgan Larsson, on his last visit?'

'Of course.'

Jacobsson scanned the list of names. She didn't see anything. She compared the names with the list from Morgan's previous visits. No name seemed to appear more than once.

'Can I have a copy?'

'Just a sec.'

He got up and went into an adjacent room. Jacobsson heard a good deal of rattling and clattering before he came back with a grimy photocopy.

'Thanks,' she said as he handed her the paper. 'Can

you tell me your impression of Morgan Larsson? And what did he do while he was here?'

The head ranger leaned back and clasped his hands.

'He was always alone whenever I ran into him. I didn't notice anything in particular about him, except that he seemed quite reserved.'

'Did he behave strangely?'

'No, not exactly. Although he seemed to be quite a person of habit. On the day after he arrived, he left the campsite very early in the morning with a rucksack, so I assume that he did what so many others do here – hike around the island.'

'How long does it take?'

'Hmm . . . the perimeter is about 30 kilometres, so not everybody makes it all the way round. You can choose different options. Some people start by going straight across the island through the woods and then follow the path along the shore back home. Others start at the lighthouse and take the shoreline path, or else they turn off by Tärnudden on the other side and take the forest path back.'

'If you choose the coastal path all the way round the island, how long does it take?'

'Nine or ten hours, if you're used to hiking. Parts of the shoreline are rocky and difficult, and in a number of places you have to turn inland; for instance, out by Säludden, which is a protected area.'

'Are there any seals out there?'

'Yes, we almost always see seals out there. The biggest

chance is in the morning or the evening, when they lie on the rocks out in the water.'

'Do you know which route Morgan Larsson chose?'

'I actually ran into him early on Saturday morning, on the path that goes straight through the woods and down to the Las Palmas beach on the east side of the island. And I know that others saw him coming back in the evening from the south, on the west side. Since he seemed to be such a man of habit, I would guess that he took one of the more common routes, which take seven or eight hours.'

'Could you show me on a map?'

'Sure.'

Again he got up and went into the next room, returning with a map labelled: 'County Administrative Board'. He pointed out the route.

'If I take the same route tomorrow, what do I need to keep in mind?'

'Get up early and eat a good breakfast. Pack light, but remember that you need to take along enough water and food to last you all day. Wear sturdy shoes, shorts and a sunhat. Take a swimming costume. It can be quite a strenuous hike if the sun is as hot as it is today. Down on the southern side, here' – he used a ballpoint pen to circle a spot on the map – 'you'll find a pump with fresh water that's OK to drink. That's about the halfway point, and you can fill up your water bottles.'

'Thanks for your help. Is there anything else you can tell me about Morgan Larsson?'

'Yes, there's one other thing he always did. He visited the chapel.'

'There's a chapel on the island?' asked Jacobsson in surprise, at the same time embarrassed by her ignorance.

'Yes, it's close to the campsite. You'll pass right by it if you take this path. It's always open. And if you'd like to go there tonight, there's going to be a service at nine o'clock.'

'Thanks.'

'If you need any more information about the island, the museum and library are upstairs. Feel free to go up there and browse,' the ranger suggested helpfully.

Jacobsson thanked him again and left the office.

She was looking forward to following in Morgan Larsson's footsteps.

GOTSKA SANDÖN, THE NIGHT OF 22 JULY, 1985

*T*he search for Tanya went on all night. At the campsite, every single person turned out to help find the missing young woman. The core group of the Folklore Society on the island had gathered a number of people together and gone out in their own vehicle. In all, a hundred people took part, organized into different search parties that left from the campsite. The police would arrive as soon as it was light.

Vera was in the group searching on the western side. She felt numb, moving mechanically, staring at the ground, shining her torch into crevices and groves of trees. She wanted to find her sister, and yet she didn't. The dread got worse with every step. Oleg and Sabine walked hand in hand about ten yards ahead of her, seeking support and solace from each other. She was locked out. The injustice of it all burned inside her. As if it was her fault. Her parents were punishing her by closing themselves off in their own bubble, and she was not allowed to enter. They were so focused on the search for their younger daughter that they hardly even noticed Vera. She continued doggedly on, *shouting until she was hoarse, walking without a pause across the forest floor, the beaches and the rocky cliffs.*

Suddenly she tripped over an invisible tree root on the ground. Then she lay on the ground in the dark, sobbing. She didn't have the energy to get up. She had a horrible feeling she was never going to see her little sister again. Maybe it didn't matter whether she got up. What she really wanted to do was to walk right out into the sea and let herself drown. Just disappear.

'What's the matter?'

The man appeared out of nowhere and leaned over her. At first she was scared, but she calmed down as soon as she saw the look in his eyes.

'I'm sorry, I don't understand.'

'OK.'

He switched to English. He wanted to know if she was OK and offered to help. He didn't know who she was, probably assumed she was just an ordinary summer visitor who was taking part in the search for the missing young woman. He helped Vera to her feet. They were standing in the middle of the woods, utterly alone. The others had already moved on. The moon was spreading a pale light that trickled through the trees and cast ghostlike shadows.

'Are you hurt?' he asked.

'No, I'm OK.' She brushed off the dirt that was clinging to her clothes.

'Are you cold?'

She shook her head.

'Where are you from? Germany?'

322

'Yes, Hamburg. We got here a few days ago. It's my sister who's missing.'

He didn't say anything for a moment, just put his arm around her shoulders.

'Are you able to keep searching?'

'Sure. Of course.'

Silently, they walked side by side. He didn't ask any questions, and she was grateful for that. It just felt comforting to walk next to somebody.

The hours passed, and every once in a while they would sit down to rest. He'd brought along a rucksack containing water and biscuits. The sun started coming up, and then it was time to head back to camp.

When they arrived, people had begun to gather, coming from every direction. More police had arrived, with dogs on leads, and they were in the process of organizing another search. Oleg and Sabine were nowhere in sight.

'You need to rest,' said her new-found friend. 'Which cabin are you staying in?'

'I don't want to go there.'

The thought of sleeping in a room that she had shared with Tanya horrified her.

'Would you like to come with me?'

'Yes, thanks.'

They walked past the tents. Vera could feel everyone staring at her. None of the police officers seemed to know who she was.

They quickly passed the crowd. He was holding her by the arm and leading her away from the Folklore Society cottages.

They stopped in front of a red-painted wooden house with white trim at the edge of the settlement. Vera was so tired she could hardly stand up.

A narrow stairway led up to the top floor. He made her hot chocolate and several sandwiches, which he coaxed her to eat. They sat across from each other at the little table. He looked out of the window.

'There's the police helicopter.'

Vera couldn't bring herself to reply.

The museum was deserted when Jacobsson went in. It consisted of only two rooms. One of them housed displays of objects from the sea and the island, with texts describing their history. The other room was used as a library. Along the wall were rows of books about Gotska Sandön, the lighthouses and the fisheries. On a table stood file folders with different labels: the lighthouse-keepers' diaries, newspaper clippings from various periods, general facts. Jacobsson leafed through them and was again struck by how little she'd known before coming here. She sat down and began going through the folders. From the lighthouse-keepers' diaries she learned what a hard life it must have been for them, and she was shocked by the large number of ships that had gone down in the vicinity over the years. There was even a cemetery on the island, near Franska Bukten, where Russian sailors had been buried after their ship sank.

Suddenly she caught sight of a folder with the title 'Crimes on the Island'. The first page showed newspaper clippings from the early twentieth century, when a lighthouse-keeper's assistant was suspected of murdering the lighthouse-keeper by pouring arsenic into his box of macaroni. The pages continued with stories of burglaries, the plundering of wrecked ships, and a man who had heaved an enemy overboard during the crossing to the island.

An article about a missing young woman caught Jacobsson's attention. The text described the search for a German woman who had disappeared in the 1980s after an outing with her sister at Franska Bukten, where the two young women had spent the night. The family had notified the police the following evening, and a patrol had come over the next morning. A search party was organized, but without result. The headline of the next article announced: 'Missing woman found dead.' Jacobsson read with growing interest. A police helicopter had flown over the island, and that was when Tanya Petrov's body was found in the water a short distance out in Franska Bukten.

At first the theory was that her death was an ordinary drowning accident. Then came a series of articles recounting how the story had developed. It was discovered that the woman hadn't drowned at all. She'd been murdered, and then her body was thrown into the water. The post mortem showed that she was killed by a blow to the head delivered with a blunt instrument, that someone had gripped her throat in a stranglehold, and that she had most likely been raped. Jacobsson shivered as she read on. The police had put out a nationwide alert for a boat with two men, probably Stockholmers. According to the interview with the sister, the young women had met the men when they anchored their sailboat in Franska Bukten. They had partied together on the beach, and later the older sister had gone off to bed. In the morning her little sister and both men were gone, and the boat was too. Twenty-four hours later, the woman's body was found in the water of Franska Bukten.

The evening newspapers couldn't get enough of the story, reporting on the lives of the entire Petrov family, how the father had fled from the Soviet Union and created a new life for himself in the West. How Tanya was missed by her classmates, and how the sunny story of the happy family that was finally going to make their dream trip to Gotska Sandön had ended in a tragedy as black as night.

In spite of intensive investigative work, neither man had ever been found. The case was eventually shelved.

Jacobsson leafed through the rest of the folder, looking for more articles. What had happened to the family? She had a vague memory of hearing something about the case when it happened. She had some scattered images in her mind of the newspaper headlines and photographs of Gotska Sandön. That was even before she'd started at the Police Academy, in 1985.

She closed up the folder and left the museum with an uneasy churning in her stomach.

TUESDAY, 25 JULY

It felt unreal to be waking up in the double bed in Roma next to Emma. It took Johan a moment to comprehend that he was really there. Only now, as he lay in bed, did he realize how intense his longing had been. She lay on her side, turned away from him. Gently he stroked the small of her back. How fragile she was, both inside and out. Suddenly he felt so strong. And then he had a great yearning to see Elin. He wanted to drive out and get her at once. But his work was waiting for him; they hadn't sent over another reporter from the national news, so he was responsible for the continuing coverage of the murder of the explosives expert.

In the shower, he thought about the homicide. It couldn't be a coincidence that Morgan Larsson had been killed at the Cementa site in Slite, so close to the harbour where the sale of illegal booze took place. Booze that Peter Bovide had also purchased. There had to be some sort of connection: the Cementa factory – the transactions at the harbour – Russia. Everything fitted together. Plenty of indications that the key to the motive for the murders would be found down at the harbour. The first thing he had to do was to find a link between Peter Bovide and Morgan Larsson.

His thoughts were interrupted when Emma appeared in the doorway to the bathroom and let her dressing gown fall to the floor. How beautiful she was. Although thinner than usual. He held out his hand.

'Come here.'

He'd never found it so difficult to leave her. It was as if the time they'd spent apart had now brought them closer together than ever before.

'What's happened to your mouth?' he asked with a laugh when they kissed on the way out to his car. 'It's like a suction cup.'

'You should talk.'

He took her face between his hands.

'I love you, Emma.'

'I love you too.'

'I want to see Elin. When can you bring her home?'

'I'm driving out there today, so why don't you come back here after work and spend the night?'

'When can I move in?'

'Now.'

'Are you sure?'

'Yes, I'm sure.'

She looked so serious he had to laugh.

'Too bad we can't get married tomorrow.'

At five thirty, the alarm clock rang. Karin Jacobsson felt as if she hadn't slept more than an hour. She had to make a real effort to get herself out of bed. Outside the window it was utterly quiet. She packed her rucksack, drank a cup of coffee and forced herself to eat a couple of sandwiches. She was definitely not a breakfast person, and she didn't much like eating anything so early in the morning, but the words of the ranger were still echoing in her ears. She had a long hike ahead of her, and there was no food to be found along the way.

The rising sun was just becoming visible between the trees, but it was still the early light of dawn as she set off. There wasn't a sound in the woods; all she heard was the soft tramping of her own feet.

On the map, she'd seen where the chapel was located, and she caught sight of it after only a few minutes. The door stood open, and she went inside, sat down in one of the back rows, and let her eyes scan the blue-painted wooden pews. The furnishings were simple, and a lovely light came in through the windows. She wondered if there was some special reason Morgan Larsson had always come here.

She lit one of the candles that were affixed to the pews, studying it for a moment before she blew it out, and then left the chapel.

The hike through the woods took longer than she'd thought. On the other side, the beach called Las Palmas opened up before her. She'd read that the name came from a Spanish ship which had capsized long ago.

The shore was rocky and uneven, which made it difficult to walk. When she reached Säludden, she fought an inner battle with herself. Either she could choose to follow the instructions on the little sign and turn right so as not to disturb the seals, or she could ignore what it said and continue along the water. The decision was easy to make. If for once in her life she was going to see seals in their natural habitat, then she wanted to see them up close.

As she approached, she saw big, ungainly shapes moving slowly back and forth, way out in the sun-glinting water. She raised her binoculars to her eyes and was amazed when she counted fifteen chubby grey seals frolicking in the morning sun. Soon she could see them with the naked eye.

She sat down cautiously at the very end of the promontory, took out the sandwiches she'd brought along, and then poured herself some coffee. The seals were swimming, playing and drying themselves off in the sun. Even though she was breaking the law, she didn't regret for a moment coming this way. She sat there for half an hour, fascinated by the spectacle. Just her and the seals.

After walking for three hours, Franska Bukten opened out before her. It was hard to imagine that a young woman had been raped and murdered in this peaceful spot.

In the middle of the beach, Karin stopped, stripped off her clothes and walked naked into the water. She knew she was alone. Presumably, she'd left long before all the others, and it was at least a three-hour walk from the campsite. Nobody was going to turn up for at least an hour.

After her swim, she lay down on the beach to dry off. She drank a bottle of water and looked at the map. So it was here that she'd find the Russian cannons from the sunken ship. She looked around, but couldn't see anything. According to the map, they were a bit higher up on the shore, near the Russian cemetery.

She pulled on her shirt and shorts and walked up towards the woods. There it was. Slowly, an idea was taking shape in her mind. She stopped short. The Russian cemetery. Of course. The murders had nothing at all to do with illegal workers or Russian coal transports. The key was here, on Gotska Sandön. Right in front of her eyes. How could she have been so stupid? She ran down to the beach and grabbed her things.

She thought about Morgan Larsson's visits to Gotska Sandön. When was it he'd come here? Always on the

same date, over the past fifteen years. She got her notebook out of the rucksack. He was usually here between
21 and 23 July. When was Tanya murdered? It was in
the summer, but she couldn't remember the exact date.
She cursed herself for not writing it down. She pulled
out her mobile to ring the head ranger. It was dead. No
coverage. Shit. That meant she couldn't ring Knutas
either.

She checked the map to find the quickest route back
to camp.

By the time Jacobsson finally reached the campsite, she was parched and drenched with sweat. She was dying for a drink of water, but there was no time for that. First she had to do two things: get in touch with Knutas, and then find out the date that Tanya was murdered. She also wanted to get home as fast as possible. Her mobile still wasn't working. Near the rows of outhouses, she ran into a couple of young guys who were emptying the latrines. They told her that the next boat to Gotland was leaving in fifteen minutes.

She dashed into the cabin and threw all her things into the rucksack, then raced over to the museum. Luckily, it was open. Not a soul was in sight. She bounded up the stairs and grabbed the folder she was looking for. Five minutes until the boat left.

On her way down to the beach, she saw that the mobile phone signal was back, and she rang Knutas. He answered immediately.

'Hi,' she panted. 'I've worked out how everything fits together. The murders have to do with an old case. A German girl who came here to Gotska Sandön on holiday with her family, an unsolved homicide from 1985.'

Her mobile beeped, warning her that the battery was almost used up.

'Damn it. If we get cut off, I'll ring from the boat. I'm going on board right now; it leaves in a few minutes. I think the father is the killer. He's Russian.'

'OK, start over. I'm not following you.'

'You remember the case, don't you? It was in the middle of the summer, a German family whose daughter was murdered, in 1985.'

'Oh right, I do now. Although I was working in uniform back then, so I don't recall much about it. But good God, that was twenty years ago, and the case was never solved.'

'Exactly, but now I've . . .'

The connection was broken. The battery was dead. Karin swore as she ran down towards the boat, where the gangway was being pulled on board.

'Wait!' she shouted, waving her arms.

A boy standing on shore, who was tossing the last bag on to the ship's deck, signalled to the captain.

Jacobsson thanked him as she stumbled on board, gasping for breath.

It was with relief that she recognized the captain, Stefan Norrström, from before, and she quickly went up to the wheelhouse.

'Hi again. Could I borrow your phone?'

'Absolutely. Has something happened?'

'Yes, you might say that,' replied Jacobsson as she opened the folder containing the old newspaper clippings.

She wanted to find out the date that the German woman was murdered before she talked to Knutas. The captain cast a curious glance at the folder over her shoulder.

'I have to ring the police. My crappy mobile isn't working.'

'Sometimes there are problems with coverage out here.'

'The battery's dead, and I left the charger back home in Visby,' she said, with a gesture of resignation.

She had reached the pages with the clippings about the murder of Tanya Petrov. In her mind, she went over what she knew. Morgan Larsson always travelled to Gotska Sandön on the same date. He'd visited the island every few years over the past fifteen years. And each time he'd been here from 21 July until 23 July.

Her eyes fell on the date of the murder. Tanya had been killed in the early hours of 22 July 1985. Her body had been found on the twenty-third. Jacobsson took a deep breath. The connection was crystal clear.

'What do you have there?' asked the captain as he handed her the phone. 'Is that about the girl who was murdered out here?'

'Yes,' said Jacobsson curtly as she took the phone. She had neither the time nor the desire to tell an outsider about what she'd discovered.

She began punching in Knutas's number.
'Do you have any water?' she asked.
'Of course.'
Stefan Norrström got up from his chair and turned
away to get a bottle of water out of the refrigerator.
Jacobsson happened to catch a glimpse of his
expression. It had changed completely.

At police headquarters in Visby, Knutas contacted the German police and asked them to find out what had happened to the family from Hamburg that had spent a holiday on Gotska Sandön in July 1985. A holiday that had ended in tragedy. Could it be the father, Oleg Petrov, who had finally decided to avenge his daughter's death?

While he waited to hear back from the Germans, he summoned to his office everyone from the investigative team who was available. He told them the facts that Karin Jacobsson had managed to tell him before their conversation was cut off.

'So it's the father who's supposedly the murderer?' said Kihlgård, sounding dubious. 'After such a long time? Why now?'

'Yes, that's the big question,' said Wittberg. 'Something must have triggered the whole chain of events.'

'I remember that case,' interjected Prosecutor Smittenberg. 'The girl went missing, and at first a search party was organized; a lot of officers from here helped look for her. Then her body was found in the water off the coast of Gotska Sandön; she'd been raped and murdered. A terrible story. There was something about some young men who had come ashore from a boat and later disappeared. They were never caught.'

'I can't understand why Karin hasn't reported in again,' said Knutas, annoyed. 'She was supposed to ring me as soon as she was on board.'

'Why don't you try the boat?' suggested Wittberg. 'Ask them to call her on the loudspeakers.'

'Oh, right. Good idea.'

Knutas looked a bit embarrassed, but he got the police switchboard on the line, and was connected to the M/S *Gotska Sandön*. A man's deep voice could be heard over a crackling sound.

'M/S *Gotska Sandön*. Captain Stefan Norrström speaking.'

Knutas introduced himself.

'Would it be possible to contact a specific individual on board, by using the loudspeaker system, for example?'

'Who do you want to speak to?'

'A police officer named Karin Jacobsson.'

'Do you want to wait on the line or ring back in a few minutes?'

'I'd like to wait.'

'OK.'

Knutas heard the captain announcing Karin's name, asking her to come to the wheelhouse immediately. Then he was back on the phone.

'If she's on board, she should be here in a minute. This boat isn't very big.'

'OK.'

Several minutes passed.

'Shouldn't she have responded by now?'

'Yes. She can't be on board.'

'Could you try one more time?'

The captain hesitated.

'Is that really necessary?'

'I think it is. Just to be sure.'

Again the captain announced Karin's name. After another couple of minutes, Knutas gave up.

'I guess she didn't make it on board.'

'I guess not.'

'Thanks for your help.'

'Not at all.'

An uneasy feeling had settled in Knutas's chest during the conversation. Karin had found a link between the murder on Gotska Sandön and the two current homicide cases. And now she was missing. He asked the operator to phone the head ranger on Gotska Sandön. When he was connected, Knutas explained why he was calling.

'She left on the two-thirty boat. Apparently she was in a real hurry.'

'Are you sure she made it on board?'

'Absolutely. I was down at the dock helping with the loading, and I saw her go on board.'

'Are you a hundred per cent sure? I mean, do you

know what Karin Jacobsson looks like? Petite, thin, about forty, although she looks younger, with short dark hair, brown eyes, a big gap between her front teeth, quite attractive . . .'

He heard the ranger sigh with impatience.

'Yes, of course I know what she looks like. She interviewed me yesterday about that man named Morgan Larsson who was murdered.'

'OK. When does the boat arrive at Fårösund?'

'At four thirty. The crossing takes two hours.'

Knutas had barely put down the phone before the operator rang to say that he had the Germans on the line. Knutas pushed his uneasiness about Jacobsson aside.

The other members of the investigative team listened intently to his stumbling English. Knutas looked at them with an inscrutable expression as he slowly put down the phone.

'That was our German colleagues. Oleg Petrov can't be the killer, because he's dead. Three months after Tanya was found murdered, he committed suicide by throwing himself in front of a train.'

Everyone in the room exchanged puzzled looks.

'What about the mother and sister? What happened to them, and where are they now?' asked Wittberg.

'The mother still lives in Hamburg, but wait until you hear this: the sister lives here on Gotland. She's married to a Gotlander and they live in Kyllaj.'

'Kyllaj,' Wittberg repeated, a pensive look coming

over him. 'That woman on the ferry, the first ferry on the morning the murder was committed. She lived in Kyllaj. She was pregnant and married. But she had an alibi – that's why we didn't question her further. Her husband provided her with an alibi.'

Knutas leaned forward. 'That's right, her husband. She's married to a man by the name of Stefan Norrström. He's the captain that I was just talking to!'

Knutas's brain now went into high gear. The captain had claimed that Karin wasn't on board his boat. And now she was missing.

It all started that day in early June when she went shopping at the ICA supermarket. It was a lovely, warm day, full of promise for the coming summer. She'd gone to Slite and parked near the ICA, where she usually shopped. She grabbed a cart outside and then went in to buy some food.

They were planning to have a barbecue that evening. Strangely enough, she had a particular craving for strongly spiced meat now that she was pregnant. She picked up a couple of big potatoes which she was going to bake and fill with the special herbed butter that Stefan liked so much. She spent a long time in the fruit and vegetable section, carefully selecting green peppers, tomatoes and fresh mushrooms. They could grill the steaks separately and then make some vegetable skewers. She put some cobs of sweetcorn in her cart. Suddenly she felt a kicking inside of her, then another. She stood still. She loved feeling the child moving around. She rested for a moment, leaning on the shopping cart and running her hand gently over her stomach. She still couldn't believe she was going to be a mother. It looked as if her life was finally going to work out. So often in the past she'd had her doubts. But every time, Stefan had persuaded her not to give up. Of course they were meant to be together. Surely she understood that. 'Don't even think of objecting,' he'd say. 'Don't even think of it.'

And in the end she'd begun to believe him. Really believe him, deep in her heart. To her surprise, she realized that she was actually on her way to feeling safe. From the outside, she appeared to have had a stable upbringing, but the pain and insecurity had never gone away. She'd been marginalized by her parents, constantly compared to her sister. She'd never felt good enough just the way she was. She'd never felt a real sense of security. To be utterly secure, no matter how she looked, what she did, or what happened around her. Stefan loved her like no one ever had before. But she still had wounds she would have to live with to the end of her days. It helped a lot that he knew everything, and had even been present when the very worst had happened to her. He understood her like no one else did.

The kicking stopped for the moment, and she went back to her shopping. She put some beer in her cart for Stefan; she herself drank only mineral water.

There was a long queue at both check-outs. It was Friday afternoon, and everyone was out shopping. She stood at the back of one of the queues and let her eyes slide over the people patiently waiting their turn with baskets and carts full of shopping. Several people were chatting with each other, and every once in a while someone laughed. Most people knew each other here, since Slite wasn't a big place.

She hadn't made any friends of her own yet, and she didn't really feel the need to do so. Occasionally, they got together with Stefan's relatives and acquaintances. She also talked to her classmates at the Swedish lessons she was taking, and she made regular visits to the ante-natal clinic. All in all, that was more than enough socializing for her.

Suddenly she noticed a man who looked familiar standing in the queue. He was talking to a boy who couldn't be more than five or six. She looked more closely, scanning the man's face.

The man, who looked to be a few years older than her, had a unique appearance. He had a prominent high forehead, light-blue eyes, and seemed to have no eyelashes or eyebrows at all. He also had a slightly pro-truding jaw. His hair was cut short, and he was wearing carpenter overalls. There was something self-conscious about him, a slight nervousness. Maybe it was the child's constant questions; maybe it was something else.

He was standing a few yards in front of her, in the queue for the other check-out, but she had a clear view of him because he'd turned round to talk to the boy, who she assumed was his son. All of a sudden he glanced up, and she looked away. He must have noticed that she was watching him; maybe he thought she was flirting.

She couldn't help taking another look at him. He was staring straight at her as he replied to a question his son had asked. When their eyes met and she simultaneously heard his voice, her body turned to ice. She'd heard that high-pitched, slightly nasal voice before. A long, long time ago. In an entirely different context.

As if struck by a whip, she felt a stinging blow to her forehead. She shut her eyes and opened them again. He was still there, continuing to talk to his son, unaffected. He glanced at her and smiled faintly. He hadn't recognized her. In reality, that wasn't so strange. Not strange at all. It was twenty years ago that they'd last met. She had changed more than he had.

She felt sick, overcome by dizziness as her legs began to wobble. She couldn't bear to stand there any longer. She had to get out. She left the queue and pushed her way past the check-out. Outside the supermarket, she sank down on to a bench. Tears filled her eyes, but she did her best to hold them back. She took long, deep breaths. The terrible pressure she felt in her chest frightened her; she felt as if she was going to die. She was hyperventilating.

A young woman came out and asked her if she was OK. She managed to say she was fine. The woman brought her some water and asked if she was going into labour. Should she ring for an ambulance?

No, she wasn't going into labour. She just needed to

rest for a moment. The woman sat down next to her and held her hand. How considerate she was.

Thoughts were flying through her mind. It was him. There was absolutely no doubt about it. What was he doing here?

She was still having a hard time breathing, and appreciated the concern of the woman, who remained sitting next to her. Not saying anything, not asking any questions.

Suddenly the doors of the supermarket opened and he came out. He didn't notice her as he walked past with his son and bags of shopping. With the woman's help, she got to her feet and stared after him. He went over to a white van. On the door it said: Slite Construction, with a phone number.

That was enough.

When Karin Jacobsson regained consciousness, everything was quiet. She couldn't hear the sound of any engine. She was lying in a terribly uncomfortable position, leaning forward, with her back hunched and her head stuck between her knees. Tape had been placed over her mouth, and her wrists and ankles burned from the rope tied around them. It was pitch dark in the small space. Her body ached. She had a splitting headache, and she could taste blood. He must have really hit her hard. It took a moment before she even tried to move, which turned out to be nearly impossible; she felt as if she were held in a vice.

Take it easy, she thought. *Stay calm. Keep a cool head. You're locked up somewhere, and you need to find a way out.*

She wondered how much time had passed since she was knocked out. A few minutes? Half an hour? Several hours?

She made an effort to try and make out the shapes in the dark. She managed to lift her head enough to pull herself into an upright position. The headache felt like a migraine and was almost unbearable. She touched the wall with her elbow. The surface felt hard and smooth. She could tell that she was still on the boat, but the silence was so complete that all the passengers must have disembarked by now; presumably, they had reached the harbour in Fårösund. How long would the boat stay docked? Maybe twenty-four hours? How long would it be before Knutas began to wonder why she hadn't reported back? And before he or any of the others worked out what had happened to her?

Who was Captain Stefan Norrström, and how was he involved in these events? Why had he knocked her out and then locked her up in here? Thoughts whirled through her mind without making any sort of coherent picture.

Jacobsson desperately tried to move her arms and legs, but the rope refused to budge. A sea captain would know knots, of course. It felt impossible for her to get free. She tried rocking back and forth. There was a little space next to her, and she tried to tap on the wall, but she couldn't hear anything.

To top it all off, she needed to pee.

She listened for some sound. She had no idea where she was on the boat.

Suddenly she heard a ruckus on the other side of the wall. The door opened, and a strong light blinded her. There he stood, right in front of her. He stared at her for a couple of seconds, then slammed the door shut again. She heard the clack of the lock turning.

Wasn't he even going to let her use the toilet? Give

her anything to drink? She felt terribly thirsty after her long hike on Gotska Sandön in the blazing sun. She'd been in such a hurry back at the campsite that she hadn't filled her water bottles. It had been a long time since she'd had anything to drink, much less any food. Her head felt heavy, and she was starting to feel dizzy. Was he going to leave her here to die? She tried again to loosen the ropes, to move her fingers, hands and feet, but nothing did any good.

For a long time after the door closed, she sat there trying to make out any noises. She heard nothing. It was utterly quiet. Thirst and dizziness were making her confused. She closed her eyes, and her body went numb.

Knutas and Kihlgård took the lead, followed closely by two other police vehicles. They drove north-east at top speed, heading for Kyllaj. Kihlgård had managed to bring along the report on what the police had dug up so far about the investigation into Tanya Petrov's death.

'Tell us everything you know,' commanded Knutas, concentrating on keeping his eyes on the road.

'Let's take it from the beginning,' said Kihlgård. 'A week after Tanya's murder, the family returned to Hamburg. Vera had been studying languages at the university, but she gave it up and took a job in a supermarket. Both parents, Sabine and Oleg Petrov, went on sick leave. When autumn came, more specifically, on 22 October 1985, Oleg committed suicide. He threw himself in front of an express train that was just pulling into Hamburg Hauptbahnhof. He died instantly.'

'What an awful way to die.'

'After that, things starting going downhill for the mother too. She became addicted to painkillers, and she never returned to her job. The following year, in February 1986, she retired on a disability pension. She moved to a smaller flat in a suburb of Hamburg, but her daughter Vera didn't move with her. She lived in several different places in the city while she worked at the supermarket. Two years after the murder, in August 1987, she went back to university and completed her studies. After that, she spent many years working as a language teacher at a school in Hamburg. Until she moved to Sweden, that is, two years ago.'

'Why did she move here?' asked Knutas.

He was just in the process of overtaking a long-distance tractor-trailer that seemed to go on and on, and he really couldn't see far enough ahead. Kihlgård winced but went on with his report.

'I suppose she moved here because she got married to Stefan Norrström.'

'How did they happen to meet?'

'I have no idea. All I know is that they were married last summer. And now they're about to have a baby.'

'OK. We're almost there.'

Kyllaj was only ten kilometres from Slite, but its location seemed very remote, all the way out by the sea. Nowadays, it consisted mostly of summer visitors, but for centuries Kyllaj had been an important town because of its stone quarry and port. The harbour was lined with boathouses and piers. Towering above the houses that had been built on the slope leading down to the harbour and Valleviken was the bare, rocky cliff with its magnificent view of the sea and the islets

Klausen, Fjögen and Lörgeholm. As far back as the seventeenth century, limestone had been heated in kilns here, and traces of them still remained.

The police cars drew a good deal of attention as they arrived, one after the other, disrupting the idyllic atmosphere.

The house that Stefan Norrström and his wife had built stood in lonely majesty high up on a huge plot of land that sloped gently down towards the water. Great expanses of lawn with carefully arranged shrubs and trees surrounded the big white limestone house. *The land must have been passed down through the family*, thought Knutas. The place looked much too aristocratic to belong to an ordinary sea captain.

After parking their cars at a safe distance, the officers spread out and surrounded the house. They were dealing with someone who had already killed twice, and it was impossible to know what awaited them.

Knutas and Kihlgård took the lead and crept up to the front door. Knutas rang the bell. Waited. No response. He rang the bell again.

They waited a moment longer. Knutas was sweating in the heat. The tension was also taking its toll. When nothing happened, he gave the order to go in.

One of the officers broke down the door, and they all stormed inside.

Karin Jacobsson was getting really desperate. She dozed off for a while, exhausted as she was, and by now very dehydrated. She couldn't change position other than to move sideways a few inches. She did that now and then so that her body wouldn't go completely numb. She wondered how long she'd be able to hold out. She started losing hope that anyone would ever find her. The boat still wasn't moving, and she couldn't hear a single sound from outside. She'd lost all sense of time and could no longer tell how long she'd been taped and tied up like some sort of package.

Her thoughts focused on Knutas. Why wasn't he doing anything? By now he must have realized that she was on board. After all, she'd told him she would ring from the ship. Maybe the captain had fed him some lies that meant nobody was going to come to her rescue.

Strangely enough, she no longer needed to pee. It was as if her body was already in retreat. Turning off its functions, slowing down until it would gradually shut down completely. No, she shouldn't be thinking like that.

It was pitch dark as she sat there with her legs tucked up and her arms held in front of her as if she were praying.

Suddenly she heard a thud. At first she thought she'd imagined it. Then there was another thud, and one more. Voices shouting. She repeatedly tried to throw herself against the wall to make some sort of noise, at the same time doing her best to slam her feet against the door.

Miraculously, she heard someone turning the lock outside. When the door opened, the light was so blinding she had to squint.

The house in Kyllaj was empty. They searched the garden and outbuildings as well but, obviously, the Norrströms had taken off. Knutas got out his mobile to sound the alarm, but before he could do that, it rang.

'Hi, it's Thomas,' said Wittberg, his voice agitated. 'We've just found Karin. She was tied up and locked in a cargo space on board the M/S *Gotska Sandön*. It was Stefan Norrström who knocked her out and threw her in there.'

'Bloody hell! How is she?' shouted Knutas.

'She's exhausted, but otherwise there doesn't seem to be anything wrong with her. Just very dehydrated. We're in the car on our way to the hospital. What's going on out there?'

'We're at the house in Kyllaj right now, but the place is deserted. I assume they're going to try to leave the island, so I need to notify headquarters. I'll talk to you later.'

'OK, I'll phone you after I drop Karin off.'

* * *

Knutas issued orders quickly to his colleagues. The airport had to be alerted, as well as the ferry system. Suddenly he noticed that Kihlgård had disappeared, but then he saw him coming out of the kitchen with a cordless phone in his hand.

'I think we can forget about the airport. I checked the last number that was called, and it's the number for a boat company called Destination Gotland. The next boat leaves at eight o'clock, which means in twenty minutes.'

Fortunately, the ferry to the mainland hadn't yet left the dock, but all 1,500 passengers were already on board. Not wanting to cause a panic, the crew had informed everyone that the delay was due to a minor technical problem that would soon be fixed. Only plainclothes officers boarded the ship. The ferry had two levels in addition to the car deck, and the police spread out to make their search.

Knutas and Kihlgård went to the information counter to get help checking the passenger cabins. The crew member behind the counter gave them four key cards that would serve as master keys.

Just at that moment, Knutas noticed out of the corner of his eye two people rushing towards him. He turned round and was surprised to see Wittberg and Jacobsson.

'What are you doing here?' he asked Karin. 'Shouldn't you be at the hospital?'

Jacobsson looked worn out, but there was nothing wrong with her tongue.

'Did you really think I was going to miss out on all the

fun? I was just a little dehydrated. I poured about half a gallon of water down my throat on the way over here, plus an equal amount of juice. That should be sufficient.'

Wittberg threw out his arms. 'She refused to go to hospital. What are we doing now?'

'OK, well, we've spread out to search the ship. We're almost positive that they're on board. The whole terminal has been blocked off, so there's no chance of them escaping. Now we just have to find them. Martin and I were just about to start checking the cabins.'

They each took a key card and split up. Jacobsson started with the cabins on the port side, one level up. She didn't bother to knock, but just yanked open the doors.

'Police!' she shouted each time, her gun drawn.

The first cabin was empty; the second one was too. In the third, an elderly man was sound asleep. In the fourth cabin, some young guys were in the middle of playing cards and drinking beer. They stared in surprise at Jacobsson standing in the doorway. Then came a long series of cabins that all turned out to be empty.

Finally, she reached the end of the corridor. Only two cabins remained to be checked. By now she was out of breath, and her head was pounding. When she stuck the card in the door slot, the lock jammed. She tried several times without success.

Suddenly she heard a sound from inside the cabin. Someone was whimpering. It sounded like a half-stifled scream, as if someone were wearing a muzzle. Damn it all, she thought. She was alone on this level; her colleagues were on the deck below. She pulled out her mobile to ring Knutas. Shit, it wasn't charged.

She stood there for several seconds, uncertain what to do. Should she run downstairs and get the others and maybe risk losing the Norrströms, if they were the ones inside the cabin? They must have heard her shouting and trying to open the door.

She tried the key card again, shoving it into the slot. At last, it worked, and she pressed down the door handle.

When Karin looked into Vera Norrström's panic-stricken, staring eyes, all the remembered images came back to her. Fragmentary, incoherent, but razor-sharp, they sliced into her consciousness. Assaulting her, ruthlessly, violently. As they always did. She stood in the narrow doorway, frozen to the spot. Breathing hard, with a fierce band of pressure on her forehead; her legs began to buckle and she could hardly stay on her feet. The images were familiar; she woke up to them every morning, and they were in her mind when she was about to fall asleep at night. Every day for twenty-five years she had struggled to make those memories disappear.

Vera Norrström lay on the narrow lower bunk. Her face was as white as chalk and contorted with pain. She was biting down on a towel, which prevented her from screaming aloud. Her legs were apart, with one foot hanging off the side of the bed. She was pressing that foot against a chair placed next to the bunk. A cotton sheet barely covered her. She was going to give birth at any moment.

Karin knew all about that. She had just turned fifteen.

The pain is wracking her body. She can hardly understand what's happening. Both her mother and father have refused to be present at the birth. They're waiting outside until it's over. As if they're pretending that she's suffering from some serious illness. Something bad that requires an operation and has to be surgically removed, like a cancerous tumour.

A nurse dressed in green is standing next to her. Karin wants to take her hand, but she doesn't dare. She thinks she's going to be torn apart. Terrified. She's only a child.

One last violent push. Her own wail is replaced by the newborn's hesitant, tremulous voice. Hardly a scream, merely a cry. In the dimly lit room she feels the warm, alive body next to her bare skin. A piece of herself in another human being. A girl.

Karin secretly gives her the name Lydia. She closes her eyes, places her hand carefully on the baby's back. Time stops, the world stops spinning, all activity comes to a halt. Just her and Lydia, nothing else. Just the two of them.

She doesn't know how much time passes before the nurse dressed in green takes the baby away from her. She will never see her again. Forever miss her. Forever long for her.

Next to Vera sat her husband, Stefan, who had assaulted

Karin a few hours earlier. His eyes were terrified and desperate. Karin swallowed hard, trying to pull herself together and control the dizziness.

Then she stepped inside the cabin and closed the door behind her.

The search proved fruitless. After going over the ferry with a fine-tooth comb, the police officers returned to the aft salon, where they gathered to consider the situation. Jacobsson was the last to join the others. She paused in the doorway, explained that she wasn't feeling well and needed to go home. No one even had time to react before she was gone.

The concern that Knutas felt was mixed with tenderness. She always had to be so tough and strong. Now she'd finally been forced to give in. He felt like going home himself and pulling the covers over his head. The disappointing results of the search irked him. He cursed himself for allowing the Norrströms to get away.

He turned to his colleagues as he ran his hand through his hair and said wearily, 'The Norrströms' car was apparently just found at the airport car park. They checked in for the last flight to Stockholm this evening. Our efforts here seem to have been in vain.'

Maybe the couple's phone call to Destination Gotland was just a diversionary tactic. Maybe they'd been checking all the possible ways to flee when they realized that the police were on Stefan Norrström's trail. It was a bitter feeling to have been so close to catching them; now the police would have to leave the boat empty-handed. After a two-hour delay, it would now depart for Nynäshamn.

Somehow, the story had leaked out, and the usual band of journalists was waiting on the dock. They were hoping to get pictures of the arrested couple, but that wasn't going to happen. Instead, the reporters showered the police with questions about the failed action. Knutas pushed his way through the crowd without even glancing at the journalists.

He couldn't help thinking about what had gone wrong. Of course, he shouldn't have staked everything on one effort; he should have had half the police officers go out to the airport, since that was the most likely escape option. The patrol officers had discovered too late that Stefan Norrström's car was there and then sounded the alarm. Now Knutas could only hope that the police at Arlanda airport in Stockholm would confirm that they'd taken the couple into custody.

When Knutas got back to his office at police headquarters, his mobile rang. His pulse quickened.

'Yes?'

His colleagues out at the airport reported, to his surprise, that Vera and Stefan Norrström never boarded the plane to Stockholm. After checking in, they had vanished without a trace.

Knutas swore, cursing himself again. Thoughts whirled through his head, but nothing made sense. Should he have stopped the ferry from leaving? Every nook and cranny had been searched, and yet maybe . . . At any rate, it was too late now to call the boat back. But to be on the safe side, he was thinking of contacting the Stockholm police, who could take in the Norrströms if, against all odds, it turned out that they were actually on board.

The possibility that they were still on Gotland sparked new hope in Knutas. His energy revived. He ordered a continued search of all ferries leaving Gotland the following morning and sent officers over to Visby airport. In cooperation with the NCP, the other Swedish airports and border stations were also alerted. An all-points bulletin was sent out to the entire country for Vera and Stefan Norrström, and the police also made a point of contacting taxi and bus drivers. Since Vera was in her ninth month of pregnancy, all the hospital emergency rooms and maternity clinics were contacted as well. Extreme stress might send her into labour.

Maybe there was still a chance of catching Stefan Norrström. As long as there were actions to take and information to collect, Knutas had no intention of going home. Fatigue washed over him in waves, but he managed to keep it at bay with coffee and an occasional puff on his pipe.

He opened the window. Stood there, exhaling smoke.

Stared out into the Visby night, pondering his failure. Had he been blind? Karin had discovered how everything fitted together during her visit to Gotska Sandön. Shouldn't he have been able to work things out earlier? The police had made a list of all the Russians living on Gotland. On the other hand, it hadn't been easy to discover Vera Norrström's Russian heritage. She was from Germany, after all, and she had a Swedish surname.

He should go home. They could just as easily reach him there if anything happened, but he didn't want to leave. Something was bothering him. He put out his pipe and went back to his desk, where he randomly picked up a document from the investigation and began wracking his brain, trying to work out what he had missed.

At two in the morning, he sat up with a jolt. He must have dozed off in his chair, but he was suddenly wide awake when he realized that the phone was ringing. His heart pounded as he reached for the receiver.

'Hi, this is Eva Dahlberg, the reception manager for Destination Gotland. We met earlier when you were over here searching the ship.'

'Yes?'

'I apologize for ringing in the middle of the night like this, but you gave me your card, and I think I may have something important to tell you. Weren't you looking for a pregnant woman?'

'Yes, that's correct.'

'Well, the cleaners have found something that looks like a placenta in a waste basket near one of the exits on the ship. It was wrapped in a plastic bag.'

Knutas felt his blood turn cold.

'Are you sure?'

'Well, I've had seven children, and I really think it does look like a placenta.'

'OK.'

Knutas quickly considered what to do next. He had to come up with a new plan.

'The ship needs to be evacuated, and it will have to stay docked in Nynäshamn.'

'But . . .'

'Don't argue!' he shouted. 'And for God's sake, don't throw away the placenta. Put it in a plastic bag in the refrigerator for the time being.'

Shit, he thought as he put down the phone. They were on the ship after all.

The search shifted immediately to Nynäshamn and the Stockholm area. The couple now had a newborn child, but presumably no car, so they were going to have a hard time fleeing.

All fatigue was gone. Disappointment had now changed to hope.

Erik Sohlman rang from the house in Kyllaj, which had been cordoned off and vacuum-cleaned for evidence. He reported that they'd found a gun in a hatch under the basement floor. Just as they'd suspected, it was a Russian army pistol, a Korovin from the 1920s, and they could confirm that the gun had been used recently.

After that, only silence. Nothing new was heard for several hours regarding the couple wanted by the police. At five o'clock, Knutas gave up and went home. His head felt completely empty. He went straight to bed, slipping under the covers next to his slumbering wife and putting his arm around her.

It was a while before he finally fell asleep.

SATURDAY, 19 AUGUST

Kyrkviken in the middle of Fårö was bathed in reddish-yellow afternoon light. The meadows and pastures shimmered. Johan arrived at the church along with his best friend, Andreas Eklund, who was also a journalist for Swedish TV.

He was going to be Johan's best man, and they had spent the past hour having a few beers in the garden of Fåröhus restaurant, philosophizing about the fact that Johan's bachelor days had now definitely come to an end. Emma hadn't wanted him to see her before the wedding. If they were going to get married in a church, she said, they might as well do it properly.

Previously when they'd talked about getting married, Emma had completely rejected the idea of a big church wedding, as she'd already done that once before. But this time she hadn't offered the slightest objection. They were going to be married in Fårö church and then have the celebration at Fåröhus. There would be wine and grilled lamb and dancing all night long. The next day, they would leave for a honeymoon on the Italian Riviera.

When they arrived at the church, Johan saw all the guests dressed in their finest, and he was suddenly seized by a feeling of unreality. There stood his mother in a dove-blue silk dress, laughing with Emma's parents. His brothers, decked out in morning suits, were conversing with Emma's Gotland relatives. Pia Lilja's coal-black hair was sticking up, as usual, and she was wearing a bright-red, tight-fitting dress and patent-leather shoes with stiletto heels. She was talking to Peter Bylund, and Johan wondered with amusement whether something was going on between the two. Elin, wearing a pink dress with a silk ribbon, and Emma's daughter, Sara, in a matching dress, were the bridesmaids.

Filip was running around, getting into mischief with some other boys, throwing pebbles that they'd picked up from the ground. Johan let his gaze rest on Sara and Filip for a moment. His 'bonus children', or whatever he should call them. He reflected that his relationship with them had been good so far, especially with Sara; everything was going to be all right. Or rather, he would make sure that it was all right. He refused to let anything get in the way.

Together with Andreas, he slipped past the guests standing in front of the church and went into the sacristy. He said hello to the pastor, a pleasant woman in her fifties. The sexton patted him on the shoulder.

'By the way, there's a cameraman here.'

'What? From where?'

'From Swedish TV. He wants to know whether it's OK for him to videotape the ceremony.'

Johan went into the church to have a look. There stood Peter Bylund, holding a camera on his shoulder.

'Is this OK?' he asked. 'It was Grenfors who thought we should document such a major event. It'll be a great souvenir, right?'

'I'll take care of the camera, so it's done properly.' Pia was standing next to Peter, grinning.

Johan was touched by their thoughtfulness. Now he regretted not inviting the editor-in-chief to the wedding.

'Sure, that's great. Of course.'

The guests had started streaming in, taking their places in the pews. Anders Knutas came walking up the aisle, arm in arm with his wife Lina. Johan went over to say hello.

'Hi, how nice of you to come.'

'We're glad to be here.'

Knutas didn't look entirely comfortable. The last time they'd met, they had stood on the dock at Slite yelling at each other. Johan was glad the superintendent had decided to come. He wondered how Knutas, as the head of the investigation, was feeling about the fact that they hadn't caught the Norrströms. Maybe they would eventually. There was a hunt on for both Stefan and Vera Norrström through Interpol, but so far they seemed to have vanished without a trace.

Ten minutes remained before the bells would chime

four o'clock, the time for Johan and Emma to enter the church. He started to feel nervous. Andreas steered him outside and handed over a pocket flask of whisky.

'Here, have some.'

'Thanks. I'm feeling really shaky.'

'That's not so strange. You're about to get married. That's major.'

For the hundredth time in the past hour, Johan glanced at his watch. Five minutes left. She should be here by now.

No car in sight.

'Where the hell are they?'

Johan took out a cigarette and lit it. The area in front of the church was now deserted. Only a few minutes left.

Now even Andreas was looking worried.

'Should you try and ring her? Maybe something happened.'

He punched in Emma's mobile number. No answer.

The church bells began ringing. It was four o'clock. Why wasn't she here?

The pastor came outside and smiled with satisfaction.

'It's time.'

At that moment a car came driving along Fårövägen. Johan breathed a sigh of relief.

EPILOGUE

Karin Jacobsson walked along the deserted beach alone. The tourist season was over. She was wearing jeans with the cuffs rolled up and a light shirt. A sweater was draped over her shoulders. She walked barefoot, carrying her sandals in one hand, feeling the lukewarm water between her toes. The long hot summer had warmed up the sea to an unbelievable 79 degrees. The temperature was posted on a solitary sign in the middle of the beach. *Who's measuring the temperature now?* she thought. *And who would bother to post it on that sign? There's nobody here to read it.*

The air was warm, even though clouds were gathering over the sea. The little turquoise ice-cream stand was closed, shut down for the season, and it wouldn't open again until next year. She paused with her back to the water and studied the sand dunes and the woods higher up. Peter Bovide's caravan had been parked at the edge of the campsite. He'd jogged along this beach on that fateful morning barely two months earlier. And this was where he had met his killer.

It all seemed so long ago. She felt as if she had aged,

changed. She was carrying a secret, and she didn't know if she'd be able to continue to do so, much less share it with anyone else.

Vera had given birth to a baby girl in the cabin on the ship. Everything had gone well. The birth was over in less than ten minutes.

Before Karin left the cabin and the new parents with their baby, she had demanded to know the truth.

The killer that the police had been searching for the whole time was a woman. And a very pregnant woman. Who would ever have imagined that?

In the cramped cabin, with her blood-smeared new-born child at her breast, Vera had confessed to shooting both Peter Bovide and Morgan Larsson. Before they died, she'd forced them to their knees and then demanded to hear their remorse. Peter Bovide had pleaded and begged. He claimed that the murder was a mistake. That Tanya had started screaming when she was raped, and Morgan had hit her on the head with a rock to make her shut up. He hadn't meant to hit her so hard. Tanya died instantly, both young men were seized with panic, and without even thinking, they had tossed her body overboard. By then it was too late, and they fled back to Nynäshamn as fast as they could go.

His explanation made no difference. Vera carried out what she had intended to do.

She'd smuggled into Sweden her father's old army pistol in the moving van from Germany, keeping it as a memento. Then she had put it to use. In all these years, she had been convinced that the two men on Gotska Sandön were Stockholmers she would never see again, but by chance she'd recognized Peter Bovide in the ICA supermarket in Slite. And after that it didn't take long before she located Morgan Larsson. She guessed that he too was from Slite, and she started looking for him at the big work sites in the area. She found him in a personnel catalogue from the Cementa factory. He hadn't changed.

Without telling her husband, Vera had carried out her plan. But after Morgan Larsson was killed, Stefan had discovered that the gun was missing from the locked cabinet in the living room. He had confronted her, understood why she'd done it, and forgiven her. He loved her, and they were about to become parents.

Together they'd decided that there was little chance the police would ever figure out that the pregnant woman from Kyllaj was the murderer. So they could just go on living their lives.

But if Vera should come under suspicion for the murders, they'd devised an escape plan. When Karin Jacobsson had come on board the boat from Gotska Sandön with the old newspaper clippings, Stefan had realized that the jig was up. He rang Vera, who came to pick him up in Fårösund when the boat docked. She had packed their bags and brought along cash, passports and everything else they needed. To confuse the police, they went out to the airport and bought tickets on the last plane to Stockholm that evening. They parked the car, and even checked in for the flight. But instead of proceeding through security, they left the airport and took a cab to the ferry that was due to depart at eight o'clock for Nynäshamn. From there they planned to go out to Arlanda to catch a flight. Karin hadn't wanted to know where they were headed.

She sat down on the sand and looked out at the sea. She wondered how they'd managed to evade the police and what they were doing at this very moment.

Presumably, she ought to run away too. She'd helped a double murderer go free. She couldn't explain why she'd made that decision. Maybe it was because of the whole tragic story about the two young girls who had just wanted to sleep on the beach under the open sky on that hot July night twenty years ago – the night that shattered the entire family. The father had taken his own life, the mother became addicted to painkillers and lost all contact with Vera. Leaving her alone with the guilt.

Maybe, in her heart, Karin thought that it was a matter of justice. Maybe it had been easier to make the decision because she'd helped bring Vera's baby into the world, and most of all because of her own life-long trauma. She would probably never see her own child again, unless her daughter decided to look for her biological mother. And so far she hadn't. She would be twenty-five this year. Karin knew nothing about the people who had adopted her or where she had ended up, except that she was not living on Gotland.

She wondered how much her daughter knew about her birth. She hoped that no one would tell her the truth.

Karin thought of her as Lydia, the name she had secretly given the baby in that dimly lit maternity room at Visby hospital. The happiest hour of her life.

In all these years, she had never forgiven her parents. When she changed her mind and wanted to keep the baby, they told her it was impossible. They said all the papers had already been signed. During the whole pregnancy, they had actually never asked her what she wanted or how she felt. They'd just taken it for granted that the child had to be given away.

It was a Thursday afternoon when Karin went out riding in the woods alone. Her horse fell and ended up lame, so she had to lead him home. On the way back, she passed the riding teacher's remote farm, and she went in to borrow the phone to ring for help.

The riding teacher was home alone. He explained that his wife and children were away. They put the horse in the stable and went back to the house.

He invited her to sit in the living room and offered her a glass of juice before she used the phone.

The next second, he was on her, tearing off her sweater and riding breeches, raping her right there on the burgundy carpet. She could still remember how the rug scratched against her bare back.

Afterwards, she was allowed to use the phone. Her father came to get her and the horse. The riding teacher was very pleasant and completely unfazed.

Karin didn't tell anyone, not even her parents. Occasionally, she would run into the riding teacher in town, at the post office or in the Konsum supermarket; she felt nauseated every time she saw him. He pretended nothing had happened.

When she missed her period and began throwing up in the mornings, she repressed the whole episode. The shame was too great. In the end, she couldn't hide it any longer. Even though she wore baggy sweaters, her mother saw that her belly was sticking out and took her to the local clinic. By then she was five months pregnant, and it was too late to have an abortion.

At first it was a relief to tell her parents what had happened. Even though she felt ashamed and guilty, she knew in her heart that she wasn't to blame. But just the fact that he'd been in her knickers, and inside of her, made her feel strangely ashamed. She told herself that when her parents found out about it they would help her, take charge of everything and see to it that this terrible wrong would be redressed. They would report the riding teacher to the police, see to it that he had to answer for his actions to his family and be put in jail for the crime he'd committed. Justice in the end would prevail.

* * *

But their reaction shocked her. Not only did they refuse to report the riding teacher to the police, they refused even to talk about what had happened. They chose to pretend it had never occurred, as if, deep inside, they didn't believe her. Karin would never forget the humiliation. They told her that, since she was so far along, the only option was to give the baby up for adoption; there was nothing else to discuss. Karin didn't object; she wanted to get rid of all traces of the rape. She wanted to continue being young.

But after the birth, everything changed. That was when the worst betrayal occurred, when she regretted her decision and wanted to keep the baby. Her parents' claim that it was impossible, since the papers had already been signed, turned out to be a lie. Something died inside her on the day she gave birth to the baby and had to give her up.

This was the secret Karin had kept to herself her entire adult life. Eventually, she moved to Stockholm and stayed with relatives while she attended college.

Then she was admitted to the Police Academy. When she received her first job offer on Gotland, she hesitated at first, but in the end she accepted. She thought she needed to move on, that she'd come through the worst of it. Ten years had passed, after all. The riding teacher who had raped her was long since dead, so at least there was no chance of running into him again. Her parents, now old, still lived in Tingstäde, and she visited them now and then, out of politeness.

They never discussed the matter.

Was it disastrous that she'd allowed Vera Norrström to go free? This shattered person who was capable of shooting to death two people? What sort of mother was she going to be to her newborn daughter? But now she had finished exacting her revenge. Karin hoped that Vera would be able to put everything behind her and be happy in spite of it all, with her husband and child.

She had toyed with the idea of telling Knutas, but she realized that would be impossible. If she did, her police career would be over. Would she even be able to continue as a police officer, carrying this baggage? At the moment, she couldn't answer that question. It was just one more secret she had to hide.

She lay down on the sand and closed her eyes, listening to the waves lapping against the shore. Thunder rumbled over the sea. The rain fell slowly, one drop after another striking her face.

ACKNOWLEDGEMENTS

This story is entirely fictional. Any similarities between the characters in the novel and actual individuals are coincidental. Occasionally, I have taken artistic liberties to change things for the benefit of the book. This includes Swedish TV's coverage of Gotland, which in the book has been moved to Stockholm. I have the utmost respect for SVT's regional news programme *Östnytt*, which covers Gotland with a permanent team stationed in Visby.

The settings used in the books are usually described as they actually exist in reality, although there are a few exceptions.

Any errors that may have slipped into the story are mine alone.

First and foremost, I would like to thank my husband, journalist Cenneth Niklasson, who is always ready to be my sounding board and offer me the greatest support.

Special thanks to:

Gösta Svensson, former detective superintendent with the Visby police

Ulf Åsgård, psychiatrist
Magnus Frank, detective superintendent with the Visby police
Martin Csatlos, of the Forensic Medicine Laboratory in Solna
Johan Gardelius, crime technician, Visby police
Sonny Björk, detective superintendent, technical division, county criminal police, Stockholm
Staffan Lindblom, harbour master, Cementa in Slite
Torsten Lindqvist, captain of the M/S *Gotska Sandön*
Gotska Sandön Folklore Society
The head ranger, Gotska Sandön

I would also like to thank my dear author colleagues – thanks for being there!

Thanks also to my readers for their valuable opinions:
Lena Allerstam, journalist, Swedish TV
Lilian Andersson, editor at Bonnier Educational Books
Kerstin Jungstedt, consultant, Provins fem
Bosse Jungstedt, Surrea Design

My thanks to Albert Bonniers Förlag, and especially to my publisher Jonas Axelsson and editor Ulrika Åkerlund for all their support, encouragement and work on my books. Thanks to my agents Bengt Nordin and Maria Enberg at Nordin Agency, and to my designer, John Eyre, for the great cover on the Swedish edition.

* * *

Last, but not least, I want to thank my wonderful children, Rebecka and Sebastian, for their understanding and many encouraging comments.

Älta, May 2007
Mari Jungstedt

www.jungstedtsgotland.se
www.marijungstedt.se

Death Sentence

Mikkel Birkegaard

A murder committed on paper, safely within the confines of a novel, is one thing. To see that same crime in the real world, is something else entirely . . .

FRANK FØNS IS a successful crime writer. His novels, famed for their visceral descriptions of violent death, have made him a household name. But now someone is copying his crimes. For Frank what once seemed a clever, intriguing plot twist, has suddenly become a terrifying, blood-spattered reality.

Frank unwittingly swaps his role of writer for detective. He must find out who is using his fiction to destroy his life, and why. What had once been a game is now a matter of life and death.

In fiction, the bad guy always gets caught, but in real life there is no such guarantee. And as Frank knows no-one is promising him a happy ending . . .

9780552776806